PENGUIN

THE STRANGE CASE OF DR JEKYLL AND MR HYDE
AND OTHER TALES OF TERROR

ROBERT LOUIS STEVENSON was born in Edinburgh in 1850. The son of a prosperous civil engineer, he was expected to follow the family profession but finally was allowed to study law at Edinburgh University. Stevenson reacted violently against the Presbyterian respectability of the city's professional classes and this led to painful clashes with his parents. In his early twenties he became afflicted with a severe respiratory illness from which he was to suffer for the rest of his life; it was at this time that he determined to become a professional writer. In 1879 he travelled to California to marry Fanny Osbourne, an American ten years his senior. Together they continued his search for a climate kind to his fragile health, eventually settling in Samoa, where he died on 3 December 1894.

Stevenson began his literary career as an essayist and travel-writer, but the success of *Treasure Island* (1883) and *Kidnapped* (1886) established his reputation for tales of action and adventure. *Kidnapped*, and its sequel *Catriona* (1893), *The Master of Ballantrae* and stories such as 'Thrawn Janet' and 'The Merry Men' also reveal his knowledge and feeling for the Scottish cultural past. Stevenson's Calvinistic upbringing gave him a preoccupation with pre-destination and a fascination with the presence of evil. In *Strange Case of Dr Jekyll and Mr Hyde* he explores the darker side of the human psyche, and the character of the Master in *The Master of Ballantrae* (1889) was intended to be 'all I know of the Devil'. During the last years of his life Stevenson's creative range developed considerably and *The Beach of Falesá* brought to fiction the kind of scenes now associated with Conrad and Maugham. At the time of his death Robert Louis Stevenson was working on *Weir of Hermiston*, at once a romantic historical novel and an emotional reworking of one of Stevenson's own most distressing experiences, the conflict between father and son.

ROBERT MIGHALL completed a Ph.D. on Gothic fiction and Victorian medico-legal science at the University of Wales, and then spent three years as a post-doctoral fellow at Merton College, University of Oxford. In 1997 he became the editor of Penguin Classics, and now works in London as a consultant. His publications include an edition of Oscar Wilde's poems for Everyman Paperbacks, and a study of Victorian Gothic fiction for Oxford University Press (1999). He has also edited Oscar Wilde's *The Picture of Dorian Gray* for Penguin Classics. He is a Fellow of the Royal Society of Arts.

ROBERT LOUIS STEVENSON

THE STRANGE CASE OF
DR JEKYLL AND MR HYDE

AND OTHER TALES OF TERROR

Edited by
ROBERT MIGHALL

PENGUIN BOOKS

PENGUIN BOOKS

Published by the Penguin Group
Penguin Books Ltd, 80 Strand, London WC2R 0RL, England
Penguin Putnam Inc., 375 Hudson Street, New York, New York 10014, USA
Penguin Books Australia Ltd, 250 Camberwell Road, Camberwell, Victoria 3124, Australia
Penguin Books Canada Ltd, 10 Alcorn Avenue, Toronto, Ontario, Canada M4V 3B2
Penguin Books India (P) Ltd, 11 Community Centre, Panchsheel Park, New Delhi – 110 017, India
Penguin Books (NZ) Ltd, Cnr Rosedale and Airborne Roads, Albany, Auckland, New Zealand
Penguin Books (South Africa) (Pty) Ltd, 24 Sturdee Avenue, Rosebank 2196, South Africa

Penguin Books Ltd, Registered Offices: 80 Strand, London WC2R 0RL, England

www.penguin.com

This edition first published 2002
2

Introduction, 'Diagnosing Jekyll . . .' and notes copyright © Robert Mighall, 2002
All rights reserved

The moral right of the editor has been asserted

Set in 10/12.5 pt Monotype Baskerville
Typeset by Rowland Phototypesetting Ltd, Bury St Edmunds, Suffolk
Printed in England by Clays Ltd, St Ives plc

CONTENTS

ACKNOWLEDGEMENTS

Thanks to the British Library, the Radcliffe Science Library, Oxford, the London Library and to Tower Hamlets Local Studies Library. Many thanks to Neil Rennie, Matthew Sweet, James Morton and Simon Bradley for help with various queries. Thanks to Myrna Blumberg, and to Laura Barber, my wonderful editor.

1850   Born Robert Lewis Balfour Stevenson (he would later adopt
        the French form 'Louis') on 13 November 1850, in Edinburgh.
        His father Thomas came from a long line of engineers (famous
        in Scotland for their lighthouses), and his mother Margaret
        Isabella Balfour was from a family of lawyers.

1857   Moves to 17 Heriot Row in Edinburgh's New Town district.

1867   Enrols at Edinburgh University to follow in the family tradi-
        tion and study engineering, but soon abandons this to study
        law.

1875   Passes 'advocate' and is called to the Scottish Bar, but never
        practises.

1876   Starts publishing in magazines, his early works are mostly
        travel pieces drawing on his experiences in various countries.
        Meets Fanny Osbourne, an American of thirty-six who was
        separated from her husband.

1877   *An Inland Voyage* published, an account of a journey by canoe
        in northern France.

1878   *Travels with a Donkey in the Cevennes* is published recounting his
        adventures in southern France.

1879   Joins Fanny in California, an account of which he later pub-
        lished as *The Amateur Emigrant* (1894).

1880   Marries Fanny.

1881   *Virginia Puerisque* (essays) published.

1882   *New Arabian Nights*, a collection of short stories published.

1883   *The Silverado Squatters* published, which recounts his honeymoon
        in a Californian silver mine. *Treasure Island*, one of the most

famous children's adventure stories, is also published, which starts to establish his reputation as a writer.

1884   Moves to Bournemouth, to a house which they re-name 'Skerrymore' in honour of one of Stevenson's ancestor's light-houses. 'The Body Snatcher' published at Christmas.

1885   *Prince Otto* and *The Dynamiter* published. 'Olalla' published at Christmas.

1886   *Strange Case of Dr Jekyll and Mr Hyde* published in January, originally intended for Christmas 1885, but withdrawn owing to a rather full market. First editions of this novel retain the 1885 date on the title page. This was the work that made Stevenson's reputation. *Kidnapped* published.

1887   *The Merry Men and Other Fables* published. Death of Thomas Stevenson.

1888   The Stevensons' first trip to the South Seas. (The Whitechapel Murders take place in East London while a stage version of *Dr Jekyll and Mr Hyde* is playing on the London stage. It is withdrawn out of public delicacy.)

1889   *The Master of Ballantrae* published. *The Wrong Box*, written with his stepson Lloyd Osbourne, published. Settles in the Samoan Islands.

1892   'The Beach of Falsea' published.

1893   *Island Nights' Entertainments* and *Catriona* (the sequel to *Kidnapped*) published.

1894   *The Ebb-Tide* published. Dies in Samoa in December of tuberculosis.

1896   The unfinished *Weir of Hermiston* published.

1914   Death of Fanny Stevenson.

INTRODUCTION

Robert Louis Stevenson's *Strange Case of Dr Jekyll and Mr Hyde* (1886) is one of the most famous works of horror fiction of all time. Like Mary Shelley's *Frankenstein* (1818) and Bram Stoker's *Dracula* (1897), *Jekyll and Hyde*, or at least a version of its central idea, resides in the collective consciousness. It has been the subject of many films, featured in countless sketches, cartoons and parodies, and the term 'Jekyll-and-Hyde personality' has entered our language, describing someone who lives a double-life of outward sanctity and secret iniquity. If the popular press discovers that the latest serial killer, homicidal maniac or even petty fraudster did not spend all his daylight hours pursuing these activities, and occasionally acted like his neighbours, chances are it will suggest that X is displaying 'Jekyll-and-Hyde' tendencies, a useful shorthand for sensationalist reportage, and perhaps a way of making us scrutinize our neighbours more closely. It is testimony to Stevenson's inventiveness as a writer that his creation has this independent existence over a hundred years after his tale was first published. And yet, despite this almost universal familiarity with the *idea* of Jekyll and Hyde, it is also true that Stevenson's story is more known about than actually known, and that many of those who believe they know what it is about, have not actually *read* the hundred pages that comprise the tale. They would find there something different from what they imagined: a more complex, rewarding and disturbing story than the version that has been handed down in popular cultural form. Those who are about to read the *Strange Case* and the other tales collected here for the first time, would do best to return to this Introduction after they have read them, as it is necessary to reveal specific plot details for the purposes of discussion. New readers will also find the experience more rewarding if they forget all their preconceptions, and put themselves in the position of Stevenson's first readers who knew nothing about 'Jekyll and Hyde'.

Christmas Crawlers

Robert Louis Stevenson wrote his most famous story in October 1885 when he was thirty-five. He was living in Bournemouth with his wife Fanny and Lloyd Osbourne, her son from an earlier marriage. Stevenson's letters along with some observations in 'A Chapter on Dreams' (abridged in this volume), reveal that he was finding himself under financial constraint at the time. He had been a professional writer since the age of twenty-one, but was still dependent on his father, a matter of some embarrassment. The tale was written for a commercial market, so that he could pay the likes of 'Byles the butcher'.[1] It was his first really successful work, enabling him to be financially independent for the first time.

To ensure its success, Stevenson turned his fertile imagination to creating a 'fine bogey tale' to satisfy a large market for such literature. Stevenson's editor at Longmans asked him to write a 'shilling shocker' for Christmas 1885, a season traditionally associated with supernatural and creepy tales. Charles Dickens's most famous ghost story 'A Christmas Carol', was just one of many he produced in this tradition, whilst Stevenson himself wrote 'The Body Snatcher' and 'Olalla' for publication for Christmas 1884 and 1885. As it turned out, the Christmas 1885 book market was crowded, so publication was delayed until January; but from the start the *Strange Case* was conceived as a 'crawler', a sensational tale of supernatural incident designed to produce a pleasurable chill in its readers. It is worth considering this tradition, as it helps us understand how his tale conforms to, but also departs from and innovates within, a mode upon which it would have enormous influence.

Horror fiction really started with Horace Walpole's Gothic novel *The Castle of Otranto* published on Christmas Eve 1764. His tale of spectres, portents, family curses and bizarre supernatural occurrences was written partly as a joke, being presented as a medieval manuscript that had been 'discovered' by an eighteenth-century antiquarian and presented as a curiosity for a modern enlightened readership. Many were taken in by Walpole's ruse, and many enjoyed the new experience of reading material associated with folk legends and chivalric romances in the pages of a novel, a form hitherto concerned with the modern and the everyday, the probable and the realistic. Others followed, and by the turn of the nineteenth century critics were complaining that fiction was inundated with stories of diabolical revenges and family curses, set in ancient castles or monasteries deep in gloomy forests, and involving proud Italian or Spanish nobles and the machinations of corrupt ecclesiastics. Most early Gothic stories, even the best by Ann Radcliffe, Matthew Lewis or Charles Maturin, were set in distant times, and/or (usually Catholic) countries. There was an understanding, held by author and reader alike, that such horrors were far removed from those who avidly consumed such fictions (middle-class Protestants in London, Edinburgh or Bath), that they could only take place in 'less civilized' ages or places.

Stevenson himself writes within this tradition in his short story 'Olalla', which he published a few weeks before *Jekyll and Hyde*. This story of atavism and a form of pathological 'vampirism' set in an ancient aristocratic mansion in a remote part of Spain is a typical Gothic tale. Its opening conforms to what Victor Sage has called 'the paradigm of the horror-plot: the journey from the capital ... to the provinces'.[2] Its long description of the journey from the city to the remote mountainous domicile creates atmosphere and builds expectations of suspense and the supernatural through a technique that would serve horror fiction from Ann Radcliffe's *Mysteries of Udolpho* (1794) to Bram Stoker's *Dracula* (1897) and beyond: 'The country through which we went was wild and rocky, partially covered with rough woods, now of the cork-tree, and now of the great Spanish chestnut, and frequently intersected by the beds of mountain torrents ...' The narrator travels to the residencia in this remote region to recover from his war wounds, and (ironically, given the outcome) to 'renew [his] blood'. He finds there a typically labyrinthine, ruinous and picturesque old edifice, which he compares with the 'sleeping palace of the legend', home to an aristocratic family as decayed as their ancestral mansion. As with Poe's 'House of Usher' (1839), and Nathaniel Hawthorne's *House of the Seven Gables* (1851), 'house' (building) is the physical expression of 'House' (family or lineage). Chris Baldick, in a very useful introduction to the Gothic, observes that this 'fiction is characteristically obsessed with old buildings as the sites of human decay. The Gothic castle or house is not just an old and sinister building; it is a house of degeneration, even of decomposition . . .'³ Geography and environment thus go beyond providing atmospheric effects, and offer a suitable location to explore the themes of the tale. These also conform to Gothic type according to Baldick's definition. For, 'typically a Gothic tale will invoke the tyranny of the past (a family curse, the survival of archaic forms of despotism and of superstition) with such weight as to stifle the hopes of the present . . .' (p. xix). This is the defining property of the Gothic mode, which is characterized by its attitude to the past, its tyrannies, legacies and unwelcome survivals or returns. In 'Olalla' the unwelcome legacy takes a very precise form, and provides a modern and materialist application of this central concern. On meeting his strange hostess and her simpleton son, the narrator makes the connection between architecture and ancestry: 'The family blood had been impoverished, perhaps by long inbreeding, which I knew to be a common error among the proud and the exclusive.' The ancestral 'curse' was a staple theme of Gothic fiction from *The Castle of Otranto* onwards. But whilst Walpole depicts a supernatural mechanism avenging ancestral crime through a number of generations, Stevenson's emphasis is biological. The burden of the past is carried in the bodies of descendants. 'Evil' becomes a reproductive issue, which blights the happiness of the innocent girl Olalla, compelled to renounce her romantic attachment to the gallant soldier who intrudes upon her secluded detachment from the modern world, through a fear that the hereditary taint will afflict their offspring. Pointing to a portrait of a distant ancestor of evil reputation whom both she and her mother resemble, Olalla reasons with the besotted protagonist:

. . . Others, ages dead, have wooed other men with my eyes; other men have heard the pleading of the same voice that now sounds in your ears. The hands of the dead are in my bosom; they move me, they pluck me, they guide me; I am a puppet at their command; and I but reinform features and attributes that have long been laid aside from evil in the quiet of the grave. Is it me you love, friend? or the race that made me? . . . individual succeeds to individual, mocked with a semblance of self-control, but they are nothing. We speak of the soul, but the soul is in the race . . .

Here Stevenson provides a modern twist to the conventional Gothic theme of aristocratic family curses and ancestral returns, adapting it to the concerns of mental pathology or what was termed 'social hygiene' at the time, making Olalla's mother a biological revenant and perhaps even the first post-Darwinian 'vampire'.[4] For this emphasis on lineal repetition as a form of extended generational life provides a chilling hint of the 'vampirism' displayed by the hostess of this remote castle. The soldier has cut himself, and seeks help from the usually lethargic mother:

Her great eyes opened wide, the pupils shrank into points; a veil seemed to fall from her face, and leave it sharply expressive and yet inscrutable. And as I still stood, marvelling a little at her disturbance, she came swiftly up to me, and stooped and caught me by the hand; and the next moment my hand was at her mouth, and she had bitten me to the bone. The pang of the bite, the sudden spurting of blood, and the monstrous horror of the act, flashed through me all in one, and I beat her back; and she sprang at me again and again, with bestial cries . . .

There is no evidence beyond the superstitions of the local peasantry that the mother actually belongs to the Undead. Here, 'vampirism', like the suggestion of extended life through lineal repetition figured in the portrait, is largely metaphorical, supposedly a manifestation of her pathological inheritance. The 'blood' is impoverished, so it seeks renewal from healthy stock. In this way Stevenson cleverly adapts, and innovates within, the conventional framework of Gothic fiction. He uses the stock features of the mode to explore contemporary concerns and emphases, something he would take even further in the

Strange Case of Dr Jekyll and Mr Hyde, which is also concerned with forms of atavistic return, but which dispenses altogether with the remote geographical setting of the conventional Gothic tale.

However, before examining what made *Jekyll and Hyde* so original, it is worth briefly considering one further horror story, which offers a contrast to, but also anticipates aspects of, that more famous tale published two years later. Stevenson's 'The Body Snatcher' (1884) was also written for the Christmas ghost story market, and is in many ways an even more traditional example of that form. Its opening conforms to the narrative convention of grisly deeds recounted in hushed voices around the fireside on a winter's night. Fettes, the local drunk, is roused from his habitual stupor by the reference to a name he has not heard spoken for many years, but which has evidently haunted his memory in the intervening decades: 'Fettes became instantly sober; his eyes awoke, his voice became clear, loud, and steady, his language forcible and earnest; we were all startled by this transformation, as if a man had risen from the dead.' This analogy (which is also partly a pun) is ironic in a number of ways, for the transformation of this 'deadbeat' into lively sobriety is triggered by an association with exactly that: the ghostly return of a 'long-dead and long-dissected' corpse. This actual supernatural occurrence is saved for the chilling denouement of the story, but is pre-figured by the subject matter of the tale which Fettes relates to the anonymous narrator. This final, literal haunting finds its metaphorical counterpart in the return of the man who was Fettes's fellow witness to the resurrection of Gray, and the way both of them have obviously been haunted by its horrible memory ever since: 'Fettes clutched him by the arm, and these words came in a whisper, and yet painfully distinct, "Have you seen it again?"' 'It' is the ghost of Gray, the man Macfarlene murdered, who returns in the place of a body the two students had disinterred from a lonely rural grave for the purposes of dissection for surgical instruction. Fettes 'rising from the dead' at the start, and the return of Gray at the shocking conclusion, provide literal and metaphorical frames to a narrative about the exploits of what were called 'resurrection men', traders in human corpses.

It is in these central incidents, recalling dark deeds from the annals of true crime from the 'bad old days' of the early part of the century, that we find prefigurations of the concerns which Stevenson would develop fully in *Jekyll and Hyde*, but in a contemporary context. 'The Body Snatcher' is a fictionalized account of events that occurred in Edinburgh in the 1820s, but which were still notorious in the popular imagination. Burke and Hare posed as body snatchers, supposedly supplying resurrected corpses to the anatomical schools, but turned out to be murderers, selling bodies that had never been buried. (For full details of the historical background to this tale see note 6 to 'The Body Snatcher'). Robert Knox, a famous, and then infamous, surgeon whom these two supplied with 'subjects', was publicly implicated in this scandal and appears in the sidelines of Stevenson's tale. His representative, the fictional 'Dr Wolfe Macfarlene', takes a more central role, and is shown to be actually guilty of murder like the notorious grave robbers with whom he deals. Through this shift in emphasis from the avowedly criminal Burke and Hare (portrayed fleetingly), to the guilty secrets of the young medical students, Stevenson appears to be more interested in exploring the theme of a double life that he would make his own in his most famous tale. For Macfarlane (and to an extent Fettes) can be considered in part ancestors of Jekyll. The narrator describes Fettes when a student at the medical school:

Cold, light, and selfish in the last resort, he had that modicum of prudence, miscalled morality, which keeps a man from inconvenient drunkenness or punishable theft. He coveted besides a measure of consideration from his masters and his fellow-pupils, and he had no desire to fail conspicuously in the external parts of life. Thus he made it his pleasure to gain some distinction in his studies, and day after day rendered unimpeachable service to his employer, Mr K—. For his day of work he indemnified himself by nights of roaring blackguardly enjoyment; and, when the balance had been struck, the organ that he called his conscience declared itself content.

Fettes is a profound 'double-dealer': seeking 'consideration' from his professional peers in the light of day, but offsetting this with what would be considered the exact opposite behaviour – blackguardly enjoyment – in the hours of darkness (sounding very much like Jekyll, who believes that he is personally absolved from all of Hyde's crimes). This inverted logic ironically infers that his dishonourable behaviour 'indemnified' him for his daylight industry and sobriety, achieving a form of ethical balance. But this is undermined by the knowledge that part of his 'service' to his employer involves supplying the corpses upon which the anatomy school depended. This detail disrupts the neat dichotomy between daylight and nocturnal behaviour, and decidedly tips the moral equilibrium Fettes believes he maintains. It is tipped further when he is encouraged by Macfarlane to turn a blind eye to the murder of Gray, who Fettes receives as another 'subject' for dissection, full-knowing its provenance. The final return of Gray's ghostly corpse on a body-snatching expedition finally overturns Fettes's contrived compact with his conscience, and accounts for the ruined state he presents at the start of the tale, having abandoned all claims to respectability. Not so his fellow witness, the man who actually murdered Gray, and offered him up to surgical dissection. Wolfe Macfarlane, 'the great London Doctor', who visits the George Inn many years after that terrible night

. . . was richly dressed in the finest of broadcloth and the whitest of linen, with a great gold watch chain and studs and spectacles of the same precious material; . . . and he carried on his arm a comfortable driving-coat of fur. There was no doubt but he became his years, breathing, as he did, of wealth and consideration; and it was a surprising contrast to see our parlour sot [drunk], bald, dirty, pimpled, and robed in an old camlet cloak, confront him at the bottom of the stairs.

'Macfarlane,' he said, somewhat loudly, more like a herald than a friend.

This contrasts the two parts of duplicitous personality – roaring blackguardly excess; and sober and respectable industry – that the narrative dissects and explores. This confrontation between the representatives of the daylight and the nocturnal hours could be seen as a prefiguration of Jekyll seeing the features of Hyde for the first time. For what Macfarlane beholds is his exact counterpart in the ruined features of Fettes, who acts as his suppressed conscience. The true 'haunting' is this bringing to account of a long-buried crime of a respectable and successful man.

This pattern of suppressed guilt, of a double life of daylight respect-ability and nocturnal transgression, of the 'ghost' of old crimes over-taking their perpetrators, contained here within a fairly conventional supernatural tale, would be developed in a far more subtle and dis-turbing way in the next story Stevenson wrote for the Christmas Crawler market. Written exactly a year later, *Strange Case of Dr Jekyll and Mr Hyde* dispenses entirely with the distancing devices of the traditional Gothic – set 'over there' in southern Spain, or 'back then' in the near or distant past. It is set in London in the present day, and situates horror *within* a respectable individual, with its vision of evil reflecting on a much broader section of society than had perhaps been hitherto suggested in popular fiction. While the 'supernatural' element is given a degree of plausibility, coming close to the techniques of 'Science Fiction' in the inference that Jekyll's experiment might be repeated if he had only supplied the formula. Finally, its narrative method of collected contemporaneous testimony gives it a greater sensational immediacy, and authenticity than the fireside recollections of the traditional ghost story form. The following pages will explore what makes this story one of the most important and influential horror stories since *The Castle of Otranto*; starting with its narrative technique.

Testimony

Horror fiction has a tradition of narrative complexity. From Charles Robert Maturin's *Melmoth the Wanderer* (1820) and James Hogg's *Memoirs and Confessions of a Justified Sinner* (1824) to *Dracula* (1897) the tale of terror has rarely been presented 'straight'. Narratives often purport to be assembled from a number of discreet manuscripts, letters or testimonies, which combined provide a (more or less) coherent account of events. This technique became the trade mark of the so-called 'Sensation' school of fiction (a form of suburban Gothic) which emerged in the 1860s when writers like Wilkie Collins constructed thrilling narratives out of letters, diaries and individual testimonies and confessions. Stevenson's tale in part conforms to this pattern, where two of the most important revelatory chapters (the ninth and tenth) are discreet documents written by protagonists, while a third (the fourth) is partly presented as a newspaper report of a grisly crime. Such a technique serves the interests of veracity, as the various documents are supposedly more 'real' than the overtly artificial observations of an omniscient narrator who has no existence within the world of the fiction. It serves suspense, as the individual contributors do not know the full outcome of events, delaying complete explanation until the final pages. And it helps to heighten the emotional impact of the narration, as Dr Lanyon's own account of the shocking spectacle of Hyde turning into Jekyll, or Jekyll's terrors of Hyde's usurpation of his identity are more immediate and thrilling than would be possible if they were reported second hand.

The supposed veracity of the testimonies is further endorsed by the fact that they are produced by, or concern the interests of, highly reliable witnesses: two physicians and one lawyer, who use their professional expertise to investigate the mystery that confronts them. This heightens the shock when their investigations fail, but it also determines their preoccupations and expectations. Stevenson's tale is presented as a 'Case', evoking the procedures of both legal and medical knowledge and testimony; but it is a *strange* case, its strangeness deriving from its disruption of the very expectations associated with these procedures and forms of writing.

Strange Case of Dr Jekyll and Mr Hyde is constructed as a mystery in many ways resembling a detective story. Eight of its ten chapters are concerned with getting to the bottom of the mysterious circumstances surrounding Jekyll's will, and his dealings with a most unlikely individual, Mr Edward Hyde. We should remember that until the ninth chapter, when Dr Lanyon witnesses the transformation of Hyde into his friend Jekyll, the story involves two individuals, Jekyll and Hyde. The characters within the story, and its very first readers, believed this to be the case, and this should influence our reading, especially our understanding of the suspicions and expectations of those who investigate the mystery. Let us consider appearances, for they are all the first readers had to go on. The respectable bachelor Dr Jekyll and the 'damnable' young man Edward Hyde are the most unlikely companions. When pressed by Utterson the lawyer to 'make a clean breast of' the trouble he imagines him in, Jekyll confesses to taking 'a great, a very great interest' in a 'young man' who is not his son, and is a total stranger to his oldest friends. Hyde is allowed full range of Jekyll's house, has his own special back door and has his cheques honoured by the older man. As Utterson declares: 'It turns me cold to think of this creature stealing like a thief to Harry's bedside.' It is later learned that Hyde hangs around by the river at night, and that Jekyll has set him up with his own house in Soho, a place that appears to be appointed more for Jekyll's own refined tastes than Hyde's. It is supposed throughout that Hyde is blackmailing Jekyll. 'It isn't what you fancy; it is not so bad as that,' Jekyll assures Utterson. But what *was* this unspoken bad fancy tacitly understood by both Utterson and his client? These circumstances appear to be carefully plotted to point to, without actually specifying, a suspicion that some erotic attachment is at the bottom of Jekyll's relationship with Hyde. Blackmail and homosexuality have a long history of association. According to Rictor Norton; 'Before the passing of the 1967 Sexual Offences Act the law prohibiting homosexual intercourse was described as a "Blackmailers' Charter", for very many – perhaps even "most" – blackmail attempts involved a threat to expose a man as a homosexual, whether or not he were in fact gay (*sic*).'[5] The 'Blackmailers' Charter' was the law passed in 1885 (the year Stevenson wrote his tale), outlawing all erotic acts between males whether in public or private, and was responsible for Oscar Wilde's imprisonment in 1895.[6] But even before this new legal definition of outlawed sexuality, the much older offence of 'sodomy' had made blackmail a highly lucrative enterprise. As Norton suggests: 'Professional blackmail rings were . . . common, especially in the 1810s–1820s, and gay men who blackmailed their partners were not unknown. The threat of exposure as a sodomite is the basis of more than half of the prosecutions throughout the eighteenth century . . .' Oscar Wilde had himself been subject to a number of blackmail attempts, most of them by rent boys with whom he, or his lover Alfred Douglas, had consorted. Given this association it is likely that suspicions of some form of erotic connection between Dr Jekyll and Edward Hyde might have been entertained by Stevenson's first readers, who also wondered about Jekyll's 'very great interest' in Hyde.

A suggestion of homosexuality provides a plausible hypothesis until the truth is revealed that two men are actually one.[7] Of course, Stevenson could not describe or directly refer to what was called 'unnatural' and deemed unspeakable in the pages of prose fiction designed for a popular readership; but he could, and perhaps did, manipulate the expectations and suppositions of his readers who could not complain if their own imaginations had supplied what Stevenson had refused to actually state.[8] An 'unspeakable vice' provides a particularly effective sub-text for a sensational plot about secrets, where what looks like an 'unnatural' relationship eventually turns out to be a supernatural or preternatural one. This is an effect of the framework of expectations upon which the narrative is built: the use of legal and medical procedures and forms of knowledge (which, apart from pornography, constituted almost the sole place where homosexuality was discussed in print), and their corresponding adherence to the rationalist principles which the supernatural explanation brilliantly overturns.

This overturning of expectations has its greatest effect in Dr Lanyon's Narrative, when the fantastic explanation that two people are in fact one is first revealed. If Utterson's investigations evoke the expectations and procedures of legal inquiry, then Lanyon's narrative is even more self-consciously structured according to the methods of his profession. Lanyon has responded to Jekyll's plea to assist him in an urgent matter, to collect his chemicals and to admit a stranger (Hyde) to his house late at night. When Hyde arrives, he receives him in his consulting room as if he were one of his patients, and attempts to turn Hyde into a 'case':

as there was something abnormal and misbegotten in the very essence of the creature that now faced me – something seizing, surprising and revolting . . . to my interest in the man's nature and character there was added a curiosity as to his origin, his life, his fortune and status in the world . . . [Therefore I] sat down myself in my customary seat and with as fair an imitation of my ordinary manner to a patient, as the lateness of the hour, the nature of my preoccupations, and the horror I had of my visitor, would suffer me to muster.

Lanyon's preoccupations and procedures are characteristic of medical writing at the time. The origin, life, fortune and status of 'abnormal' subjects contributed important information to clinical case-studies.[9] Lanyon believes he has an insane patient before him, 'wrestling against the approaches of hysteria'. But before he has time to compile his notes, this monstrosity turns into his friend Henry Jekyll, a fellow member of his profession, who has, at least to appearances, impeccable 'life, origin and status'; and yet contained within him the misbegotten, abnormal, revolting murderer, Hyde. The transformation of 'patient' into physician; abnormal hysteric into respectable member of the middle classes; two people into one, stages a narrative and 'epistemological' revolution also. For as medical, legal, or rational forms of understanding collapse, the *case* of Jekyll and Hyde becomes the *Strange Case* of one of the most original horror tales ever written.

The horror of my other self

That Stevenson's *Strange Case of Dr Jekyll and Mr Hyde* is something more than just a shilling shocker, a creepy tale for Christmas 1885, was noticed immediately. Reviewers stated that 'the story has a much larger and deeper interest than that belonging to mere skilful narrative. It is a marvellous exploration into the recesses of human nature', and referred to it as a 'parable' with a 'profound allegory', while a Christian paper stated that it was an 'allegory based on the two-fold nature of man, a truth taught us by the Apostle Paul in Romans 7'.[10] Indeed, his tale provided the text for a sermon that was preached from the pulpit of St Paul's Cathedral. Pared down to its essentials it is about the fight between good and evil, duty and temptation, in the human 'soul': a story as old as Genesis. Jekyll considers his dilemma in these terms, referring to 'the perennial war among my members', and the fact that 'the terms of this debate are as old and commonplace as man'. Stevenson's own upbringing inculcated in him a strong sense of sin, which emerges in the moral foundation of his tale. As he wrote to Edward Purcell in February 1886: 'I have the old Scotch Presbyterian preoccupation with these [moral] problems . . . The Scotch side came out plain in *Dr Jekyll*'[11]. However, this 'moral' extrapolation from his tale is one of the first simplifications it has undergone, and needs to be put into context.

When Adam and Eve clothed themselves in shame they did not immediately don frock coats and crinoline. In other words, Stevenson's tale, despite its 'perennial' moral framework, is very much a product of its time, and if it is an allegory it is constructed out of historical circumstances and class relations. Edward Hyde is the embodiment of what Jekyll refers to as his 'lower elements', but he also makes clear that this hierarchical relationship is formed by Jekyll's excessive conformity to the codes of respectability and public opinion. As he explains, 'the worst of my faults was a certain impatient gaiety of disposition, such as has made the happiness of many, but such as I found it hard to reconcile with my imperious desire to carry my head high, and wear a more than commonly grave countenance before the public'. The simple opposition between good and evil breaks down at this point. He continues: 'Many a man would have blazoned such irregularities as I was guilty of; but from the high views that I had set before me, I regarded and hid them with an almost morbid sense of shame.' It is his overdeveloped sense of sinfulness that constructs Hyde. The more Jekyll sought to do *and appear to be* 'good', the more 'evil' he made Hyde. His Hyde is imaginary and potential until Jekyll discovers a potion that will *embody* these divisions. It is here that the moral allegory starts to wear the vestments of class and history:

If each, I told myself, could but be housed in separate identities, life would be relieved of all that was unbearable; the unjust might go his way, delivered from the aspirations and remorse of his more upright twin; and the just could walk steadfastly and securely on his upward path, doing the good things in which he found his pleasure, and no longer exposed to disgrace and penitence by the hands of this extraneous evil.

Jekyll appears to be observing the behaviour of two distinct individuals that happen to coexist in his consciousness. The potion makes this idea a reality. On 'releasing' his Hyde, Jekyll starts to characterize him, clothe him, classify him, and to moralize on him, appalled but also thrilled by his behaviour. Hyde is the bodily expression of his relationship to Jekyll's more exalted principles – lower in stature and uglier in aspect than his 'more upright twin' Jekyll, who we are told is a fine figure of a man, with a 'handsome face'. Once his imagined divisions are externalized and made concrete, Jekyll could give his righteousness full rein:

The pleasures which I made haste to seek in my disguise were, as I have said, undignified; I would scarce use a harder term. But in the hands of Edward Hyde, they soon began to turn towards the monstrous. When I would come back from these excursions, I was often plunged into a kind of wonder at my vicarious depravity . . . Henry Jekyll stood at times aghast before the acts of Edward Hyde; but the situation was apart from ordinary laws, and insidiously relaxed the grasp of conscience.

Thus even when we are told that two people are one, Jekyll's testimony still divides them, denying responsibility for Hyde's actions. Such distinctions allow Henry Jekyll to act with all propriety as a member of his class, and castigate the behaviour of Hyde, his social, and what could be termed his 'anthropological', opposite and inferior. For Jekyll, as much as his friends, views Hyde the monstrous criminal in distinctive terms, fashioned according to the theories of crime and immorality at the time.

Apes and Angels

Jekyll conceives of Hyde as his 'lower element'. Whilst this is principally a moral or even metaphysical designation, it is also strongly suggested that Hyde is also lower on the evolutionary scale (as it was perceived) than his more upright twin Henry Jekyll. Jekyll's reference to treading the 'upward path' also refers to his perceived position on what was considered the 'ladder' of cultural and biological development. A less upright individual evokes suggestions of the simian, and Hyde is certainly that. Utterson found him both dwarfish and 'troglodytic', whilst another remarks upon the 'ape-like' fury of his attack on Carew, and Jekyll himself refers to Hyde's 'ape-like spite', his 'bestial' nature, and remarks how hairy his opposite is. This inference eventually culminates in a frightening vision of primordial immorality: 'This was the shocking thing; that the slime of the pit seemed to utter cries and voices; and that the amorphous dust gesticulated and sinned; and what was dead, and had no shape, would usurp the offices of life.' This emphasis on criminality or sinfulness being a *primitive* condition or impulse corresponds with that found in a number of writings from the period which employed evolutionary models to understand criminality and mental disorder. The idea of 'reversion', which helped explain immoral behaviour in scientific terms, also provided possibilities for Gothic representation, which could now figure unwelcome ancestral legacies on a greatly extended scale, reaching back to the origins of human life itself. This can be seen by comparing the psychiatrist Henry Maudsley's 'Remarks on Crime and Criminals' from 1888 with Stevenson's depiction of Jekyll and Hyde:

The sense of moral relations, or so-called moral feeling . . . are the latest and the highest products of mental evolution; being the least stable, therefore, they are the first to disappear in mental degeneration, which is in the literal sense an *unkinding* or undoing of mind; and when they are stripped off the primitive and more stable passions are exposed – naked and not ashamed, just as they were in the premoral ages of animal and human life on earth.[12]

Maudsley's reasoning sounds very like Jekyll's, who thinks of Hyde as 'lower', and as the 'animal within' him, who allows him to 'strip off these lendings [of moral sense] and spring headlong into the sea of liberty'. Jekyll's potion effects the 'unkinding' to which the psychiatrist refers; a release from the bonds of acquired civilized behaviour, and thus a return to 'primitive' pre-moral indulgence. When embodied, Hyde naturally resembles the simian and 'degenerate', hardly human form of the criminal type described by medico-legal experts. In short, Hyde is the physical expression of moral lowness according to post-Darwinian thought.[13] (A much fuller discussion of these aspects of Stevenson's story is offered in the essay 'Diagnosing Jekyll' at the end of this volume.)

A world of ordinary secret sinners

In Mr Hyde Stevenson created a new fictional monster; a Franken-stein's creature, fabricated from the beliefs of evolutionary anthropol-ogy and scientific criminology, whom he releases into contemporary London. Jekyll marvelling at the 'monstrous' depravity of Hyde, and the witness of the Carew murder commenting on the 'ape-like' fury of his assault, sound very like the classic descriptions of the atavistic criminal type; who, according to Lombroso: 'desire[s] not only to extinguish life in the victim, but to mutilate the corpse, tear its flesh and drink its blood'.[14] But Stevenson's tale is actually more complex and disturbing than that, for he used this picture of criminal mon-strosity to reflect on that which had actually defined it: the world of respectable physicians and legislators. Hyde is *within* Jekyll, and per-haps within others too. Stevenson's story strips away all the distancing devices of the traditional Gothic, locating the horror of atavistic returns in central London, in the present and in the body and mind of a representative of the professional classes. It is this world that his tale reflects on and probes with its central concern with respectability and its discontents. Jekyll attempts to make an absolute division between the respectable and the disreputable, the righteous and the libertine, the social and the sensual/sexual. But he fails. Ostensibly because of a mistake with his chemicals; but the experiment also fails because the divisions Jekyll imagines and attempts to solidify were impossible to sustain. It is not only the chemicals that are 'impure', the differences he considers to be absolute are also decidedly mixed and confused.

Jekyll claims that he is 'a composite', like 'all human beings, as we meet them . . . commingled out of good and evil'; whereas 'Edward Hyde, alone, in the ranks of mankind, was pure evil.' And yet Hyde appears to have some elements of Jekyll in him. Jekyll's original plan is that Hyde would act as an 'alibi'. Like a contract killer or 'bravo' he would conduct the business Jekyll was ashamed of, and if there were any reprisals, Jekyll would not be implicated:

Let me but escape into my laboratory door, give me but a second or two to mix and swallow the draught . . . and whatever he had done, Edward Hyde would pass away like the stain of breath upon a mirror; and there in his stead, quietly at home, trimming the midnight lamp in his study, a man who could afford to laugh at suspicion, would be Henry Jekyll.

If Jekyll 'hired' Hyde for this peace of mind and security, then he was short changed. For if Hyde is pure evil, and Jekyll believed he could laugh at suspicion, Hyde himself does not share this view. Indeed, the very first words we hear him speak, recounted by Enfield in his anecdote about Hyde trampling on the child, show Hyde acting in a very Jekyll-like way. As Enfield recalls:

. . . and there was the man in the middle, with a kind of black, sneering coolness – frightened too, I could see that – but carrying it off, sir, really like Satan. 'If you choose to make capital out of this accident,' said he, 'I am naturally helpless. No gentleman but wishes to avoid a scene,' says he. 'Name your figure.'

Hyde's 'Satanic' sneering scarcely disguises an overriding concern with his reputation. Would Satan truly attempt to convince the witnesses that the incident with the child was an 'accident'? Why should he care what they think if he was pure evil? Hyde appears to be performing no useful function here. For he costs Jekyll a hundred pounds (a very considerable sum at the time), and the necessity of drawing the cheque which implicates his own name in the business, the very thing he wished to avoid. Enfield told Hyde: 'If he had any friends of credit . . . he should lose them' unless he pays up. But it is Jekyll's 'credit' (meaning reputation) that he should preserve here by *not* drawing on his funds. Far from laughing at suspicion, Jekyll's 'bravo' leads him into an inquiry that eventually spells his ruin. On hearing this anecdote, Utterson, already unhappy about the will, resolves to discover what hold Hyde has over Jekyll.

Indeed, the will that alerted Utterson's suspicions in the first place also contributes to the failure of Jekyll's plans. Jekyll draws up a will 'so that if anything befell me in the person of Dr Jekyll, I could enter on that of Edward Hyde without pecuniary loss'. It is significant that

Jekyll uses the first person when he refers to Hyde continuing without pecuniary loss. Jekyll wishes to enjoy all the comforts and privileges of the position he has gained in the world *as himself*, even if he has to do so in the person of Hyde, supposedly pure evil and disassociated from, and indifferent to, the interests of Jekyll. By drawing up a will Jekyll clings to the financial support systems and observes the sanctioned procedures of the class whose moral codes and values he attempts to escape with his experiment. This wanting to have it both ways, renouncing and preserving bourgeois values, is in effect a hypocritical continuation of the duplicity Jekyll originally sought to evade, and entangles him in the very network of secret sins and their reprisals that he attempted to escape. Jekyll is never really free as Hyde because Hyde is never really free of Jekyll and all he represents.[15] In short, perhaps the strangest (and certainly the most disturbing) thing about the case of Jekyll and Hyde, is that it turns out not to be so strange at all. Appearances would suggest that if we read the confessions of others in his circle we would appreciate how ordinary his case is.

Secrets everywhere

Following the Carew murder Jekyll renounces Hyde, and attempts to settle back into a life of respectability once more. After a while the temptations return and he becomes an 'ordinary secret sinner' again, without the help of Hyde. This phrase captures something that is glimpsed repeatedly in the narrative: that the 'ordinary' condition of his society is for individuals to sin in secret, but also to hold, hide or attempt to discover or reveal secrets. There are a good many secrets that are never revealed. Enfield (a well-known man about town) returns home from 'some place at the end of the world, about three o'clock of a black winter morning', but neglects to mention exactly where or what he was doing. Both he and Utterson have a policy that 'the more it looks like Queer Street, the less I ask'. Enfield predicts what happens when this rule is broken: 'You start a question, and it's like starting a stone. You sit quietly on the top of a hill; and away the stone goes, starting others; and presently some bland old bird (the last you would have thought of) is knocked on the head in his own back garden, and the family have to change their name.' One such 'bland old bird' might be the elderly MP Sir Danvers Carew, whose death down by the river late at night is rather suspicious. The maid:

became aware of an aged and beautiful gentleman with white hair, drawing near along the lane; and advancing to meet him, another and very small gentleman, to whom at first she paid less attention. When they had come within speech . . . the older man bowed and accosted the other with a very pretty manner of politeness. It did not *seem* as if the subject of his address were of great importance; indeed, from his pointing, it *sometimes appeared* as if he were only inquiring his way; but the moon shone on his face as he spoke . . . [and] it *seemed* to breathe such an *innocent* and old-world kindness of disposition, yet with something high too, as of a well-founded self-content. [my italics]

If we look at what the maid says we find that it is qualified and highly speculative. Why mention that he *seemed* innocent? And what is he doing 'accosting' young men in a 'pretty' manner down by the river late at night? Surely when directions are asked it is the knowledgeable addressee who does the pointing. When the police officer learns that the victim of this crime is Sir Danvers Carew, his response: ' "Good God, sir!' exclaimed the officer, 'is it possible?" ' appears somewhat excessive. Why is he so amazed? What are the circumstances that trouble him about the identity of such a victim in such a crime – 'some bland old bird (*the last you would have thought of*)' as Enfield puts it? What was in the letter he was carrying addressed to Utterson, seeking his professional help? We will never know. But are we right to be so suspicions?[16] According to the text we are. We are actively encouraged to imagine secrets where there might be none, and be suspicious perhaps without cause. Stevenson's story actively demonstrates that you can never trust appearances.

Seek and hide

This lack of trust also affects our belief in the testimony of others, and undermines our faith in the veracity of what we read. From the very first page we are introduced to a world governed by public opinion, and by a fear of revelation and blackmail. In fact, it could be argued that the real 'monster' in *Jekyll and Hyde* is opinion. It casts an ominous shadow across the entire narrative and is responsible for stunted lives, and two, or even three deaths. The fear of exposure is so powerful it even scares Hyde, who pays a hundred pounds to keep a good name he doesn't even have. Enfield and the doctor blackmail Hyde: 'killing being out of the question, we did the next best. We told the man we could and would make such a scandal out of this, as should make his name stink from one end of London to the other.'[17] When Hyde produces the cheque in another's name Enfield assumes Hyde is blackmailing Jekyll; on hearing this Utterson resolves to have a go himself and see what Hyde has to hide. They are all motivated by the need to maintain appearances and to protect the system that works on 'credit', however bankrupt this appears to be. It is this that encourages Utterson to turn amateur detective and investigate the mystery of Jekyll and Hyde. However, whilst most detectives investigate secrets in order to solve crimes and bring the details to light, Utterson is driven by the opposite motives.[18] He is a questor who doesn't actually want to know, whose ruling passion is to preserve his friend from scandal, to save his 'credit'. If he can find out what Hyde's secrets are he can trade them for Jekyll's being forgotten. Or so he thinks. When Hyde commits a murder Utterson accompanies the police officer, whose job it is to make a thorough investigation and publicize all facts if necessary. Utterson assists the investigation, but only up to a point. He technically obstructs the course of justice, for he fails to mention someone who is intimately connected with the murderer, and has supposedly received a communication from him subsequent to the crime. Indeed, the murder weapon actually belongs to Jekyll, having been given to him many years before by Utterson. Jekyll confesses to Utterson that he is only 'thinking of [his] own character, which this hateful business has rather exposed'. His friend shares this concern; fearing that 'the good name of [Jekyll] should be sucked down in the eddy of a scandal'. To the very end this is his objective. When all is lost, Hyde is dead, Jekyll has been murdered, or has disappeared, Utterson still hopes that 'we may at least save his credit'. Even Lanyon, who has been killed by the shock of Jekyll's 'moral turpitude', puts restrictions on his disclosures, stipulating that if Utterson predeceases him the document which we eventually read should be 'destroyed unread'.

How near we came to not having the full facts of the case, from Lanyon or from Jekyll. As the latter observes in his final paragraph: 'if my narrative has hitherto escaped destruction, it has been by a combination of great prudence and great good luck'. But do we have the full facts? Lanyon recalls 'What [Jekyll] told me in the next hour, I cannot bring my mind to set on paper.' We have no way of knowing whether this actually corresponds with Jekyll's final confession. And even this encourages doubt. For if Utterson has spent the whole time attempting to hide or withhold information – 'can we venture to declare this suicide? O, we must be careful. I foresee that we may yet involve your master in some dire catastrophe' – why does he release these documents? Can we be sure they are presented unaltered or unedited? There appears to be a conflict of interests between content and form. The narrative attempts full revelation, the agents of its publication concealment. At the core of the text are silences, evasions, suppressions. Stevenson's tale is effective as horror fiction because it creates more questions than it answers. As a result it lives and grows in the imaginations of those who read and reread it over a hundred years after Dr Jekyll first concocted his potion.

Unreal City

Stevenson's tale put the modern city, and specifically London, firmly on the map of Gothic horror. In this it had an immediate influence on writers like Oscar Wilde, Arthur Conan Doyle and Arthur Machen, and is perhaps largely responsible for creating the late-Victorian

London of our cinematic imaginations; a foggy, gaslit labyrinth where Mr Hyde easily metamorphoses into Jack the Ripper, and Sherlock Holmes hails a hansom in pursuit of them both. There had been examples of 'Urban Gothic' fiction earlier in the century, when writers like Charles Dickens and the popular novelist G. W. M. Reynolds depicted scenes of crime and horror in the rookeries of outcast London in narratives as sprawling and labyrinthine as the districts which they haunt.[19] However, Stevenson's hundred pages, which draw on the imagery of these earlier writers, convey in a more intense and succinct form a cityscape transformed by what could be termed the psychological focus of the narrative. He was perhaps the first 'psychogeographer', laying the foundations of an imaginative topography that would be explored by writers from Arthur Machen to Iain Sinclair. Consider Stevenson's representation of a specific London locale, Soho:

It was by this time about nine in the morning, and the first fog of the season. A great chocolate-coloured pall lowered over heaven, but the wind was continually charging and routing these assembled vapours; so that as the cab crawled from street to street, Mr Utterson beheld a marvellous number of degrees and hues of twilight . . . The dismal quarter of Soho seen under these changing glimpses, with its muddy ways, and slatternly passengers, and its lamps, which had never been extinguished or had been kindled afresh to combat this mournful reinvasion of darkness, seemed, in the lawyer's eyes, like a district of some city in a nightmare. The thoughts on his mind, besides, were of the gloomiest dye . . .

As the cab drew up before the address indicated, the fog lifted a little and showed him a dingy street, a gin palace, a low French eating house, a shop for the retail of penny numbers and twopenny salads, many ragged children huddled in the doorways, and many women of many different nationalities passing out, key in hand, to have a morning glass; and the next moment the fog settled down again on that part, as brown as umber, and cut him off from his blackguardly surroundings. This was the home of Henry Jekyll's favourite; of a man who was heir to a quarter of a million sterling.

This passage (in both senses), invites comparison with the famous opening of Charles Dickens's consummate Urban Gothic novel, *Bleak House* (1853), where the whole of London is enveloped in fog, mud and mire. But whilst Dickens uses fog to comment on the obfuscation of political and legal procedure (a reflection of the muddled state of Britain at the time), Stevenson's use of a similar setting can be characterized as more directly 'psychological'. And whilst Dickens's description manages to convey a recognizable and identifiable London floating in his sea of fog, Stevenson's cityscape is conspicuous for its unreality. It is truly a district from a 'nightmare', no more real than the city figured in Utterson's earlier dream of a lamplit labyrinth crawling with murderous Hydes. The use of 'pall' to describe the fog manages to suggest both a theatrical scene, the lowering of a stage curtain, and (with its funeral associations) the metaphysical implication that 'heaven' and its influences are being blotted out as they descend into an infernal region. The descent into this abyss is for Utterson a confrontation with the heart of darkness that we later learn resides within Jekyll himself. For him location reinforces the supposed dichotomy between the 'blackguardly' Hyde, and the prosperous and respectable Jekyll; but in truth it provides an allegorical reflection of Jekyll's true relationship with Hyde. Soho was an enclave of poverty and criminality (which was by then principally associated with the East End), residing within the more salubrious Western end of London. It thus provides a suitable location for Hyde's dwelling, but also a geographical expression of the Hyde within Jekyll.

This 'allegorical' approach to London geography is typical of a text that specifies very few identifiable locations, and is reinforced by the description of Jekyll's own house:

Round the corner from the bystreet, there was a square of ancient, handsome houses, now for the most part decayed from their high estate and let in flats and chambers to all sorts and conditions of men: map-engravers, architects, shady lawyers and the agents of obscure enterprises. One house, however, second from the corner, was still occupied entire . . . [and] wore a great air of wealth and comfort . . .

In other words, this is the architectural equivalent of Jekyll's character and relationship with his fellow men. The other houses are fragmented, openly proclaiming that they are made up of many parts, and many conditions. Jekyll's, however, must 'wear' (with an emphasis on seeming and disguise) a great air of integrity as well as respectability. But, as we know, Jekyll has his back door, tucked away in obscurity and seemingly unconnected with his 'stately' official residence. Hyde's special door is the architectural equivalent of Jekyll's condition: he can only preserve his house 'entire' on the square because he has Hyde, his backdoor man, to do his dirty work for him. So landscape is transformed, serving allegorical and psychological more than strictly geographical purposes, and creating an Urban Gothic stageset for late-Victorian horror.

The return of Mr Hyde

Strange Case of Dr Jekyll and Mr Hyde was an enormous success for Stevenson. It sold 40,000 copies in six months in Britain alone, and appears to have been read by everyone including the prime minister and Queen Victoria herself. It struck a chord with the late-Victorian public, and very soon entered the collective imagination. *Punch* parodied it, preachers pontificated on it, and Oscar Wilde has Vivian in 'The Decay of Lying' (1889) recount an anecdote about an unfortunate individual who happens to be called Mr Hyde finding himself reproducing all the incidents of the first chapter of Stevenson's tale. This Hyde is horrified at what is happening, takes to his heels, and finally finds refuge from the child's family in a doctor's surgery: 'the name on the brass door-plate of the surgery caught his eye. It was "Jekyll". At least it should have been.'[20]

Stevenson's tale was also very influential on writers of imaginative and supernatural fiction. Wilde's own novel *The Picture of Dorian Gray* (1890–91) bears some points of resemblance. Also set in a foggy London, with excursions into low-life neighbourhoods, it too is about appearances and reputations, and involves an individual who lives a double life of outward purity and secret corruption. As Jekyll uses the ugly deformed Hyde as his body double, so Dorian Gray has a magic portrait that bears all the consequences of a sinful life. As Stevenson refused to specify what Jekyll's or Hyde's 'monstrous' crimes were, so Wilde keeps Dorian's sins similarly vague, allowing him to be surrounded by 'hideous' rumours that are never fully disclosed. Wilde describes a similar world of secrets, rumours and speculations:

Curious stories became current about him . . . It was rumoured that he had been seen brawling with foreign sailors in a low den in the distant parts of Whitechapel . . . His extraordinary absences became notorious, and, when he used to reappear again in society, men would whisper to each other in corners, or pass him with a sneer, or look at him with cold searching eyes, as though they were determined to discover his secret.[21]

As a character tells Dorian, 'Every gentleman is interested in his reputation' (p. 143), a circumstance that necessitates the supernatural stratagems employed by both Wilde's and Stevenson's characters.

But perhaps the main thing that both stories have in common, and where Stevenson's influence on horror fiction can be felt most, is the focus on the body and brain of the individual as the location for horror. Jekyll's metamorphosis into the grotesque, misshapen Hyde (who bears the physical 'stamp' of his evil impulses) finds its counterpart in the description of Dorian's portrait: 'Through some strange quickening of inner life the leprosies of sin were slowly eating the thing away. The rotting of a corpse in a watery grave was not so fearful' (p. 150). If the first generation of Gothic novelists located fictional terror in the forests and castles of Italy and Spain, then the tradition that developed after Stevenson betrayed a distinct physiological interest, demonstrating that the body and mind of individuals could provide horrors of their own, the site for unwelcome legacies and returns. Bram Stoker's five-hundred-year-old Count Dracula is, like Hyde, partly an atavistic 'criminal type', conspicuous for his grotesque features, who is also glimpsed through the collected testimonies of the lawyers and physicians who track him down. H. G. Wells's Doctor Moreau conducts experiments in accelerated evolution, attempting to extract the man out of beasts as Jekyll had released the beast out of a man (*The Island of Doctor Moreau* (1896)). Arthur Machen's *The Great God Pan* (1894) and *The Three Impostors* (1895), involve strange experiments, and fragmented testimonies recalling hideous bodily transformations, unspeakable sins and indescribable individuals. Jekyll, a pioneer in 'transcendental medicine', had prophesied that 'Others will follow, others will outstrip me on the same lines.' This turns out to be true, for Machen's own Dr Raymond in *The Great God Pan*, also described as a practitioner in 'transcendental medicine', uses surgery on a certain group of nerve-cells in the brain to explore 'the unknowable gulf that yawns profound between two worlds, the world of matter and the world of spirit',[22] and releases from these experiments primitive horrors far exceeding Stevenson's in their grotesque hyperbole. After Stevenson, horror fiction repeatedly explored these worlds, devising fanciful, but still plausible, pseudo-scientific theories about the horrors that lurked within seemingly ordinary individuals, in their bodies, brains or memories. This domain has proven to be extremely fertile; from H. P. Lovecraft to *Psycho*, *Nightmare on Elm Street* and *The Silence of the Lambs*, versions of Mr Hyde have leaped forth from the pages and screens of the horror industry.

Notes

1. Stevenson, letter to F. W. H. Myers, 1 March 1886, in *Collected Letters*, vol. 5, edited by Bradford A. Booth and Ernest Mehew (1995), p. 216. Byles stands for a generic creditor, and was not actually the name of his butcher.

2. Victor Sage, *Horror Fiction in the Protestant Tradition* (1988), p. 8.

3. Baldick, 'Introduction' to *The Oxford Book of Gothic Tales* (1993), p. xx.

4. She is 'atavistic' in as far as her character and condition appear to derive from her distant ancestors (*atavus* means ancestor), and therefore like a vampire she, or her ancestors, has lived and died many times. There is an echo here of Walter Pater's famous description of Da Vinci's 'La Gioconda' (known as the Mona Lisa), which offered a template for prose stylists and a model for femmes fatales at the end of the nineteenth century: 'She is older than the rocks among which she sits; like the vampire, she has been dead many times, and learned the secrets of the grave; and been a diver in deep seas, and keeps their fallen day about her . . . ; and as Leda, was the mother of Helen of Troy, and, as Saint Anne, the mother of Mary; and all this has been to her but as the sound of lyres and flutes, and lives only in the delicacy with which it has moulded the changing lineaments, and tinged the eyelids and the hands', Pater, from *Studies in the History of the Renaissance* (1873). Bram Stoker would make an explicit connection between the extended life of the supernatural vampire (a Victorian embellishment of the folkloric original who had only lasted a few days in his or her Undead state) and the theory of biological atavism when he suggests that Count Dracula might be considered analogous to Lombroso's atavistic criminal types. On Stoker's possible debt to Stevenson's tale see the Notes to 'Olalla'.

5. Rictor Norton, 'A (longish) pre-Victorian digression on blackmail', posted to the Victoria Web (http://www.listserv.indiana.edu) (March 1998).

6. This statute was an amendment to an Act 'to make further provision for the Protection of Women and Girls, the suppression of brothels and other purposes'. The principal aim of the Act was to protect young girls from the exploitation of brothel-keepers who ran a trade in virgins, by raising the age of consent from thirteen to sixteen years. Section II, however, dealt with intimate acts between male persons, a more precise and comprehensive legal proscription of homosexual activities than had hitherto been implemented. The Act outlawed any and all 'acts of gross indecency with another male person', whether in public or in private, and carried a maximum penalty of two years imprisonment with hard labour, Wilde's own sentence.

7. For a more detailed discussion of the aura of homosexuality that pervades Stevenson's tale see William Veeder, 'Children of the Night: Stevenson and Patriarchy', in Hirsch and Veeder (1988), pp. 107–60.

8. A comment by Gerard Manley Hopkins shows that Stevenson's 'coded' or suggestive plotting had some success; as he observes to Robert Bridges: 'The trampling scene is perhaps a convention: he was talking of something unsuitable for fiction', reproduced in *Robert Louis Stevenson: The Critical Heritage*, edited by Paul Maixner (1981), p. 229.

9. The following opening to one of Krafft-Ebing's cases (of sadism) is typical in this respect: 'Case 24. Mr. X., aged 25; father syphilitic, died of paretic dementia; mother hysterical and neurasthenic. He is a weak individual, constitutionally neuropathic, and presents several anatomical signs of degeneration', *Psychopathia Sexualis* (1886; 1892), 71. Hyde's own case, if it were written up, might very well resemble this, demonstrating 'the connection between lust and cruelty'. Hyde the sadist is discussed in 'Diagnosing Jekyll' in the present volume.

10. Maixner (1981), pp. 204, 223, 224.

11. Booth and Mehew (1995), pp. 212–13. On Stevenson's religious upbringing see J. C. Furnas's biography, *Voyage to Windward: The Life of Robert Louis Stevenson* (1952), pp. 28–33. For its influence on *Jekyll and Hyde* and the anecdote about the sermon, see Christopher Frayling, *Nightmare: The Birth of Horror* (1996), pp. 125–9.

12. Henry Maudsley, 'Remarks on Crime and Criminals', *Journal of Mental Science* (1888), pp. 34, 162.

13. That Stevenson subscribed to evolutionary tenets, and that these contributed to his depiction of Jekyll's relation to Hyde is suggested by an essay he published in 1887 called 'The Manse'. Here he wonders whether it is 'more strange, that I should carry about with me some fibres of my minister-grandfather; or that in him, as he sat there in his cool study, grave, reverend, contented gentleman, there was an aboriginal frisking of the blood that was not his; tree-top memories, like undeveloped negatives, lay dormant in his mind; tree-top instincts awoke and were trod down; and Probably Arboreal [Darwin's term for humankind's ape ancestor] (scarce to be distinguished from a monkey) gambolled and chattered in the brain of the old divine', *Memoirs and Portraits*, in vol. IX, *Works*, edited by Andrew Lang (1912), p. 67. Jekyll is another such 'grave' gentleman, who lets his ape out.

14. In Gina Lombroso-Ferrero, *Criminal Man According to the Classifications of Cesare Lombroso* (1911), p. xxv.

15. A similar emphasis is found in one of the most original readings of *Jekyll and Hyde* for a good many years, Stephen Arata's chapter on Stevenson in *Fictions of Loss in the Victorian 'Fin de Siècle'* (1996). His excellent close reading of the text suggests that Hyde is educated into bourgeois codes through the course of the narrative, growing into Jekyll's respectable clothes as he overcomes his personality.

16. One of Stevenson's first readers also found these circumstances suspicious or puzzling. Frederick W. H. Myers, who sent him a long list of queries and ways in which Stevenson could improve the tale (none of which he carried out), pointed out the 'Ambiguity as to house where maid was. Was it in Westminster? How did Baronet need to ask way to post so close to Parliament or to his own house? If house in a low district how did Baronet come there?', in Maixner (1981), p. 215.

17. Following the Carew murder we learn that it does: 'tales came out of the man's cruelty, at once so callous and violent, of his vile life, of his strange associates, of the hatred that seemed to have surrounded his career'.

18. On the forms and motivations of blackmail narratives see Alexander Welsh's excellent introductory chapters to *George Eliot and Blackmail* (1985).

19. Dickens's 'Urban Gothic' episodes can be found principally in *Oliver Twist*, *Bleak House*, and parts of *Little Dorrit* and *Our Mutual Friend*. G. W. M. Reynolds's *Mysteries of London*, and its sequel *Mysteries of the Court of London* (1844–56) were extremely popular series depicting a city as mysterious and terrifying as any forest or mountain of the earlier Gothic mode.

20. Oscar Wilde, 'The Decay of Lying', in *The Soul of Man Under Socialism and Other Critical Writings*, edited by Linda Dowling (Penguin, Harmondsworth, 2001), p. 82.

21. Oscar Wilde, *The Picture of Dorian Gray*, edited by Robert Mighall (Penguin, Harmondsworth, 2000), p. 136.

22. Arthur Machen, *The Great God Pan* (1895; 1993), p. 27.

FURTHER READING

Works

The Annotated Dr Jekyll and Mr Hyde, edited by Richard Dury (Guerini, Milan, 1993)

'A Chapter on Dreams', *Scribner's Magazine* (January 1888)

'The Manse', in *Works*, IX edited by Andrew Lang (Chatto & Windus, London, 1912)

Biography and letters

Aldington, Richard, *Portrait of a Rebel: The Life and Works of Robert Louis Stevenson* (Evans, London, 1957)

Balfour, Graham, *The Life of Robert Louis Stevenson*, sixth edn (Methuen, London, 1911)

Booth, Bradford A., and Mehew, Ernest (eds.), *The Letters of Robert Louis Stevenson*, vol. 5 (Yale University Press, New Haven and London, 1995)

Furnas, J. C., *Voyage to Windward: The Life of Robert Louis Stevenson* (Faber and Faber, London, 1952)

Criticism

Arata, Stephen D., *Fictions of Loss in the Victorian 'Fin de Siècle'* (Cambridge University Press, Cambridge, 1996)

Baldick, Chris, *In Frankenstein's Shadow: Myth, Monstrosity and Nineteenth-Century Writing* (Oxford University Press, Oxford, 1987)

Block, Ed, Jnr, 'James Sully, Evolutionary Psychology, and Late Victorian Gothic Fiction', *Victorian Studies*, 25 (1982), pp. 443–67.

Dury, Richard, 'Stevenson's *Strange Case of Dr Jekyll and Mr Hyde*: Textual Variants', *Notes and Queries* (Dec. 1993), vol. 40, pp. 490–92

Eigner, Edwin, *Robert Louis Stevenson and the Romantic Tradition* (Princeton University Press, Princeton NJ, 1966)

Frayling, Christopher, *Nightmare: The Birth of Horror* (BBC Books, London, 1996)

Heath, Stephen, 'Psychopathia Sexualis: Stevenson's *Strange Case*', *Critical Quarterly*, 28 (1986), pp. 93–108

Hirsch, Gordon and Veeder, William, *Dr Jekyll and Mr Hyde After One Hundred Years* (Chicago University Press, Chicago, 1986)

Maixner, Paul, *Robert Louis Stevenson: The Critical Heritage* (Routledge and Kegan Paul, London, 1981)

Swearingen, Roger G., *The Prose Writings of Robert Louis Stevenson: A Guide* (Macmillan, Basingstoke, 1980)

Background

Bailey, Brian, *The Resurrection Men: A History of the Trade in Corpses* (Macmillan & Co., London, 1991)

Baldick, Chris (ed.), *The Oxford Book of Gothic Tales* (Oxford University Press, Oxford, 1993)

Byron, Glennis and Punter, David, *Spectral Readings: Towards a Gothic Geography* (Macmillan, Basingstoke, 1999)

Cameron, Deborah, and Frazer, Elizabeth, *The Lust to Kill: A Feminist Investigation of Sexual Murder* (New York University Press, New York, 1987)

Doyle, Arthur Conan, *The Hound of the Baskervilles*, edited by Christopher Frayling (Penguin, Harmondsworth, 2001)

Evans, Stewart P. and Skinner, Keith, *The Ultimate Jack the Ripper Sourcebook: An Illustrated Encyclopaedia* (Constable & Robinson, London, 2000)

Galton, Francis, *Inquiries into Human Faculty*, 2nd edn (Dent, London, 1906)

Huysmans, Joris Karl, *Against Nature*, translated by Robert Baldick (1884; Penguin, Harmondsworth, 1959)

Krafft-Ebing, Richard Von, *Psychopathia Sexualis. With Especial Reference to the Antipathic Sexual Instinct: A Medico-Legal Study*, 1st English edn (1886; F. A. Davis and Co., Philadelphia, 1892)

Lombroso-Ferrero, Gina, *Criminal Man According to the Classification of Cesare Lombroso* (G. P. Putnams' Sons, New York, 1911)

Machen, Arthur, *The Great God Pan* (1895; Creation Press, London, 1993)

Maudsley, Henry, *Responsibility in Mental Disease* (Henry S. King, London, 1874)

— *Body and Mind: An Inquiry into Their Connection and Mutual Influence, Specially in Reference to Mental Disorders . . .* 2nd edn (Macmillan & Co., London, 1873)

— 'Remarks on Crime and Criminals', *Journal of Mental Science*, 34 (1888), pp. 159–67

— *Pathology of Mind*, 3rd edn (Macmillan & Co., London, 1895)

McIntosh, W. C., *On Morbid Impulse* (J. E. Adland, London, 1863)

Mighall, Robert, *A Geography of Victorian Gothic Fiction: Mapping History's Nightmares* (Oxford University Press, Oxford, 1999)

Myers, Fredrick W. H., 'Multiplex Personality', *Nineteenth Century*, 20 (1886)

Nisbet, J. F., *Marriage and Heredity: A View of Psychological Evolution* (Ward & Downey, London, 1889)

Otis, Laura, *Organic Memory: History and the Body in the Late Nineteenth and Early Twentieth Centuries* (Nebraska University Press, Lincoln, 1994)

Prichard, James Cowles, *A Treatise on Insanity and Other Disorders Affecting the Mind* (Sherwood & Piper, London, 1835)

Rae, Isobel, *Knox the Anatomist* (Oliver & Boyd, London and Edinburgh, 1964)

Ribot, Theodule, *Diseases of Memory: An Essay in Positive Psychology* (Kegan Paul, Trench & Co., London, 1882)

Richardson, Ruth, *Death, Disease and the Destitute* (Routledge and Kegan Paul, London, 1987)

Rumbelow, Donald, *The Complete Jack the Ripper* (Penguin, Harmondsworth, 1988)

Sage, Victor, *Horror Fiction in the Protestant Tradition* (Macmillan, Basingstoke, 1988)

Spitzka, Edward Charles, 'Cases of Masturbation (Masturbatic Insanity)', *Journal of Mental Science*, 34 (1888), pp. 52–61

— 'The Whitechapel Murders: Their Medico-Legal and Historical Aspects', *Journal of Nervous and Mental Disease*, 13 (1888), pp. 765–78

Stoker, Bram, *Dracula*, edited by Maurice Hindle (1897; Penguin, Harmondsworth, 1993)

Tissot, Samuel, *A Treatise on the Diseases Produced by Onanism* (1760; Collins & Hannay, New York, 1832)

Tomaslli, Sylvia, and Porter, Roy (eds.), *Rape* (Basil Blackwell, Oxford, 1986)

Tuke, Daniel Hack, 'Case of Moral Insanity, or Congenital Moral Defect. With Commentary', *Journal of Mental Science*, 31 (1885), pp. 360–66

Welsh, Alexander, *George Eliot and Blackmail* (Harvard University Press, Cambridge MA, 1985)

Wilde, Oscar, *The Picture of Dorian Gray*, edited by Robert Mighall (Penguin, Harmondsworth, 2000)

— *The Soul of Man Under Socialism and Other Critical Writings*, edited by Linda Dowling (Penguin, Harmondsworth, 2001)

A NOTE ON THE TEXTS

The text of *Strange Case of Dr Jekyll and Mr Hyde* (as it was first entitled) reproduced here is based upon the first edition published by Longmans, Green and Co. on 9 January 1886; the US edition was published on 5 January by Scribners' Sons from the Longmans' plates. There are many accounts of the conception and revision of this tale, and the history of its composition has attained something of a mythical status. I will not comment on it here, but direct interested readers to Stevenson's own account of the conception of his story 'A Chapter on Dreams' (abridged in this volume). A full account of the various revisions Stevenson made to the texts, based upon the known surviving fragments of earlier drafts, and transcriptions of those drafts is very usefully provided by William Veeder in Gordon Hirsch and William Veeder (eds.), *Dr Jekyll and Mr Hyde After One Hundred Years* (1986), pp. 3–56. Richard Dury supplements this with his 'Stevenson's *Dr Jekyll and Mr Hyde*: Textual Variants', in *Notes and Queries*, 40 (1993), pp. 490–92. Christopher Frayling offers a very useful, balanced and sceptical overview of the various accounts of the tale's composition in his chapter on Stevenson in *Nightmare: The Birth of Horror* (1996), pp. 114–16. I have retained Stevenson's varying uses of Dr and Doctor but, to conform to Penguin house style, I have silently modernized a few spellings.

'The Body Snatcher' was published as a 'Christmas Extra' of the *Pall Mall Gazette* for 1884, and is reproduced here from that version. 'Olalla' first appeared in the *Court and Society Review* for Christmas 1885, and was written while Stevenson was working on the proofs of *Jekyll and Hyde*. It was later reproduced in *The Merry Men and Other Tales and Fables* (Chatto & Windus, London, 1887), upon which the current text is based.

STRANGE CASE OF
DR JEKYLL AND MR HYDE

TO

KATHARINE DE MATTOS[1]

It's ill to loose the bands that God decreed to bind;
Still will we be the children of the heather and the wind.
Far away from home, O it's still for you and me
That the broom is blowing bonnie in the north countrie.

Contents

Strange Case of
Dr Jekyll and Mr Hyde

STORY OF THE DOOR

Mr Utterson the lawyer was a man of a rugged countenance, that was never lighted by a smile; cold, scanty and embarrassed in discourse; backward in sentiment; lean, long, dusty, dreary and yet somehow lovable. At friendly meetings, and when the wine was to his taste, something eminently human beaconed from his eye; something indeed which never found its way into his talk, but which spoke not only in these silent symbols of the after-dinner face, but more often and loudly in the acts of his life. He was austere with himself; drank gin when he was alone, to mortify a taste for vintages; and though he enjoyed the theatre, had not crossed the doors of one for twenty years. But he had an approved tolerance for others; sometimes wondering, almost with envy, at the high pressure of spirits involved in their misdeeds; and in any extremity inclined to help rather than to reprove. 'I incline to Cain's heresy,'¹ he used to say quaintly: 'I let my brother go to the devil in his own way.' In this character, it was frequently his fortune to be the last reputable acquaintance and the last good influence in the lives of down-going men. And to such as these, so long as they came about his chambers, he never marked a shade of change in his demeanour.

No doubt the feat was easy to Mr Utterson; for he was undemonstrative at the best, and even his friendships seemed to be founded in a similar catholicity of good-nature. It is the mark of a modest man to accept his friendly circle ready-made from the hands of opportunity; and that was the lawyer's way. His friends were those of his own blood or those whom he had known the longest; his affections, like ivy, were the growth of time, they implied no aptness in the object. Hence, no doubt, the bond that united him to Mr Richard Enfield, his distant kinsman, the well-known man about town. It was a nut to crack for many, what these two could see in each other or what subject they could find in common.[2] It was reported by those who encountered them in their Sunday walks, that they said nothing, looked singularly dull, and would hail with obvious relief the appearance of a friend. For all that, the two men put the greatest store by these excursions, counted them the chief jewel of each week, and not only set aside occasions of pleasure, but even resisted the calls of business, that they might enjoy them uninterrupted.

It chanced on one of these rambles that their way led them down a bystreet in a busy quarter of London. The street was small and what is called quiet, but it drove a thriving trade on the weekdays. The inhabitants were all doing well, it seemed, and all emulously hoping to do better still, and laying out the surplus of their gains in coquetry; so that the shop fronts stood along that thoroughfare with an air of invitation, like rows of smiling saleswomen. Even on Sunday, when it veiled its more florid charms and lay comparatively empty of passage, the street shone out in contrast to its dingy neighbourhood, like a fire in a forest; and with its freshly painted shutters, well-polished brasses, and general cleanliness and gaiety of note, instantly caught and pleased the eye of the passenger.

Two doors from one corner, on the left hand going east, the line was broken by the entry of a court; and just at that point, a certain sinister block of building thrust forward its gable on the street. It was two storeys high; showed no window, nothing but a door on the lower storey and a blind forehead of discoloured wall on the upper; and bore in every feature, the marks of prolonged and sordid negligence. The door which was equipped with neither bell nor knocker, was blistered and distained. Tramps slouched into the recess and struck matches on the panels; children kept shop upon the steps; the schoolboy had tried his knife on the mouldings; and for close on a generation, no one had appeared to drive away these random visitors or to repair their ravages.

Mr Enfield and the lawyer were on the other side of the bystreet; but when they came abreast of the entry, the former lifted up his cane and pointed.

'Did you ever remark that door?' he asked; and when his companion had replied in the affirmative, 'it is connected in my mind,' added he, 'with a very odd story.'

'Indeed?' said Mr Utterson, with a slight change of voice, 'and what was that?'

'Well, it was this way,' returned Mr Enfield: 'I was coming home from some place at the end of the world, about three o'clock of a black winter morning, and my way lay through a part of town where there was literally nothing to be seen but lamps. Street after street, and all the folks asleep – street after street, all lighted up as if for a procession and all as empty as a church – till at last I got into that state of mind when a man listens and listens and begins to long for the sight of a policeman. All at once, I saw two figures: one a little man who was stumping along eastward at a good walk, and the other a girl of maybe eight or ten who was running as hard as she was able down a cross street. Well, sir, the two ran into one another naturally enough at the corner; and then came the horrible part of the thing; for the man trampled calmly over the child's body and left her screaming on the ground. It sounds nothing to hear, but it was hellish to see. It wasn't like a man; it was like some damned Juggernaut.[3] I gave a view halloa, took to my heels, collared my gentleman, and brought him back to where there was already quite a group about the screaming child. He was perfectly cool and made no resistance, but gave me one look, so ugly that it brought out the sweat on me like running. The people who had turned out were the girl's own family; and pretty soon, the doctor, for whom she had been sent, put in his appearance. Well, the child was not much the worse, more frightened, according to the Sawbones;[4] and there you might have supposed would be an end to it. But there was one curious circumstance. I had taken a loathing to my gentleman at first sight. So had the child's family, which was only natural. But the doctor's case was what struck me. He was the usual cut and dry apothecary, of no particular age and colour, with a strong Edinburgh accent, and about as emotional as a bagpipe. Well, sir, he was like the

7

rest of us; every time he looked at my prisoner, I saw that Sawbones turn sick and white with the desire to kill him. I knew what was in his mind, just as he knew what was in mine; and killing being out of the question, we did the next best. We told the man we could and would make such a scandal out of this, as should make his name stink from one end of London to the other. If he had any friends or any credit, we undertook that he should lose them. And all the time, as we were pitching it in red hot, we were keeping the women off him as best we could, for they were as wild as harpies.[5] I never saw a circle of such hateful faces; and there was the man in the middle, with a kind of black, sneering coolness – frightened too, I could see that – but carrying it off, sir, really like Satan. "If you choose to make capital out of this accident," said he, "I am naturally helpless. No gentleman but wishes to avoid a scene," says he. "Name your figure." Well, we screwed him up to a hundred pounds for the child's family; he would have clearly liked to stick out; but there was something about the lot of us that meant mischief, and at last he struck. The next thing was to get the money; and where do you think he carried us but to that place with the door? – whipped out a key, went in, and presently came back with the matter of ten pounds in gold and a cheque for the balance on Coutts's,[6] drawn payable to bearer and signed with a name that I can't mention, though it's one of the points of my story, but it was a name at least very well known and often printed. The figure was stiff; but the signature was good for more than that, if it was only genuine. I took the liberty of pointing out to my gentleman that the whole business looked apocryphal,[7] and that a man does not, in real life, walk into a cellar door at four in the morning and come out of it with another man's cheque for close upon a hundred pounds. But he was quite easy and sneering. "Set your mind at rest," says he, "I will stay with you till the banks open and cash the cheque myself." So we all set off, the doctor, and the child's father, and our friend and myself, and passed the rest of the night in my chambers; the next day, when we had breakfasted, went in a body to the bank. I gave in the cheque myself, and said I had every reason to believe it was a forgery. Not a bit of it. The cheque was genuine.'

'Tut-tut,' said Mr Utterson.

'I see you feel as I do,' said Mr Enfield. 'Yes, it's a bad story. For my man was a fellow that nobody could have to do with, a really damnable man; and the person that drew the cheque is the very pink of the proprieties, celebrated too, and (what makes it worse) one of your fellows who do what they call good.[8] Blackmail, I suppose; an honest man paying through the nose for some of the capers of his youth. Blackmail House is what I call that place with the door, in consequence. Though even that, you know, is far from explaining all,' he added, and with the words fell into a vein of musing.

From this he was recalled by Mr Utterson asking rather suddenly: 'And you don't know if the drawer of the cheque lives there?'

'A likely place isn't it?' returned Mr Enfield. 'But I happen to have noticed his address; he lives in some square or other.'

'And you never asked about – the place with the door?' said Mr Utterson.

'No, sir: I had a delicacy,' was the reply. 'I feel very strongly about putting questions; it partakes too much of the style of the day of judgment. You start a question, and it's like starting a stone. You sit quietly on the top of a hill; and away the stones goes, starting others; and presently some bland old bird (the last you would have thought of) is knocked on the head in his own back garden and the family have to change their name. No, sir, I make it a rule of mine: the more it looks like Queer Street,[9] the less I ask.'

'A very good rule, too,' said the lawyer.

'But I have studied the place for myself,' continued Mr Enfield. 'It seems scarcely a house. There is no other door, and nobody goes in or out of that one but, once in a great while, the gentleman of my adventure. There are three windows looking on the court on the first floor; none below; the windows are always shut but they're clean. And then there is a chimney which is generally smoking; so somebody must live there. And yet it's not so sure; for the buildings are so packed together about that court, that it's hard to say where one ends and another begins.'

The pair walked on again for a while in silence; and then 'Enfield,' said Mr Utterson, 'that's a good rule of yours.'

'Yes, I think it is,' returned Enfield.

'And for all that,' continued the lawyer, 'there's one point I want to ask: I want to ask the name of that man who walked over the child.'

'Well,' said Mr Enfield, 'I can't see what harm it would do. It was a man of the name of Hyde.'

'Hm,' said Mr Utterson. 'What sort of a man is he to see?'

'He is not easy to describe. There is something wrong with his appearance; something displeasing, something downright detestable. I never saw a man I so disliked, and yet I scarce know why. He must be deformed somewhere; he gives a strong feeling of deformity, although I couldn't specify the point. He's an extraordinary-looking man, and yet I really can name nothing out of the way. No, sir; I can make no hand of it; I can't describe him. And it's not want of memory; for I declare I can see him this moment.'

Mr Utterson again walked some way in silence and obviously under a weight of consideration. 'You are sure he used a key?' he inquired at last.

'My dear sir . . .' began Enfield, surprised out of himself.

'Yes, I know,' said Utterson; 'I know it must seem strange. The fact is, if I do not ask you the name of the other party, it is because I know it already. You see, Richard, your tale has gone home. If you have been inexact in my point, you had better correct it.'

'I think you might have warned me,' returned the other with a touch of sullenness. 'But I have been pedantically exact, as you call it. The fellow had a key; and what's more, he has it still. I saw him use it, not a week ago.'

Mr Utterson sighed deeply but said never a word; and the young man presently resumed. 'Here is another lesson to say nothing,' said he. 'I am ashamed of my long tongue. Let us make a bargain never to refer to this again.'

'With all my heart,' said the lawyer. 'I shake hands on that, Richard.'

That evening, Mr Utterson came home to his bachelor house in sombre spirits and sat down to dinner without relish. It was his custom of a Sunday, when this meal was over, to sit close by the fire, a volume of some dry divinity on his reading desk, until the clock of the neighbouring church rang out the hour of twelve, when he would go soberly and gratefully to bed. On this night, however, as soon as the cloth was taken away, he took up a candle and went into his business room. There he opened his safe, took from the most private part of it a document endorsed on the envelope as Dr Jekyll's Will, and sat down with a clouded brow to study its contents. The will was holograph, for Mr Utterson, though he took charge of it now that it was made, had refused to lend the least assistance in the making of it; it provided not only that, in case of the decease of Henry Jekyll, MD, DCL, LLD, FRS, &c.,[1] all his possessions were to pass into the hands of his 'friend and benefactor Edward Hyde', but that in case of Dr Jekyll's 'disappearance or unexplained absence for any period exceeding three calendar months', the said Edward Hyde should step into the said Henry Jekyll's shoes without further delay and free from any burden or obligation, beyond the payment of a few small sums to the members of the doctor's household. This document had long been the lawyer's eyesore. It offended him both as a lawyer and as a lover of the sane and customary sides of life, to whom the fanciful was the immodest. And hitherto it was his ignorance of Mr Hyde that had swelled his indignation; now, by a sudden turn, it was his knowledge. It was already bad enough when the name was but a name of which he could learn no more. It was worse when it began to be clothed upon with detestable attributes; and out of the shifting, insubstantial mists that had so long baffled his eye, there leaped up the sudden, definite presentment of a fiend.

'I thought it was madness,' he said, as he replaced the obnoxious paper in the safe, 'and now I begin to fear it is disgrace.'

With that he blew out his candle, put on a great coat and set forth in the direction of Cavendish Square,[2] that citadel of medicine, where his friend, the great Dr Lanyon, had his house and received his crowding patients. 'If anyone knows, it will be Lanyon,' he had thought.

The solemn butler knew and welcomed him; he was subjected to no stage of delay, but ushered direct from the door to the dining room where Dr Lanyon sat alone over his wine. This was a hearty, healthy, dapper, red-faced gentleman, with a shock of hair prematurely white, and a boisterous and decided manner. At sight of Mr Utterson, he sprang up from his chair and welcomed him with both hands. The geniality, as was the way of the man, was somewhat theatrical to the eye; but it reposed on genuine feeling. For these two were old friends, old mates both at school and college, both thorough respecters of themselves and of each other, and, what does not always follow, men who thoroughly enjoyed each other's company.

After a little rambling talk, the lawyer led up to the subject which so disagreeably preoccupied his mind.

'I suppose, Lanyon,' said he, 'you and I must be the two oldest friends that Henry Jekyll has?'

'I wish the friends were younger,' chuckled Dr Lanyon. 'But I suppose we are. And what of that? I see little of him now.'

'Indeed?' said Utterson. 'I thought you had a bond of common interest.'

'We had,' was the reply. 'But it is more than ten years since Henry Jekyll became too fanciful for me. He began to go wrong, wrong in mind; and though of course I continue to take an interest in him for old sake's sake as they say, I see and I have seen devilish little of the man. Such unscientific balderdash,' added the doctor, flushing suddenly purple, 'would have estranged Damon and Pythias.'[3]

This little spirt of temper was somewhat of a relief to Mr Utterson. 'They have only differed on some point of science,' he thought; and being a man of no scientific passions (except in the matter of conveyancing) he even added: 'It is nothing worse than that!' He gave his friend a few seconds to recover his composure, and then approached the question he had come to put. 'Did you ever come across a protégé of his – one Hyde?' he asked.

'Hyde?' repeated Lanyon. 'No. Never heard of him. Since my time.'

That was the amount of information that the lawyer carried back with him to the great, dark bed on which he tossed to and fro, until the small hours of the morning began to grow large. It was a night of little ease to his toiling mind, toiling in mere darkness and besieged by questions.

Six o'clock struck on the bells of the church that was so conveniently near to Mr Utterson's dwelling, and still he was digging at the problem. Hitherto it had touched him on the intellectual side alone; but now his imagination also was engaged or rather enslaved; and as he lay and tossed in the gross darkness of the night and the curtained room, Mr Enfield's tale went by before his mind in a scroll of lighted pictures. He would be aware of the great field of lamps of a nocturnal city; then of the figure of a man walking swiftly; then of a child running from the doctor's; and then these met, and that human Juggernaut trod the child down and passed on regardless of her screams. Or else he would see a room in a rich house, where his friend lay asleep, dreaming and smiling at his dreams; and then the door of that room would be opened, the curtains of the bed plucked apart, the sleeper recalled, and lo! there would stand by his side a figure to whom power was given, and even at that dead hour, he must rise and do its bidding. The figure in these two phases haunted the lawyer all night; and if at any time he dozed over, it was but to see it glide more stealthily through sleeping houses, or move the more swiftly and still the more swiftly, even to dizziness, through wider labyrinths⁴ of lamplighted city, and at every street corner crush a child and leave her screaming. And still the figure had no face by which he might know it; even in his dreams, it had no face, or one that baffled him and melted before his eyes; and thus it was that there sprang up and grew apace in the lawyer's mind a singularly strong, almost an inordinate, curiosity to behold the features of the real Mr Hyde. If he could but once set eyes on him, he thought the mystery would lighten and perhaps roll altogether away,⁵ as was the habit of mysterious things when well examined. He might see a reason for his friend's strange preference or bondage (call it which you please) and even for the startling clauses of the will. And at least it would be a face worth seeing: the face of a man who was without bowels of mercy: a face which had but to show itself to raise up, in the mind of the unimpressionable Enfield, a spirit of enduring hatred.

From that time forward, Mr Utterson began to haunt the door in the bystreet of shops. In the morning before office hours, at noon when business was plenty and time scarce, at night under the face of the fogged city moon, by all lights and at all hours of solitude or concourse, the lawyer was to be found on his chosen post.

'If he be Mr Hyde,' he had thought, 'I shall be Mr Seek.'

And at last his patience was rewarded. It was a fine dry night; frost in the air; the streets as clean as a ballroom floor; the lamps, unshaken by any wind, drawing a regular pattern of light and shadow. By ten o'clock, when the shops were closed, the bystreet was very solitary and, in spite of the low growl of London from all round, very silent. Small sounds carried far; domestic sounds out of the houses were clearly audible on either side of the roadway; and the rumour of the approach of any passenger preceded him by a long time. Mr Utterson had been some minutes at his post, when he was aware of an odd, light footstep drawing near. In the course of his nightly patrols, he had long grown accustomed to the quaint effect with which the footfalls of a single person, while he is still a great way off, suddenly spring out distinct from the vast hum and clatter of the city. Yet his attention had never before been so sharply and decisively arrested; and it was with a strong, superstitious prevision of success that he withdrew into the entry of the court.

The steps drew swiftly nearer, and swelled out suddenly louder as they turned the end of the street. The lawyer, looking forth from the entry, could soon see what manner of man he had to deal with. He was small and very plainly dressed, and the look of him, even at that distance, went somehow strongly against the watcher's inclination. But he made straight for the door, crossing the roadway to save time; and as he came, he drew a key from his pocket like one approaching home.

Mr Utterson stepped out and touched him on the shoulder as he passed. 'Mr Hyde, I think?'

Mr Hyde shrank back with a hissing intake of the breath. But his fear was only momentary; and though he did not look the lawyer in the face, he answered coolly enough: 'That is my name. What do you want?'

'I see you are going in,' returned the lawyer. 'I am an old friend of Dr Jekyll's – Mr Utterson of Gaunt Street[6] – you must have heard my name; and meeting you so conveniently, I thought you might admit me.'

'You will not find Dr Jekyll; he is from home,' replied Mr Hyde, blowing in the key. And then suddenly, but still without looking up, 'How did you know me?' he asked.

'On your side,' said Mr Utterson, 'will you do me a favour?'

'With pleasure,' replied the other. 'What shall it be?'

'Will you let me see your face?' asked the lawyer.

Mr Hyde appeared to hesitate, and then, as if upon some sudden reflection, fronted about with an air of defiance; and the pair stared at each other pretty fixedly for a few seconds. 'Now I shall know you again,' said Mr Utterson. 'It may be useful.'

'Yes,' returned Mr Hyde, 'it is as well we have met; and à propos, you should have my address.' And he gave a number of a street in Soho.

'Good God!' thought Mr Utterson, 'can he too have been thinking of the will?' But he kept his feelings to himself and only grunted in acknowledgement of the address.

'And now,' said the other, 'how did you know me?'

'By description,' was the reply.

'Whose description?'

'We have common friends,' said Mr Utterson.

'Common friends?' echoed Mr Hyde, a little hoarsely. 'Who are they?'

'Jekyll, for instance,' said the lawyer.

'He never told you,' cried Mr Hyde, with a flush of anger. 'I did not think you would have lied.'

'Come,' said Mr Utterson, 'that is not fitting language.'

The other snarled aloud into a savage laugh; and the next moment, with extraordinary quickness, he had unlocked the door and disappeared into the house.

The lawyer stood awhile when Mr Hyde had left him, the picture of disquietude. Then he began slowly to mount the street, pausing every step or two and putting his hand to his brow like a man in mental perplexity. The problem he was thus debating as he walked, was one of a class that is rarely solved. Mr Hyde was pale and dwarfish, he gave an impression of deformity without any nameable malformation,[7] he had a displeasing smile, he had borne himself to the lawyer with a sort of murderous mixture of timidity and boldness, and he spoke with a husky, whispering and somewhat broken voice; all these were points against him, but not all of these together could explain the hitherto unknown disgust, loathing and fear with which Mr Utterson regarded him. 'There must be something else,' said the perplexed gentleman. 'There *is* something more, if I could find a name for it. God bless me, the man seems hardly human! Something troglodytic,[8] shall we say? or can it be the old story of Dr Fell?[9] or is it the mere radiance of a foul soul that thus transpires through, and transfigures, its clay continent? The last, I think; for O my poor old Harry Jekyll, if ever I read Satan's signature upon a face, it is on that of your new friend.'

Round the corner from the bystreet, there was a square of ancient, handsome houses, now for the most part decayed from their high estate and let in flats and chambers to all sorts and conditions of men: map-engravers, architects, shady lawyers and the agents of obscure enterprises. One house, however, second from the corner, was still occupied entire; and at the door of this, which wore a great air of wealth and comfort, though it was now plunged in darkness except for the fan-light, Mr Utterson stopped and knocked. A well-dressed, elderly servant opened the door.

'Is Dr Jekyll at home, Poole?' asked the lawyer.

'I will see, Mr Utterson,' said Poole, admitting the visitor, as he spoke, into a large, low-roofed, comfortable hall, paved with flags, warmed (after the fashion of a country house) by a bright, open fire, and furnished with costly cabinets of oak. 'Will you wait here by the fire, sir? or shall I give you a light in the dining room?'

'Here, thank you,' said the lawyer, and he drew near and leaned on the tall fender. This hall, in which he was now left alone, was a pet fancy of his friend the doctor's; and Utterson himself was wont to speak of it as the pleasantest room in London. But tonight there was a shudder in his blood; the face of Hyde sat heavy on his memory; he felt (what was rare with him) a nausea and distaste of life; and in the gloom of his spirits, he seemed to read a menace in the flickering of the firelight on the polished cabinets and the uneasy starting of the shadow on the roof. He was ashamed of his relief, when Poole presently returned to announce that Dr Jekyll was gone out.

'I saw Mr Hyde go in by the old dissecting room door, Poole,' he said. 'Is that right, when Dr Jekyll is from home?'

'Quite right, Mr Utterson, sir,' replied the servant. 'Mr Hyde has a key.'

'Your master seems to repose a great deal of trust in that young man, Poole,' resumed the other musingly.

'Yes, sir, he do indeed,' said Poole. 'We have all orders to obey him.'

'I do not think I ever met Mr Hyde?' asked Utterson.

'O, dear no, sir. He never *dines* here,' replied the butler. 'Indeed we see very little of him on this side of the house; he mostly comes and goes by the laboratory.'

'Well, good night, Poole.'

'Good night, Mr Utterson.'

And the lawyer set out homeward with a very heavy heart. 'Poor Harry Jekyll,' he thought, 'my mind misgives me he is in deep waters! He was wild when he was young; a long while ago to be sure; but in the law of God, there is no statute of limitations. Ay, it must be that; the ghost of some old sin, the cancer of some concealed disgrace: punishment coming, *pede claudo*,[10] years after memory has forgotten and self-love condoned the fault.' And the lawyer, scared by the thought, brooded awhile on his own past, groping in all the corners of memory, lest by chance some Jack-in-the-Box of an old iniquity should leap to light there. His past was fairly blameless; few men could read the rolls of their life with less apprehension; yet he was humbled to the dust by the many ill things he had done, and raised up again into a sober and fearful gratitude by the many that he had come so near to doing, yet avoided. And then by a return on his former subject, he conceived a spark of hope. 'This Master Hyde, if he were studied,' thought he, 'must have secrets of his own: black secrets, by the look of him; secrets compared to which poor Jekyll's worst would be like sunshine. Things cannot continue as they are. It turns me cold to think of this creature stealing like a thief to Harry's bedside; poor Harry, what a wakening! And the danger of it; for if this Hyde suspects the existence of the will, he may grow impatient to inherit. Ay, I must put my shoulder to the wheel – if Jekyll will but let me,' he added, 'if Jekyll will only let me.' For once more he saw before his mind's eye, as clear as a transparency, the strange clauses of the will.

A fortnight later, by excellent good fortune, the doctor gave one of his pleasant dinners to some five or six old cronies, all intelligent, reputable men and all judges of good wine; and Mr Utterson so contrived that he remained behind after the others had departed. This was no new arrangement, but a thing that had befallen many scores of times. Where Utterson was liked, he was liked well. Hosts loved to detail the dry lawyer, when the light-hearted and the loose-tongued had already their foot on the threshold; they liked to sit awhile in his unobtrusive company, practising for solitude, sobering their minds in the man's rich silence after the expense and strain of gaiety. To this rule, Dr Jekyll was no exception; and as he now sat on the opposite side of the fire – a large, well-made, smooth-faced man of fifty, with something of a slyish cast perhaps, but every mark of capacity and kindness – you could see by his looks that he cherished for Mr Utterson a sincere and warm affection.

'I have been wanting to speak to you, Jekyll,' began the latter. 'You know that will of yours?'

A close observer might have gathered that the topic was distasteful; but the doctor carried it off gaily. 'My poor Utterson,' said he, 'you are unfortunate in such a client. I never saw a man so distressed as you were by my will; unless it were that hide-bound pedant, Lanyon, at what he called my scientific heresies. O, I know he's a good fellow – you needn't frown – an excellent fellow, and I always mean to see more of him; but a hide-bound pedant for all that; an ignorant blatant pedant. I was never more disappointed in any man than Lanyon.'

'You know I never approved of it,' pursued Utterson, ruthlessly disregarding the fresh topic.

'My will? Yes, certainly, I know that,' said the doctor, a trifle sharply. 'You have told me so.'

'Well, I tell you so again,' continued the lawyer. 'I have been learning something of young Hyde.'

The large handsome face of Dr Jekyll grew pale to the very lips, and there came a blackness about his eyes. 'I do not care to hear more,' said he. 'This is a matter I thought we had agreed to drop.'

'What I heard was abominable,' said Utterson.

'It can make no change. You do not understand my position,' returned the doctor, with a certain incoherency of manner. 'I am painfully situated, Utterson; my position is a very strange – a very strange one. It is one of those affairs that cannot be mended by talking.'

'Jekyll,' said Utterson, 'you know me: I am a man to be trusted. Make a clean breast of this in confidence; and I make no doubt I can get you out of it.'

'My good Utterson,' said the doctor, 'this is very good of you, this is downright good of you, and I cannot find words to thank you in. I believe you fully; I would trust you before any man alive, ay, before myself, if I could make the choice; but indeed it isn't what you fancy; it is not so bad as that; and just to put your good heart at rest, I will tell you one thing: the moment I choose, I can be rid of Mr Hyde. I give you my hand upon that; and I thank you again and again; and I will just add one little word, Utterson, that I'm sure you'll take in good part: this is a private matter, and I beg of you to let it sleep.'

Utterson reflected a little looking in the fire.

'I have no doubt you are perfectly right,' he said at last, getting to his feet.

'Well, but since we have touched upon this business, and for the last time I hope,' continued the doctor, 'there is one point I should like you to understand. I have really a very great interest in poor Hyde. I know you have seen him; he told me so; and I fear he was rude. But I do sincerely take a great, a very great interest in that young man; and if I am taken away, Utterson, I wish you to promise me that you will bear with him and get his rights for him. I think you would, if you knew all; and it would be a weight off my mind if you would promise.'

'I can't pretend that I shall ever like him,' said the lawyer.

'I don't ask that,' pleaded Jekyll, laying his hand upon the other's arm; 'I only ask for justice; I only ask you to help him for my sake, when I am no longer here.'

Utterson heaved an irrepressible sigh. 'Well,' said he. 'I promise.'

Nearly a year later, in the month of October 18—, London was startled by a crime of singular ferocity and rendered all the more notable by the high position of the victim. The details were few and startling. A maidservant living alone in a house not far from the river,[1] had gone upstairs to bed about eleven. Although a fog rolled over the city in the small hours, the early part of the night was cloudless, and the lane, which the maid's window overlooked, was brilliantly lit by the full moon. It seems she was romantically given[2] for she sat down upon her box, which stood immediately under the window, and fell into a dream of musing. Never (she used to say, with streaming tears, when she narrated that experience) never had she felt more at peace with all men or thought more kindly of the world. And as she so sat she became aware of an aged and beautiful gentleman with white hair, drawing near along the lane; and advancing to meet him, another and very small gentleman, to whom at first she paid less attention. When they had come within speech (which was just under the maid's eyes) the older man bowed and accosted the other with a very pretty manner of politeness. It did not seem as if the subject of his address were of great importance; indeed, from his pointing, it sometimes appeared as if he were only inquiring his way; but the moon shone on his face as he spoke, and the girl was pleased to watch it, it seemed to breathe such an innocent and old-world kindness of disposition, yet with something high too, as of a well-founded self-content. Presently her eye wandered to the other, and she was surprised to recognize in him a certain Mr Hyde, who had once visited her master and for whom she had conceived a dislike. He had in his hand a heavy cane, with which he was trifling; but he answered never a word, and seemed to listen with an ill-contained impatience. And then all of a sudden he broke out in a great flame of anger, stamping with his foot, brandishing the cane, and carrying on (as the maid described it) like a madman. The old gentleman took a step back, with the air of one very much surprised and a trifle hurt; and at that Mr Hyde broke out of all bounds and clubbed him to the earth. And next moment, with ape-like fury,[3] he was trampling his victim under foot, and hailing down a storm of blows, under which the bones were audibly shattered and the body jumped upon the roadway. At the horror of these sights and sounds, the maid fainted.

It was two o'clock when she came to herself and called for the police. The murderer was gone long ago; but there lay his victim in the middle of the lane, incredibly mangled. The stick with which the deed had been done, although it was of some rare and very tough and heavy wood, had broken in the middle under the stress of this insensate cruelty; and one splintered half had rolled in the neighbouring gutter – the other, without doubt, had been carried away by the murderer. A purse and a gold watch were found upon the victim; but no cards or papers, except a sealed and stamped envelope, which he had been probably carrying to the post, and which bore the name and address of Mr Utterson.

This was brought to the lawyer the next morning, before he was out of bed; and he had no sooner seen it, and been told the circumstances, than he shot out a solemn lip. 'I shall say nothing till I have seen the body,' said he; 'this may be very serious. Have the kindness to wait while I dress.' And with the same grave countenance he hurried through his breakfast and drove to the police station, whither the body had been carried. As soon as he came into the cell, he nodded.

'Yes,' said he, 'I recognize him. I am sorry to say that this is Sir Danvers Carew.'

'Good God, sir,' exclaimed the officer, 'is it possible?' And the next moment his eye lighted up with professional ambition. 'This will make a deal of noise,' he said. 'And perhaps you can help us to the man.' And he briefly narrated what the maid had seen, and showed the broken stick.

Mr Utterson had already quailed at the name of Hyde; but when the stick was laid before him, he could doubt no longer: broken and battered as it was, he recognized it for one that he had himself presented many years before to Henry Jekyll.

'Is this Mr Hyde a person of small stature?' he inquired.

'Particularly small and particularly wicked-looking, is what the maid calls him,' said the officer.

Mr Utterson reflected; and then, raising his head, 'If you will come with me in my cab,' he said, 'I think I can take you to his house.'

It was by this time about nine in the morning, and the first fog of the season. A great chocolate-coloured pall lowered over heaven, but the wind was continually charging and routing these embattled vapours; so that as the cab crawled from street to street, Mr Utterson beheld a marvellous number of degrees and hues of twilight; for here it would be dark like the back-end of evening; and there would be a glow of a rich, lurid brown, like the light of some strange conflagration; and here, for a moment, the fog would be quite broken up, and a haggard shaft of daylight would glance in between the swirling wreaths. The dismal quarter of Soho⁴ seen under these changing glimpses, with its muddy ways, and slatternly passengers, and its lamps, which had never been extinguished or had been kindled afresh to combat this mournful reinvasion of darkness, seemed, in the lawyer's eyes, like a district of some city in a nightmare. The thoughts of his mind, besides, were of the gloomiest dye; and when he glanced at the companion of his drive, he was conscious of some touch of that terror of the law and the law's officers, which may at times assail the most honest.

As the cab drew up before the address indicated, the fog lifted a little and showed him a dingy street, a gin palace, a low French eating house, a shop for the retail of penny numbers and twopenny salads, many ragged children huddled in the doorways, and many women of many different nationalities passing out, key in hand, to have a morning glass; and the next moment the fog settled down again upon that part, as brown as umber, and cut him off from his blackguardly surroundings. This was the home of Henry Jekyll's favourite; of a man who was heir to a quarter of a million sterling.

An ivory-faced and silvery-haired old woman opened the door. She had an evil face, smoothed by hypocrisy; but her manners were excellent. Yes, she said, this was Mr Hyde's, but he was not at home; he had been in that night very late, but had gone away again in less than an hour; there was nothing strange in that; his habits were very irregular, and he was often absent; for instance, it was nearly two months since she had seen him till yesterday.

'Very well then, we wish to see his rooms,' said the lawyer; and when the woman began to declare it was impossible, 'I had better tell you who this person is,' he added. 'This is Inspector Newcomen of Scotland Yard.'

A flash of odious joy appeared upon the woman's face. 'Ah!' said she, 'he is in trouble! What has he done?'

Mr Utterson and the inspector exchanged glances. 'He don't seem a very popular character,' observed the latter. 'And now, my good woman, just let me and this gentleman have a look about us.'

In the whole extent of the house, which but for the old woman remained otherwise empty, Mr Hyde had only used a couple of rooms; but these were furnished with luxury and good taste. A closet was filled with wine; the plate was of silver, the napery elegant; a good picture hung upon the walls, a gift (as Utterson supposed) from Henry Jekyll, who was much of a connoisseur; and the carpets were of many plies and agreeable in colour. At this moment, however, the rooms bore every mark of having been recently and hurriedly ransacked; clothes lay about the floor, with their pockets inside out; lockfast drawers stood open; and on the hearth there lay a pile of grey ashes, as though many papers had been burned. From these embers the inspector disinterred the butt end of a green cheque book, which had resisted the action of the fire; the other half of the stick was found behind the door; and as this clinched his suspicions, the officer declared himself delighted. A visit to the bank, where several thousand pounds were found to be lying to the murderer's credit, completed his gratification.

'You may depend upon it, sir,' he told Mr Utterson: 'I have him in my hand. He must have lost his head, or he would never have left the stick or, above all, burned the cheque book. Why, money's life to the man. We have nothing to do but wait for him at the bank, and get out the handbills.'

This last, however, was not so easy of accomplishment; for Mr Hyde had numbered few familiars – even the master of the servantmaid had only seen him twice; his family could nowhere be traced; he had never been photographed;[5] and the few who could describe him differed widely, as common observers will. Only on one point, were they agreed; and that was the haunting sense of unexpressed deformity with which the fugitive impressed his beholders.

It was late in the afternoon, when Mr Utterson found his way to Dr Jekyll's door, where he was at once admitted by Poole, and carried down by the kitchen offices and across a yard which had once been a garden, to the building which was indifferently known as the laboratory or the dissecting rooms.[1] The doctor had bought the house from the heirs of a celebrated surgeon; and his own tastes being rather chemical than anatomical, had changed the destination of the block at the bottom of the garden. It was the first time that the lawyer had been received in that part of his friend's quarters; and he eyed the dingy windowless structure with curiosity, and gazed round with a distasteful sense of strangeness as he crossed the theatre, once crowded with eager students and now lying gaunt and silent, the tables laden with chemical apparatus, the floor strewn with crates and littered with pack-ing straw, and the light falling dimly through the foggy cupola. At the further end, a flight of stairs mounted to a door covered with red baize; and through this, Mr Utterson was at last received into the doctor's cabinet. It was a large room, fitted round with glass presses, furnished, among other things, with a cheval-glass and a business table, and looking out upon the court by three dusty windows barred with iron. The fire burned in the grate; a lamp was set lighted on the chimney shelf, for even in the houses the fog began to lie thickly; and there, close up to the warmth, sat Dr Jekyll, looking deadly sick. He did not rise to meet his visitor, but held out a cold hand and bade him welcome in a changed voice.

'And now,' said Mr Utterson, as soon as Poole had left them, 'you have heard the news?'

The doctor shuddered. 'They were crying it in the square,' he said. 'I heard them in my dining room.'

'One word,' said the lawyer. 'Carew was my client, but so are you, and I want to know what I am doing. You have not been mad enough to hide this fellow?'

'Utterson, I swear to God,' cried the doctor, 'I swear to God I will

never set eyes on him again. I bind my honour to you that I am done
with him in this world. It is all at an end. And indeed he does not want
my help; you do not know him as I do; he is safe, he is quite safe; mark
my words, he will never more be heard of.'

The lawyer listened gloomily; he did not like his friend's feverish
manner. 'You seem pretty sure of him,' said he; 'and for your sake, I
hope you may be right. If it came to a trial, your name might appear.'

'I am quite sure of him,' replied Jekyll; 'I have grounds for certainty
that I cannot share with anyone. But there is one thing on which you
may advise me. I have – I have received a letter; and I am at a loss
whether I should show it to the police. I should like to leave it in your
hands, Utterson; you would judge wisely I am sure; I have so great a
trust in you.'

'You fear, I suppose, that it might lead to his detection?' asked the
lawyer.

'No,' said the other. 'I cannot say that I care what becomes of Hyde;
I am quite done with him. I was thinking of my own character, which
this hateful business has rather exposed.'

Utterson ruminated awhile; he was surprised at his friend's selfishness, and yet relieved by it. 'Well,' said he, at last, 'let me see the
letter.'

The letter was written in an odd, upright hand and signed 'Edward
Hyde': and it signified, briefly enough, that the writer's benefactor,
Dr Jekyll, whom he had long so unworthily repaid for a thousand
generosities, need labour under no alarm for his safety as he had
means of escape on which he placed a sure dependence. The lawyer
liked this letter well enough; it put a better colour on the intimacy
than he had looked for; and he blamed himself for some of his past
suspicions.[2]

'Have you the envelope?' he asked.

'I burned it,' replied Jekyll, 'before I thought what I was about. But
it bore no postmark. The note was handed in.'

'Shall I keep this and sleep upon it?' asked Utterson.

'I wish you to judge for me entirely,' was the reply. 'I have lost
confidence in myself.'

'Well, I shall consider,' returned the lawyer. 'And now one word more: it was Hyde who dictated the terms in your will about that disappearance?'

The doctor seemed seized with a qualm of faintness; he shut his mouth tight and nodded.

'I knew it,' said Utterson. 'He meant to murder you. You have had a fine escape.'

'I have had what is far more to the purpose,' returned the doctor solemnly: 'I have had a lesson – O God, Utterson, what a lesson I have had!' And he covered his face for a moment with his hands.

On his way out, the lawyer stopped and had a word or two with Poole. 'By the by,' said he, 'there was a letter handed in today: what was the messenger like?' But Poole was positive nothing had come except by post; 'and only circulars by that,' he added.

This news sent off the visitor with his fears renewed. Plainly the letter had come by the laboratory door; possibly, indeed, it had been written in the cabinet; and if that were so, it must be differently judged, and handled with the more caution. The newsboys, as he went, were crying themselves hoarse along the footways: 'Special edition. Shocking murder of an MP.' That was the funeral oration of one friend and client; and he could not help a certain apprehension lest the good name of another should be sucked down in the eddy of the scandal. It was, at least, a ticklish decision that he had to make; and self-reliant as he was by habit, he began to cherish a longing for advice. It was not to be had directly; but perhaps, he thought, it might be fished for.

Presently after, he sat on one side of his own hearth, with Mr Guest, his head clerk, upon the other, and midway between, at a nicely calculated distance from the fire, a bottle of a particular old wine that had long dwelt unsunned in the foundations of his house. The fog still slept on the wing above the drowned city, where the lamps glimmered like carbuncles; and through the muffle and smother of these fallen clouds, the procession of the town's life was still rolling in through the great arteries with a sound as of a mighty wind. But the room was gay with firelight. In the bottle the acids were long ago resolved; the imperial dye had softened with time, as the colour grows richer in stained windows; and the glow of hot autumn afternoons on hillside vineyards, was ready to be set free and to disperse the fogs of London. Insensibly the lawyer melted. There was no man from whom he kept fewer secrets than Mr Guest; and he was not always sure that he kept as many as he meant. Guest had often been on business to the doctor's; he knew Poole; he could scarce have failed to hear of Mr Hyde's familiarity about the house; he might draw conclusions: was it not as well, then, that he should see a letter which put that mystery to rights? and above all since Guest, being a great student and critic of handwriting, would consider the step natural and obliging? The clerk, besides, was a man of counsel; he would scarce read so strange a document without dropping a remark; and by that remark Mr Utterson might shape his future course.

'This is a sad business about Sir Danvers,' he said.

'Yes, sir, indeed. It has elicited a great deal of public feeling,' returned Guest. 'The man, of course, was mad.'

'I should like to hear your views on that,' replied Utterson. 'I have a document here in his handwriting; it is between ourselves, for I scarce knew what to do about it; it is an ugly business at the best. But there it is; quite in your way: a murderer's autograph.'

Guest's eyes brightened, and he sat down at once and studied it with passion. 'No, sir,' he said; 'not mad; but it is an odd hand.'

'And by all accounts a very odd writer,' added the lawyer.

Just then the servant entered with a note.

'Is that from Doctor Jekyll, sir?' inquired the clerk. 'I thought I knew the writing. Anything private, Mr Utterson?'

'Only an invitation to dinner. Why? do you want to see it?'

'One moment. I thank you, sir;' and the clerk laid the two sheets of paper alongside and sedulously compared their contents. 'Thank you, sir,' he said at last, returning both; 'it's a very interesting autograph.'

There was a pause, during which Mr Utterson struggled with himself. 'Why did you compare them, Guest?' he inquired suddenly.

'Well, sir,' returned the clerk, 'there's a rather singular resemblance; the two hands are in many points identical: only differently sloped.'

'Rather quaint,' said Utterson.

'It is, as you say, rather quaint,' returned Guest.

'I wouldn't speak of this note, you know,' said the master.

'No, sir,' said the clerk. 'I understand.'

But no sooner was Mr Utterson alone that night, than he locked the note into his safe where it reposed from that time forward. 'What!' he thought. 'Henry Jekyll forge for a murderer!' And his blood ran cold in his veins.

Time ran on; thousands of pounds were offered in reward, for the death of Sir Danvers was resented as a public injury; but Mr Hyde had disappeared out of the ken of the police as though he had never existed. Much of his past was unearthed, indeed, and all disreputable: tales came out of the man's cruelty, at once so callous and violent, of his vile life, of his strange associates, of the hatred that seemed to have surrounded his career; but of his present whereabouts, not a whisper. From the time he had left the house in Soho on the morning of the murder, he was simply blotted out; and gradually, as time drew on, Mr Utterson began to recover from the hotness of his alarm, and to grow more at quiet with himself. The death of Sir Danvers was, to his way of thinking, more than paid for by the disappearance of Mr Hyde. Now that that evil influence had been withdrawn, a new life began for Dr Jekyll. He came out of his seclusion, renewed relations with his friends, became once more their familiar guest and entertainer; and whilst he had always been known for charities, he was now no less distinguished for religion. He was busy, he was much in the open air, he did good; his face seemed to open and brighten, as if with an inward consciousness of service; and for more than two months, the doctor was at peace.

On the 8th of January Utterson had dined at the doctor's with a small party; Lanyon had been there; and the face of the host had looked from one to the other as in the old days when the trio were inseparable friends. On the 12th, and again on the 14th, the door was shut against the lawyer. 'The doctor was confined to the house,' Poole said, 'and saw no one.' On the 15th, he tried again, and was again refused; and having now been used for the last two months to see his friend almost daily, he found this return of solitude to weigh upon his spirits. The fifth night, he had in Guest to dine with him; and the sixth he betook himself to Doctor Lanyon's.

There at least he was not denied admittance; but when he came in, he was shocked at the change which had taken place in the doctor's appearance. He had his death-warrant written legibly upon his face. The rosy man had grown pale; his flesh had fallen away; he was visibly balder and older; and yet it was not so much these tokens of a swift physical decay that arrested the lawyer's notice, as a look in the eye and quality of manner that seemed to testify to some deep-seated terror of the mind. It was unlikely that the doctor should fear death; and yet that was what Utterson was tempted to suspect. 'Yes,' he thought; 'he is a doctor, he must know his own state and that his days are counted; and the knowledge is more than he can bear.' And yet when Utterson remarked on his ill-looks, it was with an air of great firmness that Lanyon declared himself a doomed man.

'I have had a shock,' he said, 'and I shall never recover. It is a question of weeks. Well, life has been pleasant; I liked it; yes, sir, I used to like it. I sometimes think if we knew all, we should be more glad to get away.'

'Jekyll is ill, too,' observed Utterson. 'Have you seen him?'

But Lanyon's face changed, and he held up a trembling hand. 'I wish to see or hear no more of Doctor Jekyll,' he said in a loud, unsteady voice. 'I am quite done with that person; and I beg that you will spare me any allusion to one whom I regard as dead.'

'Tut-tut,' said Mr Utterson; and then after a considerable pause, 'Can't I do anything?' he inquired. 'We are three very old friends, Lanyon; we shall not live to make others.'

'Nothing can be done,' returned Lanyon; 'ask himself.'

'He will not see me,' said the lawyer.

'I am not surprised at that,' was the reply. 'Some day, Utterson, after I am dead, you may perhaps come to learn the right and wrong of this. I cannot tell you. And in the meantime, if you can sit and talk with me of other things, for God's sake, stay and do so; but if you cannot keep clear of this accursed topic, then, in God's name, go, for I cannot bear it.'

As soon as he got home, Utterson sat down and wrote to Jekyll, complaining of his exclusion from the house, and asking the cause of this unhappy break with Lanyon; and the next day brought him a long answer, often very pathetically worded, and sometimes darkly mysterious in drift. The quarrel with Lanyon was incurable. 'I do not blame our old friend,' Jekyll wrote, 'but I share his view that we must never meet. I mean from henceforth to lead a life of extreme seclusion; you must not be surprised, nor must you doubt my friendship, if my door is often shut even to you. You must suffer me to go my own dark way. I have brought on myself a punishment and a danger that I cannot name.[1] If I am the chief of sinners, I am the chief of sufferers also. I could not think that this earth contained a place for sufferings and terrors so unmanning; and you can do but one thing, Utterson, to lighten this destiny, and that is to respect my silence.' Utterson was amazed; the dark influence of Hyde had been withdrawn, the doctor had returned to his old tasks and amities; a week ago, the prospect had smiled with every promise of a cheerful and an honoured age; and now in a moment, friendship, and peace of mind and the whole tenor of his life were wrecked. So great and unprepared a change pointed to madness; but in view of Lanyon's manner and words, there must lie for it some deeper ground.

A week afterwards Dr Lanyon took to his bed, and in something less than a fortnight he was dead. The night after the funeral, at which he had been sadly affected, Utterson locked the door of his business room, and sitting there by the light of a melancholy candle, drew out and set before him an envelope addressed by the hand and sealed with the seal of his dear friend. 'PRIVATE: for the hands of J. G. Utterson ALONE and in case of his predecease *to be destroyed unread*', so it was emphatically superscribed; and the lawyer dreaded to behold the contents. 'I have buried one friend today,' he thought: 'what if this should cost me another?' And then he condemned the fear as a disloyalty, and broke the seal. Within there was another enclosure, likewise sealed, and marked upon the cover as 'Not to be opened till the death or disappearance of Dr Henry Jekyll.' Utterson could not trust his eyes. Yes, it was disappearance; here again, as in the mad will which he had long ago restored to its author, here again were the idea of a disappearance and the name of Henry Jekyll bracketed. But in the will, that idea had sprung from the sinister suggestion of the man Hyde; it was set there with a purpose all too plain and horrible. Written by the hand of Lanyon, what should it mean? A great curiosity came on the trustee, to disregard the prohibition and dive at once to the bottom of these mysteries; but professional honour and faith to his dead friend were stringent obligations; and the packet slept in the inmost corner of his private safe.

It is one thing to mortify curiosity, another to conquer it; and it may be doubted if, from that day forth, Utterson desired the society of his surviving friend with the same eagerness. He thought of him kindly; but his thoughts were disquieted and fearful. He went to call indeed; but he was perhaps relieved to be denied admittance; perhaps, in his heart, he preferred to speak with Poole upon the doorstep and surrounded by the air and sounds of the open city, rather than to be admitted into that house of voluntary bondage, and to sit and speak with its inscrutable recluse. Poole had, indeed, no very pleasant news to communicate. The doctor, it appeared, now more than ever confined himself to the cabinet over the laboratory, where he would sometimes even sleep; he was out of spirits, he had grown very silent, he did not read; it seemed as if he had something on his mind. Utterson became so used to the unvarying character of these reports, that he fell off little by little in the frequency of his visits.

It chanced on Sunday, when Mr Utterson was on his usual walk with Mr Enfield, that their way lay once again through the bystreet; and that when they came in front of the door, both stopped to gaze on it.

'Well,' said Enfield, 'that story's at an end at least. We shall never see more of Mr Hyde.'

'I hope not,' said Utterson. 'Did I ever tell you that I once saw him, and shared your feeling of repulsion?'

'It was impossible to do the one without the other,' returned Enfield. 'And by the way what an ass you must have thought me, not to know that this was a back way to Dr Jekyll's! It was partly your own fault that I found it out, even when I did.'

'So you found it out, did you?' said Utterson. 'But if that be so, we may step into the court and take a look at the windows. To tell you the truth, I am uneasy about poor Jekyll; and even outside, I feel as if the presence of a friend might do him good.'

The court was very cool and a little damp, and full of premature twilight, although the sky, high up overhead, was still bright with sunset. The middle one of the three windows was half way open; and sitting close beside it, taking the air with an infinite sadness of mien, like some disconsolate prisoner, Utterson saw Dr Jekyll.

'What! Jekyll!' he cried. 'I trust you are better.'

'I am very low, Utterson,' replied the doctor drearily, 'very low. It will not last long, thank God.'

'You stay too much indoors,' said the lawyer. 'You should be out, whipping up the circulation like Mr Enfield and me. (This is my cousin – Mr Enfield – Dr Jekyll.) Come now; get your hat and take a quick turn with us.'

'You are very good,' sighed the other. 'I should like to very much; but no, no, no, it is quite impossible; I dare not. But indeed, Utterson, I am very glad to see you; this is really a great pleasure; I would ask you and Mr Enfield up, but the place is really not fit.'

'Why then,' said the lawyer, good-naturedly, 'the best thing we can do is to stay down here and speak with you from where we are.'

'That is just what I was about to venture to propose,' returned the doctor with a smile. But the words were hardly uttered, before the smile was struck out of his face and succeeded by an expression of such abject terror and despair, as froze the very blood of the two gentlemen below. They saw it but for a glimpse, for the window was instantly thrust down; but that glimpse had been sufficient, and they turned and left the court without a word. In silence, too, they traversed the bystreet; and it was not until they had come into a neighbouring thoroughfare, where even upon a Sunday there were still some stirrings of life, that Mr Utterson at last turned and looked at his companion. They were both pale; and there was an answering horror in their eyes.

'God forgive us, God forgive us,' said Mr Utterson.

But Mr Enfield only nodded his head very seriously, and walked on once more in silence.

Mr Utterson was sitting by his fireside one evening after dinner, when he was surprised to receive a visit from Poole.

'Bless me, Poole, what brings you here?' he cried; and then taking a second look at him, 'What ails you?' he added, 'is the doctor ill?'

'Mr Utterson,' said the man, 'there is something wrong.'

'Take a seat, and here is a glass of wine for you,' said the lawyer. 'Now, take your time, and tell me plainly what you want.'

'You know the doctor's ways, sir,' replied Poole, 'and how he shuts himself up. Well, he's shut up again in the cabinet; and I don't like it, sir – I wish I may die if I like it. Mr Utterson, sir, I'm afraid.'

'Now, my good man,' said the lawyer, 'be explicit. What are you afraid of?'

'I've been afraid for about a week,' returned Poole, doggedly disregarding the question, 'and I can bear it no more.'

The man's appearance amply bore out his words; his manner was altered for the worse; and except for the moment when he had first announced his terror, he had not once looked the lawyer in the face. Even now, he sat with the glass of wine untasted on his knee, and his eyes directed to a corner of the floor. 'I can bear it no more,' he repeated.

'Come,' said the lawyer, 'I see you have some good reason, Poole; I see there is something seriously amiss. Try to tell me what it is.'

'I think there's been foul play,' said Poole, hoarsely.

'Foul play!' cried the lawyer, a good deal frightened and rather inclined to be irritated in consequence. 'What foul play? What does the man mean?'

'I daren't say, sir,' was the answer; 'but will you come along with me and see for yourself?'

Mr Utterson's only answer was to rise and get his hat and great coat; but he observed with wonder the greatness of the relief that appeared upon the butler's face, and perhaps with no less, that the wine was still untasted when he set it down to follow.

It was a wild, cold, seasonable night of March, with a pale moon, lying on her back as though the wind had tilted her, and a flying wrack of the most diaphanous and lawny texture. The wind made talking difficult, and flecked the blood into the face. It seemed to have swept the streets unusually bare of passengers, besides; for Mr Utterson thought he had never seen that part of London so deserted. He could have wished it otherwise; never in his life had he been conscious of so sharp a wish to see and touch his fellow-creatures; for struggle as he might, there was borne in upon his mind a crushing anticipation of calamity. The square, when they got there, was all full of wind and dust, and the thin trees in the garden were lashing themselves along the railing. Poole, who had kept all the way a pace or two ahead, now pulled up in the middle of the pavement, and in spite of the biting weather, took off his hat and mopped his brow with a red pocket-handkerchief. But for all the hurry of his coming, these were not the dews of exertion that he wiped away, but the moisture of some strangling anguish; for his face was white and his voice, when he spoke, harsh and broken.

'Well, sir,' he said, 'here we are, and God grant there be nothing wrong.'

'Amen, Poole,' said the lawyer.

Thereupon the servant knocked in a very guarded manner; the door was opened on the chain; and a voice asked from within, 'Is that you, Poole?'

'It's all right,' said Poole. 'Open the door.'

The hall, when they entered it, was brightly lighted up; the fire was built high; and about the hearth the whole of the servants, men and women, stood huddled together like a flock of sheep. At the sight of Mr Utterson, the housemaid broke into hysterical whimpering; and the cook, crying out 'Bless God! it's Mr Utterson,' ran forward as if to take him in her arms.

'What, what? Are you all here?' said the lawyer peevishly. 'Very irregular, very unseemly; your master would be far from pleased.'

'They're all afraid,' said Poole.

Blank silence followed, no one protesting; only the maid lifted up her voice and now wept loudly.

'Hold your tongue!' Poole said to her, with a ferocity of accent that testified to his own jangled nerves; and indeed, when the girl had so suddenly raised the note of her lamentation, they had all started and turned towards the inner door with faces of dreadful expectation. 'And now,' continued the butler, addressing the knife-boy, 'reach me a candle, and we'll get this through hands at once.' And then he begged Mr Utterson to follow him, and led the way to the back garden.

'Now, sir,' said he, 'you come as gently as you can. I want you to hear, and I don't want you to be heard. And see here, sir, if by any chance he was to ask you in, don't go.'

Mr Utterson's nerves, at this unlooked-for termination, gave a jerk that nearly threw him from his balance; but he re-collected his courage and followed the butler into the laboratory building and through the surgical theatre, with its lumber of crates and bottles, to the foot of the stair. Here Poole motioned him to stand on one side and listen; while he himself, setting down the candle and making a great and obvious call on his resolution, mounted the steps and knocked with a somewhat uncertain hand on the red baize of the cabinet door.

'Mr Utterson, sir, asking to see you,' he called; and even as he did so, once more violently signed to the lawyer to give ear.

A voice answered from within: 'Tell him I cannot see anyone,' it said complainingly.

'Thank you, sir,' said Poole, with a note of something like triumph in his voice; and taking up his candle, he led Mr Utterson back across the yard and into the great kitchen, where the fire was out and the beetles were leaping on the floor.

'Sir,' he said, looking Mr Utterson in the eyes, 'was that my master's voice?'

'It seems much changed,' replied the lawyer, very pale, but giving look for look.

'Changed? Well, yes, I think so,' said the butler. 'Have I been twenty years in this man's house, to be deceived about his voice? No, sir; master's made away with – he was made away with, eight days ago, when we heard him cry out upon the name of God; and *who's* in there instead of him, and *why* it stays there, is a thing that cries to Heaven, Mr Utterson!'

'This is a very strange tale, Poole; this is rather a wild tale, my man,' said Mr Utterson, biting his finger. 'Suppose it were as you suppose, supposing Dr Jekyll to have been – well, murdered, what could induce the murderer to stay? That won't hold water; it doesn't commend itself to reason.'

'Well, Mr Utterson, you are a hard man to satisfy, but I'll do it yet,' said Poole. 'All this last week (you must know) him, or it, or whatever it is that lives in that cabinet, has been crying night and day for some sort of medicine and cannot get it to his mind. It was sometimes his way – the master's, that is – to write his orders on a sheet of paper and throw it on the stair. We've had nothing else this week back; nothing but papers, and a closed door, and the very meals left there to be smuggled in when nobody was looking. Well, sir, every day, ay, and twice and thrice in the same day, there have been orders and complaints, and I have been sent flying to all the wholesale chemists in town. Every time I brought the stuff back, there would be another paper telling me to return it, because it was not pure, and another order to a different firm. This drug is wanted bitter bad, sir, whatever for.'

'Have you any of these papers?' asked Mr Utterson.

Poole felt in his pocket and handed out a crumpled note, which the lawyer, bending nearer to the candle, carefully examined. Its contents ran thus: 'Dr Jekyll presents his compliments to Messrs Maw. He assures them that their last sample is impure and quite useless for his present purpose. In the year 18 —, Dr J. purchased a somewhat large quantity from Messrs M. He now begs them to search with the most sedulous care, and should any of the same quality be left, to forward it to him at once. Expense is no consideration. The importance of this to Dr J. can hardly be exaggerated.' So far the letter had run composedly enough, but here with a sudden splutter of the pen, the writer's emotion had broken loose. 'For God's sake,' he had added, 'find me some of the old.'

'This is a strange note,' said Mr Utterson; and then sharply, 'How do you come to have it open?'

'The man at Maw's was main angry, sir, and he threw it back to me like so much dirt,' returned Poole.

'This is unquestionably the doctor's hand, do you know?' resumed the lawyer.

'I thought it looked like it,' said the servant rather sulkily; and then, with another voice, 'But what matters hand of write,' he said. 'I've seen him!'

'Seen him?' repeated Mr Utterson. 'Well?'

'That's it!' said Poole. 'It was this way. I came suddenly into the theatre from the garden. It seems he had slipped out to look for this drug or whatever it is; for the cabinet door was open, and there he was at the far end of the room digging among the crates. He looked up when I came in, gave a kind of cry, and whipped upstairs into the cabinet. It was but for one minute that I saw him, but the hair stood upon my head like quills. Sir, if that was my master, why had he a mask upon his face? If it was my master, why did he cry out like a rat, and run from me? I have served him long enough. And then . . .' the man paused and passed his hand over his face.

'These are all very strange circumstances,' said Mr Utterson, 'but I think I begin to see daylight. Your master, Poole, is plainly seized with one of those maladies that both torture and deform the sufferer;[1] hence, for aught I know, the alteration of his voice; hence the mask and his avoidance of his friends; hence his eagerness to find this drug, by means of which the poor soul retains some hope of ultimate recovery – God grant that he be not deceived! There is my explanation; it is sad enough, Poole, ay, and appalling to consider; but it is plain and natural, hangs well together and delivers us from all exorbitant alarms.'

'Sir,' said the butler, turning to a sort of mottled pallor, 'that thing was not my master, and there's the truth. My master' – here he looked round him and began to whisper – 'is a tall fine build of a man, and this was more of a dwarf.' Utterson attempted to protest. 'O, sir,' cried Poole, 'do you think I do not know my master after twenty years? do you think I do not know where his head comes to in the cabinet door, where I saw him every morning of my life? No, sir, that thing in the mask was never Doctor Jekyll – God knows what it was, but it was never Doctor Jekyll; and it is the belief of my heart that there was murder done.'

'Poole,' replied the lawyer, 'if you say that, it will become my duty to make certain. Much as I desire to spare your master's feelings, much as I am puzzled by this note which seems to prove him to be still alive, I shall consider it my duty to break in that door.'

'Ah, Mr Utterson, that's talking!' cried the butler.

'And now comes the second question,' resumed Utterson: 'Who is going to do it?'

'Why, you and me, sir,' was the undaunted reply.

'That is very well said;' returned the lawyer; 'and whatever comes of it, I shall make it my business to see you are no loser.'

'There is an axe in the theatre,' continued Poole; 'and you might take the kitchen poker for yourself.'

The lawyer took that rude but weighty instrument into his hand, and balanced it. 'Do you know, Poole,' he said, looking up, 'that you and I are about to place ourselves in a position of some peril?'

'You may say so, sir, indeed,' returned the butler.

'It is well, then, that we should be frank,' said the other. 'We both think more than we have said; let us make a clean breast. This masked figure that you saw, did you recognize it?'

'Well, sir, it went so quick, and the creature was so doubled up, that I could hardly swear to that,' was the answer. 'But if you mean, was it Mr Hyde? – why, yes, I think it was! You see, it was much of the same bigness; and it had the same quick light way with it; and then who else could have got in by the laboratory door? You have not forgot, sir, that at the time of the murder he had still the key with him? But that's not all. I don't know, Mr Utterson, if ever you met this Mr Hyde?'

'Yes,' said the lawyer, 'I once spoke with him.'

'Then you must know as well as the rest of us that there was something queer about that gentleman – something that gave a man a turn – I don't know rightly how to say it, sir, beyond this: that you felt it in your marrow kind of cold and thin.'

'I own I felt something of what you describe,' said Mr Utterson.

'Quite so, sir,' returned Poole. 'Well, when that masked thing like a monkey jumped from among the chemicals and whipped into the cabinet, it went down my spine like ice. 'O, I know it's not evidence,

Mr Utterson; I'm book-learned enough for that; but a man has his feelings, and I give you my bible-word it was Mr Hyde!'

'Ay, ay,' said the lawyer. 'My fears incline to the same point. Evil, I fear, founded – evil was sure to come – of that connection. Ay, truly, I believe you; I believe poor Harry is killed; and I believe his murderer (for what purpose, God alone can tell) is still lurking in his victim's room. Well, let our name be vengeance. Call Bradshaw.'

The footman came at the summons, very white and nervous.

'Pull yourself together, Bradshaw,' said the lawyer. 'This suspense, I know, is telling upon all of you; but it is now our intention to make an end of it. Poole, here, and I are going to force our way into the cabinet. If all is well, my shoulders are broad enough to bear the blame. Meanwhile, lest anything should really be amiss, or any mal-efactor seek to escape by the back, you and the boy must go round the corner with a pair of good sticks, and take your post at the laboratory door. We give you ten minutes, to get to your stations.'

As Bradshaw left, the lawyer looked at his watch. 'And now, Poole, let us get to ours,' he said; and taking the poker under his arm, he led the way into the yard. The scud had banked over the moon, and it was now quite dark. The wind, which only broke in puffs and draughts into that deep well of building, tossed the light of the candle to and fro about their steps, until they came into the shelter of the theatre, where they sat down silently to wait. London hummed solemnly all around; but nearer at hand, the stillness was only broken by the sound of a footfall moving to and fro along the cabinet floor.

'So it will walk all day, sir,' whispered Poole; 'ay, and the better part of the night. Only when a new sample comes from the chemist, there's a bit of a break. Ah, it's an ill-conscience that's such an enemy to rest! Ah, sir, there's blood foully shed in every step of it! But hark again, a little closer – put your heart in your ears, Mr Utterson, and tell me, is that the doctor's foot?'

The steps fell lightly and oddly, with a certain swing, for all they went so slowly; it was different indeed from the heavy creaking tread of Henry Jekyll. Utterson sighed. 'Is there never anything else?' he asked.

Poole nodded. 'Once,' he said. 'Once I heard it weeping!'

'Weeping? how that?' said the lawyer, conscious of a sudden chill of horror.

'Weeping like a woman or a lost soul,' said the butler. 'I came away with that upon my heart, that I could have wept too.'

But now the ten minutes drew to an end. Poole disinterred the axe from under a stack of packing straw; the candle was set upon the nearest table to light them to the attack; and they drew near with bated breath to where that patient foot was still going up and down, up and down, in the quiet of the night.

'Jekyll,' cried Utterson, with a loud voice, 'I demand to see you.' He paused a moment, but there came no reply. 'I give you fair warning, our suspicions are aroused, and I must and shall see you,' he resumed; 'if not by fair means, then by foul – if not of your consent, then by brute force!'

'Utterson,' said the voice, 'for God's sake, have mercy!'

'Ah, that's not Jekyll's voice – it's Hyde's!' cried Utterson. 'Down with the door, Poole.'

Poole swung the axe over his shoulder; the blow shook the building, and the red baize door leaped against the lock and hinges. A dismal screech, as of mere animal terror, rang from the cabinet. Up went the axe again, and again the panels crashed and the flame bounded; four times the blow fell; but the wood was tough and the fittings were of excellent workmanship; and it was not until the fifth, that the lock burst in sunder and the wreck of the door fell inwards on the carpet.

The besiegers, appalled by their own riot and the stillness that had succeeded, stood back a little and peered in. There lay the cabinet before their eyes in the quiet lamplight, a good fire glowing and chattering on the hearth, the kettle singing its thin strain, a drawer or two open, papers neatly set forth on the business table, and nearer the fire, the things laid out for tea: the quietest room, you would have said, and, but for the glazed presses full of chemicals, the most commonplace that night in London.

Right in the midst there lay the body of a man sorely contorted and still twitching. They drew near on tiptoe, turned it on its back and beheld the face of Edward Hyde. He was dressed in clothes far too large for him, clothes of the doctor's bigness; the cords of his face still moved with a semblance of life, but life was quite gone; and by the crushed phial in the hand and the strong smell of kernels[2] that hung upon the air, Utterson knew that he was looking on the body of a self-destroyer.

'We have come too late,' he said sternly, 'whether to save or punish. Hyde is gone to his account; and it only remains for us to find the body of your master.'

The far greater proportion of the building was occupied by the theatre, which filled almost the whole ground storey and was lighted from above, and by the cabinet, which formed an upper storey at one end and looked upon the court. A corridor joined the theatre to the door on the bystreet; and with this, the cabinet communicated separately by a second flight of stairs. There were besides a few dark closets and a spacious cellar. All these they now thoroughly examined. Each closet needed but a glance, for all were empty and all, by the dust that fell from their doors, had stood long unopened. The cellar, indeed, was filled with crazy lumber, mostly dating from the times of the surgeon who was Jekyll's predecessor; but even as they opened the door, they were advertised of the uselessness of further search, by the fall of a perfect mat of cobweb which had for years sealed up the entrance. Nowhere was there any trace of Henry Jekyll, dead or alive.

Poole stamped on the flags of the corridor. 'He must be buried here,' he said, hearkening to the sound.

'Or he may have fled,' said Utterson, and he turned to examine the door in the bystreet. It was locked; and lying near by on the flags, they found the key, already stained with rust.

'This does not look like use,' observed the lawyer.

'Use!' echoed Poole. 'Do you not see, sir, it is broken? much as if a man had stamped on it.'

'Ay,' continued Utterson, 'and the fractures, too, are rusty.' The two men looked at each other with a scare. 'This is beyond me, Poole,' said the lawyer. 'Let us go back to the cabinet.'

They mounted the stair in silence, and still with an occasional awestruck glance at the dead body, proceeded more thoroughly to examine the contents of the cabinet. At one table, there were traces of chemical work, various measured heaps of some white salt being laid on glass saucers, as though for an experiment in which the unhappy man had been prevented.

'That is the same drug that I was always bringing him,' said Poole; and even as he spoke, the kettle with a startling noise boiled over.

This brought them to the fireside, where the easy chair was drawn cosily up, and the tea things stood ready to the sitter's elbow, the very sugar in the cup. There were several books on a shelf; one lay beside the tea things open, and Utterson was amazed to find it a copy of a pious work, for which Jekyll had several times expressed a great esteem, annotated, in his own hand, with startling blasphemies.

Next, in the course of their review of the chamber, the searchers came to the cheval glass, into whose depths they looked with an involuntary horror. But it was so turned as to show them nothing but the rosy glow playing on the roof, the fire sparkling in a hundred repetitions along the glazed front of the presses, and their own pale and fearful countenances stooping to look in.

'This glass have seen some strange things, sir,' whispered Poole.

'And surely none stranger than itself,' echoed the lawyer in the same tones. 'For what did Jekyll' – he caught himself up at the word with a start, and then conquering the weakness: 'what could Jekyll want with it?' he said.

'You may say that!' said Poole.

Next they turned to the business table. On the desk among the neat array of papers, a large envelope was uppermost, and bore, in the doctor's hand, the name of Mr Utterson. The lawyer unsealed it, and several enclosures fell to the floor. The first was a will, drawn in the same eccentric terms as the one which he had returned six months before, to serve as a testament in case of death and as a deed of gift in case of disappearance; but in place of the name of Edward Hyde, the lawyer, with indescribable amazement, read the name of Gabriel John Utterson. He looked at Poole, and then back at the paper, and last of all at the dead malefactor stretched upon the carpet.

'My head goes round,' he said. 'He has been all these days in possession; he had no cause to like me; he must have raged to see himself displaced; and he has not destroyed this document.'

He caught up the next paper; it was a brief note in the doctor's hand and dated at the top. 'O Poole!' the lawyer cried, 'he was alive and here this day. He cannot have been disposed of in so short a space, he must be still alive, he must have fled! And then, why fled? and how? and in that case, can we venture to declare this suicide? O, we must be careful. I foresee that we may yet involve your master in some dire catastrophe.'

'Why don't you read it, sir?' asked Poole.

'Because I fear,' replied the lawyer solemnly. 'God grant I have no cause for it!' And with that he brought the paper to his eyes and read as follows.

'My dear Utterson, – When this shall fall into your hands, I shall have disappeared, under what circumstances I have not the penetration to foresee, but my instinct and all the circumstances of my nameless situation tell me that the end is sure and must be early. Go then, and first read the narrative which Lanyon warned me he was to place in your hands; and if you care to hear more, turn to the confession of

'Your unworthy and unhappy friend,

'HENRY JEKYLL'

'There was a third enclosure?' asked Utterson.

'Here, sir,' said Poole, and gave into his hands a considerable packet sealed in several places.

The lawyer put it in his pocket. 'I would say nothing of this paper. If your master has fled or is dead, we may at least save his credit. It is now ten; I must go home and read these documents in quiet; but I shall be back before midnight, when we shall send for the police.'

They went out, locking the door of the theatre behind them; and Utterson, once more leaving the servants gathered about the fire in the hall, trudged back to his office to read the two narratives in which this mystery was now to be explained.

On the ninth of January, now four days ago, I received by the evening delivery a registered envelope, addressed in the hand of my colleague and old school-companion, Henry Jekyll. I was a good deal surprised by this; for we were by no means in the habit of correspondence; I had seen the man, dined with him, indeed, the night before; and I could imagine nothing in our intercourse that should justify the formality of registration. The contents increased my wonder; for this is how the letter ran:

'10th December, 18 —[1]

'Dear Lanyon, – You are one of my oldest friends; and although we may have differed at times on scientific questions, I cannot remember, at least on my side, any break in our affection. There was never a day when, if you had said to me, "Jekyll, my life, my honour, my reason, depend upon you," I would not have sacrificed my fortune or my left hand to help you. Lanyon, my life, my honour, my reason, are all at your mercy; if you fail me tonight, I am lost. You might suppose, after this preface, that I am going to ask you for something dishonourable to grant. Judge for yourself.

'I want you to postpone all other engagements for tonight – ay, even if you were summoned to the bedside of an emperor; to take a cab, unless your carriage should be actually at the door; and with this letter in your hand for consultation, to drive straight to my house. Poole, my butler, has his orders; you will find him waiting your arrival with a locksmith. The door of my cabinet is then to be forced; and you are to go in alone; to open the glazed press (letter E) on the left hand, breaking the lock if it be shut; and to draw out, *with all its contents as they stand*, the fourth drawer from the top or (which is the same thing) the third from the bottom. In my extreme distress of mind, I have a morbid fear of misdirecting you; but even if I am in error, you may know the right drawer by its contents: some powders, a phial and a paper book. This drawer I beg of you to carry back with you to Cavendish Square exactly as it stands.

'That is the first part of the service: now for the second. You should be back, if you set out at once on the receipt of this, long before midnight; but I will leave you that amount of margin, not only in the fear of one of those obstacles that can neither be prevented nor foreseen, but because an hour when your servants are in bed is to be preferred for what will then remain to do. At midnight, then, I have to ask you to be alone in your consulting room, to admit with your own hand into the house a man who will present himself in my name, and to place in his hands the drawer that you will have brought with you from my cabinet. Then you will have played your part and earned my gratitude completely. Five minutes, afterwards, if you insist upon an explanation, you will have understood that these arrangements are of capital importance; and that by the neglect of one of them, fantastic as they must appear, you might have charged your conscience with my death or the shipwreck of my reason.

'Confident as I am that you will not trifle with this appeal, my heart sinks and my hand trembles at the bare thought of such a possibility. Think of me at this hour, in a strange place, labouring under a blackness of distress that no fancy can exaggerate, and yet well aware that, if you will but punctually serve me, my troubles will roll away like a story that is told. Serve me, my dear Lanyon, and save

'Your friend,

'H. J.

'PS I had already sealed this up when a fresh terror struck upon my soul. It is possible that the post office may fail me, and this letter not come into your hands until tomorrow morning. In that case, dear Lanyon, do my errand when it shall be most convenient for you in the course of the day; and once more expect my messenger at midnight. It may then already be too late; and if that night passes without event, you will know that you have seen the last of Henry Jekyll.'

Upon the reading of this letter, I made sure my colleague was insane; but till that was proved beyond the possibility of doubt, I felt bound to do as he requested. The less I understood of this farrago, the less I was in a position to judge of its importance; and an appeal so worded could not be set aside without a grave responsibility. I rose accordingly from table, got into a hansom, and drove straight to Jekyll's house. The butler was awaiting my arrival; he had received by the same post as mine a registered letter of instruction, and had sent at once for a locksmith and a carpenter. The tradesmen came while we were yet speaking; and we moved in a body to old Dr Denman's surgical theatre from which (as you are doubtless aware) Jekyll's private cabinet is most conveniently entered. The door was very strong, the lock excellent; the carpenter avowed he would have great trouble and have to do much damage, if force were to be used; and the locksmith was near despair. But this last was a handy fellow, and after two hours' work, the door stood open. The press marked E was unlocked; and I took out the drawer, had it filled up with straw and tied in a sheet, and returned with it to Cavendish Square.

Here I proceeded to examine its contents. The powders were neatly enough made up, but not with the nicety of the dispensing chemist; so that it was plain they were of Jekyll's private manufacture; and when I opened one of the wrappers, I found what seemed to me a simple, crystalline salt of a white colour. The phial, to which I next turned my attention, might have been about half-full of a blood-red liquor, which was highly pungent to the sense of smell and seemed to me to contain phosphorus and some volatile ether. At the other ingredients, I could make no guess. The book was an ordinary version book and contained little but a series of dates. These covered a period of many years, but I observed that the entries ceased nearly a year ago and quite abruptly. Here and there a brief remark was appended to a date, usually no more than a single word: 'double' occurring perhaps six times in a total of several hundred entries; and once very early in the list and followed by several marks of exclamation, 'total failure!!!' All this, though it whetted my curiosity, told me little that was definite. Here were a phial of some tincture, a paper of some salt, and the record of a series of experiments that had led (like too many of Jekyll's investigations) to no end of practical usefulness. How could the presence of these articles in my house affect either the honour, the sanity, or the life of my flighty colleague? If his messenger could go to one place, why could he not go to another? And even granting some impediment, why was this gentleman to be received by me in secret? The more I reflected, the more convinced I grew that I was dealing with a case of cerebral disease; and though I dismissed my servants to bed, I loaded an old revolver that I might be found in some posture of self-defence.

Twelve o'clock had scarce rung out over London, ere the knocker sounded very gently on the door. I went myself at the summons, and found a small man crouching against the pillars of the portico.

'Are you come from Dr Jekyll?' I asked.

He told me 'yes' by a constrained gesture; and when I had bidden him enter, he did not obey me without a searching backward glance into the darkness of the square. There was a policeman not far off, advancing with his bull's eye[2] open; and at the sight, I thought my visitor started and made greater haste.

These particulars struck me, I confess, disagreeably; and as I followed him into the bright light of the consulting room, I kept my hand ready on my weapon. Here, at last, I had a chance of clearly seeing him. I had never set eyes on him before, so much was certain. He was small, as I have said; I was struck besides with the shocking expression of his face, with his remarkable combination of great muscular activity and great apparent debility of constitution, and – last but not least – with the odd, subjective disturbance caused by his neighbourhood. This bore some resemblance to incipient rigor, and was accompanied by a marked sinking of the pulse. At the time, I set it down to some idiosyncratic, personal distaste, and merely wondered at the acuteness of the symptoms; but I have since had reason to believe the cause to lie much deeper in the nature of man, and to turn on some nobler hinge than the principle of hatred.

This person (who had thus, from the first moment of his entrance, struck in me what I can only describe as a disgustful curiosity) was dressed in a fashion that would have made an ordinary person laughable: his clothes, that is to say, although they were of rich and sober fabric, were enormously too large for him in every measurement – the trousers hanging on his legs and rolled up to keep them from the ground, the waist of the coat below his haunches, and the collar sprawling wide upon his shoulders. Strange to relate, this ludicrous accoutrement was far from moving me to laughter. Rather, as there was something abnormal and misbegotten in the very essence of the creature that now faced me – something seizing, surprising and revolting – this fresh disparity seemed but to fit in with and to reinforce it; so that to my interest in the man's nature and character, there was added a curiosity as to his origin, his life, his fortune and status in the world.

These observations, though they have taken so great a space to be set down in, were yet the work of a few seconds. My visitor was, indeed, on fire with sombre excitement.

'Have you got it?' he cried. 'Have you got it?' And so lively was his impatience that he even laid his hand upon my arm and sought to shake me.

I put him back, conscious at his touch of a certain icy pang along my blood. 'Come, sir,' said I. 'You forget that I have not yet the pleasure of your acquaintance. Be seated, if you please.' And I showed him an example, and sat down myself in my customary seat and with as fair an imitation of my ordinary manner to a patient, as the lateness of the house, the nature of my preoccupations, and the horror I had of my visitor, would suffer me to muster.

'I beg your pardon, Dr Lanyon,' he replied civilly enough. 'What you say is very well founded; and my impatience has shown its heels to my politeness. I come here at the instance of your colleague, Dr Henry Jekyll, on a piece of business of some moment; and I understood . . .' he paused and put his hand to his throat, and I could see, in spite of his collected manner, that he was wrestling against the approaches of the hysteria – 'I understood, a drawer . . .'

But here I took pity on my visitor's suspense, and some perhaps on my own growing curiosity.

'There it is, sir,' said I, pointing to the drawer, where it lay on the floor behind a table and still covered with the sheet.

He sprang to it, and then paused, and laid his hand upon his heart; I could hear his teeth grate with the convulsive action of his jaws; and his face was so ghastly to see that I grew alarmed both for his life and reason.

'Compose yourself,' said I.

He turned a dreadful smile to me, and as if with the decision of despair, plucked away the sheet. At sight of the contents, he uttered one loud sob of such immense relief that I sat petrified. And the next moment, in a voice that was already fairly well under control, 'Have you a graduated glass?' he asked.

I rose from my place with something of an effort and gave him what he asked.

He thanked me with a smiling nod, measured out a few minims of the red tincture and added one of the powders. The mixture, which was at first of a reddish hue, began, in proportion as the crystals melted, to brighten in colour, to effervesce audibly, and to throw off small fumes of vapour. Suddenly and at the same moment, the ebullition ceased and the compound changed to a dark purple, which faded again more slowly to a watery green. My visitor, who had watched these metamorphoses with a keen eye, smiled, set down the glass upon the table, and then turned and looked upon me with an air of scrutiny.

'And now,' said he, 'to settle what remains. Will you be wise? will you be guided? will you suffer me to take this glass in my hand and to go forth from your house without further parley? or has the greed of curiosity too much command of you? Think before you answer, for it shall be done as you decide. As you decide, you shall be left as you were before, and neither richer nor wiser, unless the sense of service rendered to a man in mortal distress may be counted as a kind of riches of the soul. Or, if you shall so prefer to choose, a new province of knowledge and new avenues to fame and power shall be laid open to you, here, in this room, upon the instant; and your sight shall be blasted by a prodigy to stagger the unbelief of Satan.'

'Sir,' said I, affecting a coolness that I was far from truly possessing, 'you speak enigmas, and you will perhaps not wonder that I hear you with no very strong impression of belief. But I have gone too far in the way of inexplicable services to pause before I see the end.'

'It is well,' replied my visitor. 'Lanyon, you remember your vows: what follows is under the seal of our profession.[3] And now, you who have so long been bound to the most narrow and material views, you who have denied the virtue of transcendental medicine, you who have derided your superiors – behold!'

He put the glass to his lips and drank at one gulp. A cry followed; he reeled, staggered, clutched at the table and held on, staring with injected eyes, gasping with open mouth; and as I looked there came, I thought, a change – he seemed to swell – his face became suddenly black and the features seemed to melt and alter – and the next moment, I had sprung to my feet and leaped back against the wall, my arm raised to shield me from that prodigy, my mind submerged in terror.

'O God!' I screamed, and 'O God!' again and again; for there before my eyes – pale and shaken, and half fainting, and groping before him with his hands, like a man restored from death – there stood Henry Jekyll!

What he told me in the next hour, I cannot bring my mind to set on paper. I saw what I saw, I heard what I heard, and my soul sickened at it; and yet now when that sight has faded from my eyes, I ask myself if I believe it, and I cannot answer. My life is shaken to its roots; sleep has left me; the deadliest terror sits by me at all hours of the day and night; I feel that my days are numbered, and that I must die; and yet I shall die incredulous. As for the moral turpitude that man unveiled to me, even with tears of penitence, I cannot, even in memory, dwell on it without a start of horror. I will say but one thing, Utterson, and that (if you can bring your mind to credit it) will be more than enough. The creature who crept into my house that night was, on Jekyll's own confession, known by the name of Hyde and hunted for in every corner of the land as the murderer of Carew.

HASTIE LANYON.

I was born in the year 18— to a large fortune, endowed besides with excellent parts, inclined by nature to industry, fond of the respect of the wise and good among my fellow-men, and thus, as might have been supposed, with every guarantee of an honourable and distinguished future. And indeed the worst of my faults was a certain impatient gaiety of disposition, such as has made the happiness of many, but such as I found it hard to reconcile with my imperious desire to carry my head high, and wear a more than commonly grave countenance before the public. Hence it came about that I concealed my pleasures; and that when I reached years of reflection, and began to look round me and take stock of my progress and position in the world, I stood already committed to a profound duplicity of life. Many a man would have even blazoned such irregularities as I was guilty of; but from the high views that I had set before me, I regarded and hid them with an almost morbid sense of shame. It was thus rather the exacting nature of my aspirations than any particular degradation in my faults, that made me what I was and, with even a deeper trench than in the majority of men, severed in me those provinces of good and ill which divide and compound man's dual nature. In this case, I was driven to reflect deeply and inveterately on that hard law of life, which lies at the root of religion and is one of the most plentiful springs of distress. Though so profound a double-dealer, I was in no sense a hypocrite; both sides of me were in dead earnest; I was no more myself when I laid aside restraint and plunged in shame, than when I laboured, in the eye of day, at the furtherance of knowledge or the relief of sorrow and suffering. And it chanced that the direction of my scientific studies, which led wholly towards the mystic and the transcendental, reacted and shed a strong light on this consciousness of the perennial war among my members.[1] With every day, and from both sides of my intelligence, the moral and the intellectual, I thus drew steadily nearer to that truth, by whose partial discovery I have been doomed to such a dreadful shipwreck: that man is not truly one, but truly two. I say two, because the state of my own knowledge does not pass beyond that point. Others will follow, others will outstrip me on the same lines; and I hazard the guess that man will be ultimately known for a mere polity of multifarious, incongruous and independent denizens. I for my part, from the nature of my life, advanced infallibly in one direction and in one direction only. It was on the moral side, and in my own person, that I learned to recognize the thorough and primitive duality of man; I saw that, of the two natures that contended in the field of my consciousness, even if I could rightly be said to be either, it was only because I was radically both; and from an early date, even before the course of my scientific discoveries had begun to suggest the most naked possibility of such a miracle, I had learned to dwell with pleasure, as a beloved daydream, on the thought of the separation of these elements. If each, I told myself, could but be housed in separate identities, life would be relieved of all that was unbearable; the unjust might go his way, delivered from the aspirations and remorse of his more upright twin; and the just could walk steadfastly and securely on his upward path, doing the good things in which he found his pleasure, and no longer exposed to disgrace and penitence by the hands of this extraneous evil. It was the curse of mankind that these incongruous faggots[2] were thus bound together – that in the agonized womb of consciousness, these polar twins should be continuously struggling. How, then, were they dissociated?

I was so far in my reflections when, as I have said, a side light began to shine upon the subject from the laboratory table. I began to perceive more deeply than it has ever yet been stated, the trembling immateriality, the mist-like transience, of this seemingly so solid body in which we walk attired. Certain agents I found to have the power to shake and to pluck back that fleshly vestment, even as a wind might toss the curtains of a pavilion. For two good reasons, I will not enter deeply into this scientific branch of my confession. First, because I have been made to learn that the doom and burden of our life is bound forever on man's shoulders, and when the attempt is made to cast it off, it but returns upon us with more unfamiliar and more awful pressure. Second, because as my narrative will make alas! too evident, my discoveries were incomplete. Enough, then, that I not only recognized my natural body for the mere aura and effulgence of certain of the powers that made up my spirit, but managed to compound a drug by which these powers should be dethroned from their supremacy, and a second form and countenance substituted, none the less natural to me because they were the expression, and bore the stamp, of lower elements in my soul.

I hesitated long before I put this theory to the test of practice. I knew well that I risked death; for any drug that so potently controlled and shook the very fortress of identity, might by the least scruple of an overdose or at the least inopportunity in the moment of exhibition, utterly blot out that immaterial tabernacle which I looked to it to change. But the temptation of a discovery so singular and profound, at last overcame the suggestions of alarm. I had long since prepared my tincture; I purchased at once, from a firm of wholesale chemists, a large quantity of a particular salt which I knew, from my experiments, to be the last ingredient required; and late one accursed night, I compounded the elements, watched them boil and smoke together in the glass, and when the ebullition had subsided, with a strong glow of courage, drank off the potion.

The most racking pangs succeeded: a grinding in the bones, deadly nausea, and a horror of the spirit that cannot be exceeded at the hour of birth or death. Then these agonies began swiftly to subside, and I came to myself as if out of a great sickness. There was something strange in my sensations, something indescribably new and, from its very novelty, incredibly sweet. I felt younger, lighter, happier in body; within I was conscious of a heady recklessness, a current of disordered sensual images running like a mill race in my fancy, a solution of the bonds of obligation, an unknown but not an innocent freedom of the soul. I knew myself, at the first breath of this new life, to be more wicked, tenfold more wicked, sold a slave to my original evil; and the thought, in that moment, braced and delighted me like wine. I stretched out my hands, exulting in the freshness of these sensations; and in the act, I was suddenly aware that I had lost in stature.

There was no mirror, at that date, in my room; that which stands beside me as I write, was brought there later on and for the very purpose of these transformations. The night, however, was far gone into the morning – the morning, black as it was, was nearly ripe for the conception of the day – the inmates of my house were locked in the most rigorous hours of slumber; and I determined, flushed as I was with hope and triumph, to venture in my new shape as far as to my bedroom. I crossed the yard, wherein the constellations looked down upon me, I could have thought, with wonder, the first creature of that sort that their unsleeping vigilance had yet disclosed to them; I stole through the corridors, a stranger in my own house; and coming to my room, I saw for the first time the appearance of Edward Hyde.

I must here speak by theory alone, saying not that which I know, but that which I suppose to be most probable. The evil side of my nature, to which I had now transferred the stamping efficacy, was less robust and less developed than the good which I had just deposed. Again, in the course of my life, which had been, after all, nine tenths a life of effort, virtue and control, it had been much less exercised and much less exhausted. And hence, as I think, it came about that Edward Hyde was so much smaller, slighter and younger than Henry Jekyll. Even as good shone upon the countenance of the one, evil was written broadly and plainly on the face of the other. Evil besides (which I must still believe to be the lethal side of man) had left on that body an imprint of deformity and decay. And yet when I looked upon that ugly idol in the glass, I was conscious of no repugnance, rather of a leap of welcome. This, too, was myself. It seemed natural and human. In my eyes it bore a livelier image of the spirit, it seemed more express and single, than the imperfect and divided countenance, I had been hitherto accustomed to call mine. And in so far I was doubtless right. I have observed that when I wore the semblance of Edward Hyde, none could come near to me at first without a visible misgiving of the flesh. This, as I take it, was because all human beings, as we meet them, are commingled out of good and evil: and Edward Hyde, alone in the ranks of mankind, was pure evil.

I lingered but a moment at the mirror: the second and conclusive experiment had yet to be attempted; it yet remained to be seen if I had lost my identity beyond redemption and must flee before daylight from a house that was no longer mine; and hurrying back to my cabinet, I once more prepared and drank the cup, once more suffered the pangs of dissolution, and came to myself once more with the character, the stature and the face of Henry Jekyll.

.That night I had come to the fatal cross roads. Had I approached my discovery in a more noble spirit, had I risked the experiment while under the empire of generous or pious aspirations, all must have been otherwise, and from these agonies of death and birth, I had come forth an angel instead of a fiend. The drug had no discriminating action; it was neither diabolical nor divine; it but shook the doors of the prisonhouse of my disposition; and like the captives of Philippi,³ that which stood within ran forth. At that time my virtue slumbered; my evil, kept awake by ambition, was alert and swift to seize the occasion; and the thing that was projected was Edward Hyde. Hence, although I had now two characters as well as two appearances, one was wholly evil, and the other was still the old Henry Jekyll, that incongruous compound of whose reformation and improvement I had already learned to despair. The movement was thus wholly toward the worse.

Even at that time, I had not yet conquered my aversion to the dryness of a life of study. I would still be merrily disposed at times; and as my pleasures were (to say the least) undignified, and I was not only well known and highly considered, but growing towards the elderly man, this incoherency of my life was daily growing more unwelcome. It was on this side that my new power tempted me until I fell in slavery. I had but to drink the cup, to doff at once the body of the noted professor, and to assume, like a thick cloak, that of Edward Hyde. I smiled at the notion; it seemed to me at the time to be humorous; and I made my preparations with the most studious care. I took and furnished that house in Soho, to which Hyde was tracked by the police; and engaged as housekeeper a creature whom I well knew to be silent and unscrupulous. On the other side, I announced to my servants that a Mr Hyde (whom I described) was to have full liberty and power about my house in the square; and to parry mishaps, I even called and made myself a familiar object, in my second character. I next drew up that will to which you so much objected; so that if anything befell me in the person of Doctor Jekyll, I could enter on that of Edward Hyde without pecuniary loss. And thus fortified, as I supposed, on every side, I began to profit by the strange immunities of my position.

Men have before hired bravos to transact their crimes, while their own person and reputation sat under shelter. I was the first that ever did so for his pleasures. I was the first that could thus plod in the public eye with a load of genial respectability, and in a moment, like a schoolboy, strip off these lendings and spring headlong into the sea of liberty. But for me, in my impenetrable mantle, the safety was complete. Think of it – I did not even exist! Let me but escape into my laboratory door, give me but a second or two to mix and swallow the draught that I had always standing ready; and whatever he had done, Edward Hyde would pass away like the stain of breath upon a mirror; and there in his stead, quietly at home, trimming the midnight lamp in his study, a man who could afford to laugh at suspicion, would be Henry Jekyll.

The pleasures which I made haste to seek in my disguise were, as I have said, undignified; I would scarce use a harder term. But in the hands of Edward Hyde, they soon began to turn towards the monstrous. When I would come back from these excursions, I was often plunged into a kind of wonder at my vicarious depravity. This familiar that I called out of my own soul, and sent forth alone to do his good pleasure, was a being inherently malign and villainous; his every act and thought centered on self; drinking pleasure with bestial avidity from any degree of torture to another; relentless like a man of stone. Henry Jekyll stood at times aghast before the acts of Edward Hyde; but the situation was apart from ordinary laws, and insidiously relaxed the grasp of conscience. It was Hyde, after all, and Hyde alone, that was guilty. Jekyll was no worse; he woke again to his good qualities seemingly unimpaired; he would even make haste, where it was possible, to undo the evil done by Hyde. And thus his conscience slumbered.

Into the details of the infamy at which I thus connived (for even now I can scarce grant that I committed it) I have no design of entering; I mean but to point out the warnings and the successive steps with which my chastisement approached. I met with one accident which, as it brought on no consequence, I shall no more than mention. An act of cruelty to a child aroused against me the anger of a passer by, whom I recognized the other day in the person of your kinsman; the doctor and the child's family joined him; there were moments when I feared for my life; and at last, in order to pacify their too just resentment, Edward Hyde had to bring them to the door, and pay them in a cheque drawn in the name, of Henry Jekyll. But this danger was easily eliminated from the future, by opening an account at another bank in the name of Edward Hyde himself; and when, by sloping my own hand backward, I had supplied my double with a signature, I thought I sat beyond the reach of fate.

Some two months before the murder of Sir Danvers, I had been out for one of my adventures, had returned at a late hour, and woke the next day in bed with somewhat odd sensations. It was in vain I looked about me; in vain I saw the decent furniture and tall proportions of my room in the square; in vain that I recognized the pattern of the bed curtains and the design of the mahogany frame; something still kept insisting that I was not where I was, that I had not wakened where I seemed to be, but in the little room in Soho where I was accustomed to sleep in the body of Edward Hyde. I smiled to myself, and, in my psychological way, began lazily to inquire into the elements of this illusion, occasionally, even as I did so, dropping back into a comfortable morning doze. I was still so engaged when, in one of my more wakeful moments, my eye fell upon my hand. Now the hand of Henry Jekyll (as you have often remarked) was professional in shape and size: it was large, firm, white and comely. But the hand which I now saw, clearly enough, in the yellow light of a mid-London morning, lying half shut on the bed clothes, was lean, corded, knuckly, of a dusky pallor and thickly shaded with a smart growth of hair. It was the hand of Edward Hyde.

I must have stared upon it for near half a minute, sunk as I was in the mere stupidity of wonder, before terror woke up in my breast as sudden and startling as the crash of cymbals; and bounding from my bed, I rushed to the mirror. At the sight that met my eyes, my blood was changed into something exquisitely thin and icy. Yes, I had gone to bed Henry Jekyll, I had awakened Edward Hyde. How was this to be explained? I asked myself; and then, with another bound of terror – how was it to be remedied? It was well on in the morning; the servants were up; all my drugs were in the cabinet – a long journey, down two pairs of stairs, through the back passage, across the open court and through the anatomical theatre, from where I was then standing horror-struck. It might indeed be possible to cover my face; but of what use was that, when I was unable to conceal the alteration in my stature? And then with an overpowering sweetness of relief, it came back upon my mind that the servants were already used to the coming and going of my second self. I had soon dressed, as well as I was able, in clothes of my own size: had soon passed through the house, where Bradshaw stared and drew back at seeing Mr Hyde at such an hour and in such a strange array; and ten minutes later, Dr Jekyll had returned to his own shape and was sitting down, with a darkened brow, to make a feint of breakfasting.

Small indeed was my appetite. This inexplicable incident, this reversal of my previous experience, seemed, like the Babylonian finger on the wall,[4] to be spelling out the letters of my judgment; and I began to reflect more seriously than ever before on the issues and possibilities of my double existence. That part of me which I had the power of projecting, had lately been much exercised and nourished; it had seemed to me of late as though the body of Edward Hyde had grown in stature, as though (when I wore that form) I were conscious of a more generous tide of blood; and I began to spy a danger that, if this were much prolonged, the balance of my nature might be permanently overthrown, the power of voluntary change be forfeited, and the character of Edward Hyde become irrevocably mine. The power of the drug had not been always equally displayed. Once, very early in my career, it had totally failed me; since then I had been obliged on more than one occasion to double, and once, with infinite risk of death, to treble the amount; and these rare uncertainties had cast hitherto the sole shadow on my contentment. Now, however, and in the light of that morning's accident, I was led to remark that whereas, in the beginning, the difficulty had been to throw off the body of Jekyll, it had of late, gradually but decidedly transferred itself to the other side. All things therefore seemed to point to this: that I was slowly losing hold of my original and better self, and becoming slowly incorporated with my second and worse.

Between these two, I now felt I had to choose. My two natures had memory in common, but all other faculties were most unequally shared between them. Jekyll (who was composite) now with the most sensitive apprehensions, now with a greedy gusto, projected and shared in the pleasures and adventures of Hyde; but Hyde was indifferent to Jekyll, or but remembered him as the mountain bandit remembers the cavern in which he conceals himself from pursuit. Jekyll had more than a father's interest; Hyde had more than a son's indifference. To cast in my lot with Jekyll, was to die to those appetites which I had long secretly indulged and had of late begun to pamper. To cast it in with Hyde, was to die to a thousand interests and aspirations, and to become, at a blow and forever, despised and friendless. The bargain might appear unequal; but there was still another consideration in the scales; for while Jekyll would suffer smartingly in the fires of abstinence, Hyde would be not even conscious of all that he had lost. Strange as my circumstances were, the terms of this debate are as old and commonplace as man; much the same inducements and alarms cast the die for any tempted and trembling sinner; and it fell out with me, as it falls with so vast a majority of my fellows, that I chose the better part and was found wanting in the strength to keep to it.

Yes, I preferred the elderly and discontented doctor, surrounded by friends and cherishing honest hopes; and bade a resolute farewell to the liberty, the comparative youth, the light step, leaping pulses and secret pleasures, that I had enjoyed in the disguise of Hyde. I made this choice perhaps with some unconscious reservation, for I neither gave up the house in Soho, nor destroyed the clothes of Edward Hyde, which still lay ready in my cabinet. For two months, however, I was true to my determination; for two months, I led a life of such severity as I had never before attained to, and enjoyed the compensations of an approving conscience. But time began at last to obliterate the freshness of my alarm; the praises of conscience began to grow into a thing of course; I began to be tortured with throes and longings, as of Hyde struggling after freedom; and at last, in an hour of moral weakness, I once again compounded and swallowed the transforming draught.

I do not suppose that, when a drunkard reasons with himself upon his vice, he is once out of five hundred times affected by the dangers that he runs through his brutish, physical insensibility; neither had I, long as I had considered my position, made enough allowance for the complete moral insensibility and insensate readiness to evil, which were the leading characters of Edward Hyde. Yet it was by these that I was punished. My devil had been long caged, he came out roaring. I was conscious, even when I took the draught, of a more unbridled, a more furious propensity to ill. It must have been this, I suppose, that stirred in my soul that tempest of impatience with which I listened to the civilities of my unhappy victim; I declare at least, before God, no man morally sane could have been guilty of that crime upon so pitiful a provocation; and that I struck in no more reasonable spirit than that in which a sick child may break a plaything. But I had voluntarily stripped myself of all those balancing instincts, by which even the worst of us continues to walk with some degree of steadiness among temptations; and in my case, to be tempted, however slightly, was to fall.

Instantly the spirit of hell awoke in me and raged. With a transport of glee, I mauled the unresisting body, tasting delight from every blow; and it was not till weariness had begun to succeed, that I was suddenly, in the top fit of my delirium, struck through the heart by a cold thrill of terror. A mist dispersed; I saw my life to be forfeit; and fled from the scene of these excesses, at once glorying and trembling, my lust of evil gratified and stimulated, my love of life screwed to the topmost peg. I ran to the house in Soho, and (to make assurance doubly sure) destroyed my papers; thence I set out through the lamplit streets, in the same divided ecstasy of mind, gloating on my crime, light-headedly devising others in the future, and yet still hastening and still hearkening in my wake for the steps of the avenger. Hyde had a song upon his lips as he compounded the draught, and as he drank it, pledged the dead man. The pangs of transformation had not done tearing him, before Henry Jekyll, with streaming tears of gratitude and remorse, had fallen upon his knees and lifted his clasped hands to God. The veil of self-indulgence was rent from head to foot, I saw my life as a whole: I followed it up from the days of childhood, when I had walked with my father's hand, and through the self-denying toils of my professional life, to arrive again and again, with the same sense of unreality, at the demand horrors of the evening. I could have screamed aloud; I sought with tears and prayers to smother down the crowd of hideous images and sounds with which my memory swarmed against me; and still, between the petitions, the ugly face of my iniquity stared into my soul. As the acuteness of this remorse began to die away, it was succeeded by a sense of joy. The problem of my conduct was solved. Hyde was thenceforth impossible; whether I would or not, I was now confined to the better part of my existence; and O, how I rejoiced to think it! with what willing humility, I embraced anew the restrictions of natural life! with what sincere renunciation, I locked the door by which I had so often gone and come, and ground the key under my heel!

The next day, came the news that the murder had been overlooked, that the guilt of Hyde was patent to the world, and that the victim was a man high in public estimation. It was not only a crime, it had been a tragic folly. I think I was glad to know it; I think I was glad to have my better impulses thus buttressed and guarded by the terrors of the scaffold. Jekyll was now my city of refuge; let but Hyde peep out an instant, and the hands of all men would be raised to take and slay him.

I resolved in my future conduct to redeem the past; and I can say with honesty that my resolve was fruitful of some good. You know yourself how earnestly in the last months of last year, I laboured to relieve suffering; you know that much was done for others, and that the days passed quietly, almost happily for myself. Nor can I truly say that I wearied of this beneficent and innocent life; I think instead that I daily enjoyed it more completely; but I was still cursed with my duality of purpose; and as the first edge of my penitence wore off, the lower side of me, so long indulged, so recently chained down, began to growl for licence. Not that I dreamed of resuscitating Hyde; the bare idea of that would startle me to frenzy: no, it was in my own person, that I was once more tempted to trifle with my conscience; and it was as an ordinary secret sinner, that I at last fell before the assaults of temptation.

There comes an end to all things; the most capacious measure is filled at last; and this brief condescension to my evil finally destroyed the balance of my soul. And yet I was not alarmed; the fall seemed natural, like a return to the old days before I had made my discovery. It was a fine, clear, January day, wet under foot where the frost had melted, but cloudless overhead; and the Regent's Park[5] was full of winter chirruppings and sweet with Spring odours. I sat in the sun on a bench; the animal within me licking the chops of memory; the spiritual side a little drowsed, promising subsequent penitence, but not yet moved to begin. After all, I reflected I was like my neighbours; and then I smiled, comparing myself with other men, comparing my active goodwill with the lazy cruelty of their neglect. And at the very moment of that vainglorious thought, a qualm came over me, a horrid nausea and the most deadly shuddering. These passed away, and left me faint; and then as in its turn the faintness subsided, I began to be aware of a change in the temper of my thoughts, a greater boldness, a contempt of danger, a solution of the bonds of obligation. I looked down; my clothes hung formlessly on my shrunken limbs; the hand that lay on my knee was corded and hairy. I was once more Edward Hyde. A moment before I had been safe of all men's respect, wealthy, beloved – the cloth laying for me in the dining room at home; and now I was the common quarry of mankind, hunted, houseless, a known murderer, thrall to the gallows.

My reason wavered, but it did not fail me utterly. I have more than once observed that, in my second character, my faculties seemed sharpened to a point and my spirits more tensely elastic; thus it came about that, where Jekyll perhaps might have succumbed, Hyde rose to the importance of the moment. My drugs were in one of the presses of my cabinet; how was I to reach them? That was the problem that (crushing my temples in my hands) I set myself to solve. The laboratory door I had closed. If I sought to enter by the house, my own servants would consign me to the gallows. I saw I must employ another hand, and thought of Lanyon. How was he to be reached? how persuaded? Supposing that I escaped capture in the streets, how was I to make my way into his presence? and how should I, an unknown and displeasing visitor, prevail on the famous physician to rifle the study of his colleague, Dr Jekyll? Then I remembered that of my original character, one part remained to me: I could write my own hand; and once I had conceived that kindling spark, the way that I must follow became lighted up from end to end.

Thereupon, I arranged my clothes as best I could, and summoning a passing hansom, drove to an hotel in Portland Street,[6] the name of which I chanced to remember. At my appearance (which was indeed comical enough, however tragic a fate these garments covered) the driver could not conceal his mirth. I gnashed my teeth upon him with a gust of devilish fury; and the smile withered from his face – happily for him – yet more happily for myself, for in another instant I had certainly dragged him from his perch. At the inn, as I entered, I looked about me with so black a countenance as made the attendants tremble; not a look did they exchange in my presence; but obsequiously took my orders, led me to a private room, and brought me wherewithal to write. Hyde in danger of his life was a creature new to me: shaken with inordinate anger, strung to the pitch of murder, lusting to inflict pain. Yet the creature was astute; mastered his fury with a great effort of the will; composed his two important letters, one to Lanyon and one to Poole; and that he might receive actual evidence of their being posted, sent them out with directions that they should be registered.

Thenceforward, he sat all day over the fire in the private room, gnawing his nails; there he dined, sitting alone with his fears, the waiter visibly quailing before his eye; and thence, when the night was fully come, he set forth in the corner of a closed cab, and was driven to and fro about the streets of the city. He, I say – I cannot say, I. That child of Hell had nothing human; nothing lived in him but fear and hatred. And when at last, thinking the driver had begun to grow suspicious, he discharged the cab and ventured on foot, attired in his misfitting clothes, an object marked out for observation, into the midst of the nocturnal passengers, these two base passions raged within him like a tempest. He walked fast, hunted by his fears, chattering to himself, skulking through the less frequented thoroughfares, counting the minutes that still divided him from midnight. Once a woman spoke to him, offering, I think, a box of lights. He smote her in the face, and she fled.

When I came to myself at Lanyon's, the horror of my old friend perhaps affected me somewhat: I do not know; it was at least but a drop in the sea to the abhorrence with which I looked back upon these hours. A change had come over me. It was no longer the fear of the gallows, it was the horror of being Hyde that racked me. I received Lanyon's condemnation partly in a dream; it was partly in a dream that I came home to my own house and got into bed. I slept after the prostration of the day, with a stringent and profound slumber which not even the nightmares that wrung me could avail to break. I awoke in the morning shaken, weakened, but refreshed. I still hated and feared the thought of the brute that slept within me, and I had not of course forgotten the appalling dangers of the day before; but I was once more at home, in my own house and close to my drugs; and gratitude for my escape shone so strong in my soul that it almost rivalled the brightness of hope.

I was stepping leisurely across the court after breakfast, drinking the chill of the air with pleasure, when I was seized again with those indescribable sensations that heralded the change; and I had but the time to gain the shelter of my cabinet, before I was once again raging and freezing with the passions of Hyde. It took on this occasion a double dose to recall me to myself; and alas, six hours after, as I sat looking sadly in the fire, the pangs returned, and the drug had to be readministered. In short, from that day forth it seemed only by a great effort as of gymnastics, and only under the immediate stimulation of the drug, that I was able to wear the countenance of Jekyll. At all hours of the day and night, I would be taken with the premonitory shudder; above all, if I slept, or even dozed for a moment in my chair, it was always as Hyde that I awakened. Under the strain of this continually impending doom and by the sleeplessness to which I now condemned myself, ay, even beyond what I had thought possible to man, I became, in my own person, a creature eaten up and emptied by fever, languidly weak both in both and mind, and solely occupied by one thought: the horror of my other self. But when I slept, or when the virtue of the medicine wore off, I would leap almost without transition (for the pangs of transformation grew daily less marked) into the possession of a fancy brimming with images of terror, a soul boiling with causeless hatreds, and a body that seemed not strong enough to contain the raging energies of life. The powers of Hyde seemed to have grown with the sickliness of Jekyll. And certainly the hate that now divided them was equal on each side. With Jekyll, it was a thing of vital instinct. He had now seen the full deformity of that creature that shared with him some of the phenomena of consciousness, and was co-heir with him to death: and beyond these links of community, which in themselves made the most poignant part of his distress, he thought of Hyde, for all his energy of life, as of something not only hellish but inorganic. This was the shocking thing; that the slime of the pit seemed to utter cries and voices; that the amorphous dust gesticulated and sinned; that what was dead, and had no shape, would usurp the offices of life. And this again, that that insurgent horror was knit to him closer than a wife, closer than an eye; lay caged in his flesh, where he heard it mutter and felt it struggle to be born; and at every hour of weakness, and in the confidence of slumber, prevailed against him, and deposed him out of life. The hatred of Hyde for Jekyll, was of a different order. His terror of the gallows drove him continually to commit temporary suicide, and return to his subordinate station of a part instead of a person; but he loathed the necessity, he loathed the despondency into which Jekyll was now fallen, and he resented the dislike with which he was himself regarded. Hence the ape-like tricks that he would play me, scrawling in my own hand blasphemies on the pages of my books, burning the letters and destroying the portrait of my father; and indeed, had it not been for his fear of death, he would long ago have ruined himself in order to involve me in the ruin. But his love of life is wonderful; I go further: I, who sicken and freeze at the mere thought of him, when I recall the abjection and passion of this attachment, and when I know how he fears my power to cut him off by suicide, I find it in my heart to pity him.

It is useless, and the time awfully fails me, to prolong this description; no one has ever suffered such torments, let that suffice; and yet even to these, habit brought – no, not alleviation – but a certain callousness of soul, a certain acquiescence of despair; and my punishment might have gone on for years, but for the last calamity which has now fallen, and which has finally severed me from my own face and nature. My provision of the salt, which had never been renewed since the date of the first experiment, began to run low. I sent out for a fresh supply, and mixed the draught; the ebullition followed, and the first change of colour, not the second; I drank it and it was without efficiency. You will learn from Poole how I have had London ransacked; it was in vain; and I am now persuaded that my first supply was impure, and that it was that unknown impurity which lent efficacy to the draught.

About a week has passed, and I am now finishing this statement under the influence of the last of the old powders. This, then, is the last time, short of a miracle, that Henry Jekyll can think his own thoughts or see his own face (now how sadly altered!) in the glass. Nor must I delay too long to bring my writing to an end; for if my narrative has hitherto escaped destruction, it has been by a combination of great prudence and great good luck. Should the throes of change take me in the act of writing it, Hyde will tear it in pieces; but if some time shall have elapsed after I have laid it by, his wonderful selfishness and circumscription to the moment will probably save it once again from the action of his ape-like spite. And indeed the doom that is closing on us both, has already changed and crushed him. Half an hour from now, when I shall again and forever reindue that hated personality, I know how I shall sit shuddering and weeping in my chair, or continue, with the most strained and fearstruck ecstasy of listening, to pace up and down this room (my last earthly refuge) and give ear to every sound of menace. Will Hyde die upon the scaffold? or will he find the courage to release himself at the last moment? God knows; I am careless; this is my true hour of death, and what is to follow concerns another than myself. Here then, as I lay down the pen and proceed to seal up my confession, I bring the life of that unhappy Henry Jekyll to an end.

THE BODY SNATCHER

The Body Snatcher

Every night in the year, four of us sat together in the small parlour of the George, at Debenham; the undertaker, and the landlord, and Fettes, and myself. Sometimes there would be more; but blow high, blow low, come rain, or snow, or frost, we four would be each planted in his own particular armchair. Fettes was an old drunken Scotchman, a man of education obviously, and a man of some property; since he lived in idleness. He had come to Debenham years ago, while still young; and by mere continuance of living had grown to be an adopted townsman. His blue camlet cloak[1] was a local antiquity, like the church spire. His place in the parlour at the George, his absence from church, his old, crapulous, disreputable vices, were all things of course in Debenham. He had some vague Radical opinions and some fleeting infidelities, which he would now and again set forth and emphasize with tottering slaps upon the table. He drank rum – five glasses regularly every evening; and for the greater portion of his nightly visit to the George sat, with his glass in his right hand, in a state of melancholy, alcoholic saturation. We called him the Doctor; for he was supposed to have some special knowledge of medicine, and had been known, upon a pinch, to set a fracture or reduce a dislocation; but beyond these slight particulars, we had no knowledge of his character and antecedents.

One dark winter night, it had struck nine some time before the landlord joined us. There was a sick man in the George, a great neighbouring proprietor suddenly struck down with apoplexy on his way to Parliament; and the great man's still greater London doctor had been telegraphed to his bedside. It was the first time such a thing

73

had happened in Debenham, for the railway was but newly open, and we were all proportionately moved by the occurrence.

'He's come,' said the landlord, after he had filled and lighted his pipe.

'He?' said I. 'Who? – not the doctor?'

'Himself,' replied our host.

'What is his name?'

'Dr Macfarlane,' said the landlord.

Fettes was far through his third tumbler, stupidly fuddled, now nodding over, now staring mazily around him; but at the last word he seemed to awaken, and repeated the name 'Macfarlane' twice, quietly enough the first time, but with a sudden emotion at the second.

'Yes,' said the landlord, 'that's his name, Doctor Wolfe Macfarlane.'

Fettes became instantly sober; his eyes awoke, his voice became clear, loud, and steady, his language forcible and earnest; we were all startled by the transformation, as if a man had risen from the dead.[2]

'I beg your pardon,' he said; 'I am afraid I have not been paying much attention to your talk. Who is this Wolfe Macfarlane?' And then, when he had heard the landlord out, 'It cannot be, it cannot be,' he added; 'and yet I would like well to see him face to face.'

'Do you know him, Doctor?' asked the undertaker, with a gasp.

'God forbid,' was the reply. 'And yet the name is a strange one; it were too much to fancy two. Tell me, landlord, is he old?'

'Well,' said the host, 'he's not a young man, to be sure, and his hair is white; but he looks younger than you.'

'He is older, though; years older. But' – with a slap upon the table – 'it's the rum you see in my face, rum and sin.[3] This man, perhaps, may have an easy conscience and a good digestion. Conscience! hear me speak. You would think I was some good, old, decent Christian, would you not? But no, not I; I never canted. Voltaire might have canted[4] if he'd stood in my shoes; but the brains' – with a rattling fillip on his bald head – 'the brains were clear and active; and I saw and I made no deductions.'

'If you know this doctor,' I ventured to remark after a somewhat awful pause, 'I should gather that you do not share the landlord's good opinion.'

Fettes paid no regard to me. 'Yes,' he said, with sudden decision, 'I must see him face to face.'

There was another pause, and then a door was closed rather sharply on the first floor and a step was heard upon the stair.

'That's the doctor,' cried the landlord; 'look sharp, and you can catch him.'

It was but two steps from the small parlour to the door of the old George inn; the wide oak staircase landed almost in the street; there was room for a Turkey rug and nothing more between the threshold and the last round of the descent; but this little space was every evening brilliantly lit up, not only by the light upon the stair and the great signal lamp below the sign, but by the warm radiance of the bar-room window. The George thus brightly advertised itself to passers-by in the cold street. Fettes walked steadily to the spot, and we, who were hanging behind, beheld the two men meet, as one of them had phrased it, face to face. Dr Macfarlane was alert and vigorous. His white hair set off his pale and placid although energetic countenance; he was richly dressed in the finest of broadcloth and the whitest of linen, with a great gold watch chain and studs and spectacles of the same precious material; he wore a broad folded tie, white and speckled with lilac, and he carried on his arm a comfortable driving-coat of fur. There was no doubt but he became his years, breathing, as he did, of wealth and consideration; and it was a surprising contrast to see our parlour sot, bald, dirty, pimpled, and robed in his old camlet cloak, confront him at the bottom of the stairs.

'Macfarlane,' he said, somewhat loudly, more like a herald than a friend.

The great doctor pulled up short on the fourth step, as though the familiarity of the address surprised and somewhat shocked his dignity.

'Toddy Macfarlane,' repeated Fettes.

The London man almost staggered; he stared for the swiftest of seconds at the man before him, glanced behind him with a sort of scare, and then in a startled whisper, 'Fettes!' he said, 'you!'

'Ay,' said the other, 'me. Did you think I was dead, too? We are not so easy shot of our acquaintance.'

'Hush, hush!' exclaimed the Doctor. 'Hush, hush! this meeting is so unexpected – I can see you are unmanned. I hardly knew you, I confess, at first; but I am overjoyed, overjoyed, to have this opportunity. For the present it must be how-d'ye-do and good-bye in one; for my fly[5] is waiting, and I must not fail the train; but you shall – let me see – yes – you shall give me your address, and you can count on early news of me. We must do something for you, Fettes; I fear you are out at elbows; but we must see to that – for auld lang syne, as once we sang at suppers.'

'Money!' cried Fettes; 'money from you! The money that I had of you is lying where I cast it in the rain.'

Dr Macfarlane had talked himself into some measure of superiority and confidence; but the uncommon energy of this refusal cast him back into his first confusion. A horrible, ugly look came and went across his almost venerable countenance. 'My dear fellow,' he said, 'be it as you please; my last thought is to offend you. I would intrude on none. I will leave you my address, however –'

'I do not wish it; I do not wish to know the roof that shelters you,' interrupted the other. 'I heard your name; I feared it might be you; I wished to know if, after all, there were a God; I know now that there is none. Begone!'

He still stood in the middle of the rug, between the stair and doorway; and the great London physician, in order to escape, would be forced to step upon one side. It was plain that he hesitated before the thought of this humiliation. White as he was, there was a dangerous glitter in his spectacles; but while he still paused uncertain he became aware that the driver of his fly was peering in from the street at this unusual scene, and caught a glimpse at the same time of our little body from the parlour, huddled by the corner of the bar. The presence of so many witnesses decided him at once to flee. He crouched together, brushing on the wainscot, and made a dart, like a serpent, striking for the door. But his tribulation was not yet entirely at an end; for even as he was passing Fettes clutched him by the arm, and these words came in a whisper, and yet painfully distinct, 'Have you seen it again?'

The great, rich London doctor cried out aloud with a sharp, thrott-ling cry; he dashed his questioner across the open space, and, with his hands over his head, fled out of the door like a detected thief. Before it had occurred to one of us to make a movement the fly was already rattling towards the station. The scene was over like a dream; but the dream had left proofs and traces of its passage. Next day the servant found the fine gold spectacles crushed and broken on the threshold, and that very night were we not all standing breathless by the bar-room window, and Fettes at our side, sober, pale, and resolute in look?

'God protect us, Mr Fettes!' said the landlord, coming first into possession of his customary senses. 'What in the universe is all this? These are strange things you have been saying.'

Fettes turned towards us: he looked us each in succession in the face. 'See if you can hold your tongues,' said he. 'That man, Macfarlane, is not safe to cross; those that have done so already, have repented it too late.'

And then, without so much as finishing his third glass, far less waiting for the other two, he bade us a good-bye and went forth, under the lamp of the hotel, into the black night.

We three returned to our places in the parlour, with the big red fire and four clear candles; and as we recapitulated what had passed the first chill of our surprise soon changed into a glow of curiosity. We sat late; it was the latest session I have known in the old George; each man, before we parted, had his theory that he was bound to prove; and none of us had any nearer business in this world than to track out the past of our contemned companion, and surprise the secret that he shared with the great London doctor. It is no great boast; but I believe I was a better hand at worming out a story than either of my fellows at the George; and perhaps there is now no other man alive who could narrate to you the following foul and unnatural events:

In his young days Fettes studied medicine in the schools of Edinburgh. He had talent of a kind, the talent that picks up swiftly what it hears and readily retails it for its own. He worked little at home; but he was civil, attentive, and intelligent in the presence of his masters. They soon picked him out as a lad who listened closely and remembered well; nay, strange as it seemed to me when first I heard it, he was in those days well favoured and pleased by his exterior. There was, at this period, a certain extramural teacher of anatomy, whom I shall here designate by the letter K—. His name was subsequently too well known. The man who bore it skulked through the streets of Edinburgh in disguise, while the mob that applauded at the execution of Burke called loudly for the blood of his employer.[6] But Mr K— was then at the top of his vogue; he enjoyed a popularity due partly to his own talent and address, partly to the incapacity of his rival, the university professor. The students, at least, swore by his name, and Fettes believed himself, and was believed by others, to have laid the foundations of success when he had acquired the favour of this meteorically famous man. Mr K— was a *bon vivant* as well as an accomplished teacher; he liked a sly allusion no less than a careful preparation. In both capacities Fettes enjoyed and deserved his notice, and by the second year of his attendance he held the half-irregular position of second demonstrator or sub-assistant in the class.

In this capacity, the charge of the theatre and lecture-room devolved in particular upon his shoulders; he had to answer for the cleanliness of the premises and the conduct of the other students; and it was a part of his duty to supply, receive, and divide the various subjects.[7] It was with a view to this last – at that time very delicate – affair that he was lodged by Mr K— in the same wynd,[8] and at last in the same building, with the dissecting rooms. Here, after a night of turbulent pleasures, his hand still tottering, his sight still misty and confused, he would be called out of bed in the black hours before the winter dawn by the unclean and desperate interlopers who supplied the table; he would open the door to these men, since infamous throughout the land; he would help them with their tragic burden, pay them their sordid price, and remain alone when they were gone with the unfriended relics of humanity. From such a scene he would return to snatch another hour or two of slumber, to repair the abuses of the night and refresh himself for the labours of the day.

Few lads could have been more insensible to the impressions of a life thus passed among the ensigns of mortality. His mind was closed against all general considerations; he was incapable of interest in the fate and fortunes of another, the slave of his own desires and low ambitions. Cold, light, and selfish in the last resort, he had that modicum of prudence, miscalled morality, which keeps a man from inconvenient drunkenness or punishable theft. He coveted besides a measure of consideration from his masters and his fellow-pupils, and he had no desire to fail conspicuously in the external parts of life. Thus he made it his pleasure to gain some distinction in his studies, and day after day rendered unimpeachable eye service to his employer, Mr K—. For his day of work he indemnified himself by nights of roaring blackguardly enjoyment;[9] and, when that balance had been struck, the organ that he called his conscience declared itself content.

The supply of subjects was a continual trouble to him as well as to his master. In that large and busy class, the raw material of the anatomists kept perpetually running out; and the business thus rendered necessary was not only unpleasant in itself, but threatened dangerous consequences to all who were concerned. It was the policy of Mr K— to ask no question in his dealings with the trade. 'They bring the body, and we pay the price,' he used to say – dwelling on the alliteration – '*quid pro quo*.'[10] And again, and somewhat profanely, 'Ask no questions,' he would tell his assistants, 'for conscience's sake.' There was no understanding that the subjects were provided by the crime of murder; had that idea been broached to him in words he would have recoiled in horror; but the lightness of his speech upon so grave a matter was, in itself, an offence against good manners, and a temptation to the men with whom he dealt. Fettes, for instance, had often remarked to himself upon the singular freshness of the bodies; he had been struck again and again by the hangdog, abominable looks of the ruffians who came to him before the dawn; and, putting things together clearly in his private thoughts, he perhaps attributed a meaning too immoral and too categorical to the unguarded counsels of his master. He understood his duty, in short, to have three branches: to take what was brought, to pay the price, and to avert the eye from any evidence of crime.

One November morning this policy of silence was put sharply to the test. He had been awake all night with racking toothache – pacing his room like a caged beast, or throwing himself in fury on his bed – and had fallen at last into that profound, uneasy slumber that so often follows on a night of pain, when he was awakened by the third or fourth angry repetition of the concerted signal. There was a thin, bright moonshine; it was bitter cold, windy, and frosty; the town had not yet awakened, but an indefinable stir already preluded the noise and business of the day. The ghouls[11] had come later than usual, and they seemed more than usually eager to be gone. Fettes, sick with sleep, lighted them upstairs; he heard their grumbling Irish voices through a dream; as they stripped the sack from their sad merchandise, he leaned, dozing, with his shoulder propped against the wall. He had to shake himself to find the men their money. As he did so his eyes lighted on the dead face. He started; he took two steps nearer, with the candle raised.

'God Almighty,' he cried, 'that is Jane Galbraith!'[12]

The men answered nothing, but they shuffled nearer towards the door.

'I know her, I tell you,' he continued. 'She was alive and hearty yesterday. It's impossible she can be dead; it's impossible you should have got this body fairly.'

'Sure, sir, you're mistaken entirely,' said one of the men.

But the other looked Fettes darkly in the eyes, and demanded his money on the spot.

It was impossible to misconceive the threat or to exaggerate the danger. The lad's heart failed him; he stammered some excuses, counted out the sum, and saw his hateful visitors depart. No sooner were they gone than he hastened to confirm his doubts; by a dozen unquestionable marks he identified the girl he had jested with the day before; he saw with horror, marks upon her body that might well betoken violence. A panic seized him, and he took refuge in his room. There he reflected at length over the discovery that he had made; considered soberly the bearing of Mr K—'s instructions, and the danger to himself of interference in so serious a business; and at last, in sore perplexity, determined to wait for the advice of his immediate superior, the class assistant.

This was a young doctor, Wolfe Macfarlane, a high favourite among all the reckless students, clever, dissipated, and unscrupulous to the last degree. He had travelled and studied abroad; his manners were agreeable and a little forward; he was an authority upon the stage, skilful on the ice or the links with skate or golf club; he dressed with nice audacity, and, to put the finishing touch upon his glory, he kept a gig and a strong, trotting horse. With Fettes he was on terms of intimacy; indeed, their relative positions called for some community of life; and when subjects were scarce, the pair would drive far into the country in Macfarlane's gig, visit and desecrate some lonely graveyard, and return before dawn with their booty to the door of the dissecting room.

On that particular morning Macfarlane arrived somewhat earlier than his wont. Fettes heard him, and met him on the stairs, told him his story, and showed him the cause of his alarm. Macfarlane examined the ecchymoses.

'Yes,' he said with a nod, 'it looks fishy.'

'Well, what should I do?' asked Fettes.

'Do?' repeated the other. 'Do you want to do anything? Least said, soonest mended, I should say.'

'Someone else might recognize her,' objected Fettes. 'She was as well known as the Castle Rock.'

'We'll hope not,' said Macfarlane, 'and if anybody does – well, you didn't, don't you see, and there's an end. The fact is, this has been going on too long. Stir up the mud, and you'll get K— into the most unholy trouble; you'll be in a shocking box yourself, so will I, if you come to that. I should like to know how anyone of us would look, or what the devil we should have to say for ourselves, in any Christian witness-box. For me, you know, there's one thing certain; that, practically speaking, all our subjects have been murdered.'

'Macfarlane!' cried Fettes.

'Come now!' sneered the other. 'As if you hadn't suspected it yourself!'

'Suspecting is one thing –'

'And proof another. Yes, I know; and I'm as sorry as you are *this* should have come here,' tapping the body with his cane. 'The next best thing for me is not to recognize it; and,' he added coolly, 'I don't. You may, if you please. I don't dictate, but I think a man of the world would do as I do; and I may add I fancy that is what K— would look for at our hands. The question is, why did he choose us two for his assistants? And I answer, because he didn't want old wives.'

This was the tone of all others to affect the mind of a lad like Fettes; he agreed to imitate Macfarlane; the body of the unfortunate girl was duly dissected, and no one remarked or appeared to recognize her.

One afternoon, when his day's work was over, Fettes dropped into a popular tavern, and found Macfarlane sitting with a stranger. This was a small man, very pale and dark, with cold black eyes. The cut of his features gave a promise of intellect and refinement which was but feebly realized in his manners; for he proved, upon a nearer acquaintance, coarse, vulgar and stupid. He exercised, however, a very remarkable control over Macfarlane; issued orders like the Great Bashaw[13] became inflamed at the least discussion or delay, and commented rudely on the servility with which he was obeyed. This most offensive person took a fancy to Fettes on the spot, plied him with drinks, and honoured him with unusual confidences on his past career. If a tenth part of what he confessed were true, he was a very loathsome rogue; and the lad's vanity was tickled by the attention of so experienced a man.

'I'm a pretty bad fellow myself,' the stranger remarked; 'but Macfarlane is the boy – Toddy Macfarlane, I call him. Toddy, order your friend another glass.' Or it might be, 'Toddy, you jump up and shut that door.' 'Toddy hates me,' he said again; 'oh, yes, Toddy, you do.'

'Don't you call me that confounded name,' growled Macfarlane.

'Hear him! Did you ever see the lads play knife? He would like to do that all over my body,' remarked the stranger.

'We medicals have a better way than that,' said Fettes. 'When we dislike a dear friend of ours, we dissect him.'

Macfarlane looked up sharply, as though this jest were scarcely to his mind.

The afternoon passed. Gray, for that was the stranger's name, invited Fettes to join them at dinner, ordered a feast so sumptuous that the tavern was thrown into commotion; and when all was done commanded Macfarlane to settle the bill. It was late before they separated; the man Gray was incapably drunk; Macfarlane, sobered by his fury, chewed the end of the money he had been forced to squander and the slights he had been obliged to swallow; Fettes, with various liquors singing in his head, returned home with devious footsteps and a mind entirely in abeyance. Next day Macfarlane was absent from the class; and Fettes smiled to himself as he imagined him still squiring the intolerable Gray from tavern to tavern. As soon as the hour of liberty had struck, he posted from place to place in quest of his last night's companions; he could find them, however, nowhere, returned early to his rooms, went early to bed, and slept the sleep of the just.

At four in the morning he was wakened by the well-known signal. Descending to the door, he was filled with astonishment to find Macfarlane with his gig, and, in the gig, one of those long and ghastly packages with which he was so well acquainted.

'What?' he cried. 'Have you been out alone? How did you manage?'

But Macfarlane silenced him roughly, bidding him turn to business. When they had got the body upstairs and laid it on the table, Macfarlane made at first as if he were going away; then he paused and seemed to hesitate; and then, 'You had better look at the face,' said he, in tones of some constraint. 'You had better,' he repeated, as Fettes only stared at him in wonder.

'But where and how and when did you come by it?' cried the other.

'Look at the face,' was the only answer.

Fettes was staggered; strange doubts assailed him; he looked from the young doctor to the body, and then back again; at last with a start, he did as he was bidden. He had almost expected the sight that met his eyes, and yet the shock was cruel. To see, fixed in the rigidity of death and naked on that coarse layer of sackcloth, the man whom he had left well clad and full of meat and sin, upon the threshold of a tavern, awoke, even in the thoughtless Fettes, some of the terrors of the conscience. It was a *cras tibi*[14] which re-echoed in his soul, that two whom he had known should have come to lie upon these icy tables. Yet these were only secondary thoughts. His first concern regarded Wolfe. Unprepared for a challenge so momentous, he knew not how to look his comrade in the face; he durst not meet his eye, and he had neither words nor voice at his command.

It was Macfarlane himself who made the first advance. He came up quietly behind and laid his hand gently but firmly on the other's shoulder.

'Richardson,' said he, 'may have the head.'

Now, Richardson was a student who had long been anxious for that portion of the human subject to dissect. There was no answer, and the murderer resumed: 'Talking of business, you must pay me; your accounts, you see, must tally.'

Fettes found a voice, the ghost of his own: 'Pay you!' he cried. 'Pay you for that!'

'Why, yes, of course you must; by all means and on every possible account you must,' returned the other. 'I dare not give it for nothing; you dare not take it for nothing: it would compromise us both. This is another case like Jane Galbraith's; the more things are wrong, the more we must act as if all were right. Where does old K— keep his money?'

'There,' answered Fettes hoarsely, pointing to a cupboard in the corner.

'Give me the key, then,' said the other calmly, holding out his hand.

There was an instant's hesitation, and the die was cast. Macfarlane could not suppress a nervous twitch, the infinitesimal mark of an immense relief, as he felt the key between his fingers. He opened the cupboard, brought out pen and ink and a paper book that stood in one compartment, and separated from the funds in a drawer a sum suitable to the occasion.

'Now, look here,' he said, 'there is the payment made. First proof of your good faith; first step to your security. You have now to clinch it by a second. Enter the payment in your book, and then you for your part may defy the devil.'

The next few seconds were for Fettes an agony of thought; but in balancing his terrors it was the most immediate that triumphed. Any future difficulty seemed almost welcome if he could avoid a present quarrel with Macfarlane. He set down the candle which he had been carrying all this time, and with a steady hand entered the date, the nature, and the amount of the transaction.

'And now,' said Macfarlane, 'it's only fair that you should pocket the lucre. I've had my share already. By-the-by, when a man of the world falls into a bit of luck, has a few extra shillings in his pocket – I'm ashamed to speak of it, but there's a rule of conduct in the case. No treating, no purchase of expensive class-books, no squaring of old debts; borrow, don't lend.'

'Macfarlane,' began Fettes, still somewhat hoarsely, 'I have put my neck in a halter to oblige you.'

'To oblige me?' cried Wolfe. 'Oh, come! You did, as near as I can see the matter, what you downright had to do in self-defence. Suppose I got into trouble, where would you be? This second little matter flows clearly from the first; Mr Gray is the continuation of Miss Galbraith; you can't begin and then stop; if you begin, you must keep on beginning; that's the truth. No rest for the wicked.'

A horrible sense of blackness and the treachery of fate seized hold upon the soul of the unhappy student.

'My God!' he cried, 'but what have *I* done? and when did *I* begin? To be made a class assistant – in the name of reason, where's the harm in that? Service wanted the position; Service might have got it. Would *he* have been where *I* am now?'

'My dear fellow,' said Macfarlane, 'what a boy you are! What harm *has* come to you? What harm *can* come to you if you hold your tongue? Why, man, do you know what this life is? There are two squads of us – the lions and the lambs. If you're a lamb, you'll come to lie upon these tables like Gray or Jane Galbraith; if you're a lion, you'll live and drive a horse like me, like K—, like all the world with any wit or courage. You're staggered at the first. But look at K—! My dear fellow, you're clever, you have pluck. I like you, and K— likes you; you were born to lead the hunt; and I tell you, on my honour and my experience of life, three days from now you'll laugh at all these scarecrows like a high-school boy at a farce.'

And with that Macfarlane took his departure, and drove off up the wynd in his gig to get under cover before daylight. Fettes was thus left alone with his regrets. He saw the miserable peril in which he stood involved; he saw, with inexpressible dismay, that there was no limit to his weakness, and that, from concession to concession, he had fallen from the arbiter of Macfarlane's destiny to his paid and helpless accomplice. He would have given the world to have been a little braver at the time, but it did not occur to him that he might still be brave. The secret of Jane Galbraith and the cursed entry in the day book closed his mouth.

Hours passed; the class began to arrive; the members of the unhappy Gray were dealt out to one and to another, and received without remark; Richardson was made happy with the head; and before the hour of freedom rang Fettes trembled with exultation to perceive how far they had already gone towards safety. For two days he continued to watch, with increasing joy, the dreadful process of disguise. On the third day Macfarlane made his appearance – he had been ill, he said; but he made up for lost time by the energy with which he directed the students; to Richardson, in particular, he extended the most valuable assistance and advice, and that student, encouraged by the praise of the demonstrator, burned high with ambitious hopes, and saw the medal already in his grasp.

Before the week was out Macfarlane's prophecy had been fulfilled. Fettes had outlived his terrors and forgotten his abasement. He began to plume himself upon his courage; and had so arranged the story in his mind that he could look back on these events with an unhealthy pride. Of his accomplice he saw but little. They met, of course, in the business of the class; they received their orders together from Mr K—; at times they had a word or two in private, and Macfarlane was from first to last particularly kind and jovial. But it was plain that he avoided any reference to their common secret; and even when Fettes whispered to him that he had cast in his lot with the lions and forsworn the lambs, he only signed to him smilingly to hold his peace.

At length an occasion arose which threw the pair once more into a closer union. Mr K— was again short of subjects; pupils were eager; and it was a part of this teacher's pretensions to be always well supplied. At the same time there came the news of a burial in the rustic graveyard of Glencorse. Time has little changed the place in question. It stood, then as now, upon a cross road, out of call of human habitations, and buried fathom deep in the foliage of six cedar trees. The cries of the sheep upon the neighbouring hills, the streamlets upon either hand, one loudly singing among pebbles, the other dripping furtively from pond to pond, the stir of the wind in mountainous old flowering chestnuts, and, once in seven days, the voice of the bell and the old tunes of the precentor,[15] were the only sounds that disturbed the silence round the rural church. The Resurrection Man – to use a by-name of the period – was not to be deterred by any of the sanctities of customary piety. It was part of his trade to despise and desecrate the scrolls and trumpets of old tombs, the paths worn by the feet of worshippers and mourners, and the offerings and the inscriptions of bereaved affection. To rustic neighbourhoods, where love is more than commonly tenacious, and where some bonds of blood or fellow-ship unite the entire society of a parish, the body snatcher, far from being repelled by natural respect, was attracted by the ease and safety of his task. To bodies that had been laid in the earth in joyful expectation of a far different awakening,[16] there came that hasty, lamp-lit, terror-haunted resurrection of the spade and mattock; the coffin was forced, the cerements torn, and the melancholy relics, clad in sackcloth, after being rattled for hours on moonless byways, were at length exposed to uttermost indignities before a class of gaping boys.

Somewhat as two vultures may swoop upon a dying lamb, Fettes and Macfarlane were to be let loose upon a grave in that green and quiet resting-place. The wife of a farmer, a woman who had lived for sixty years, and been known for nothing but good butter and a godly conversation, was to be rooted from her grave at midnight, and carried, dead and naked, to that far-away city that she had always honoured with her Sunday's best; the place beside her family was to be empty till the crack of doom; her innocent and almost venerable members to be exposed to that last curiosity of the anatomist.

Late one afternoon the pair set forth, well wrapped in cloaks, and furnished with a formidable bottle. It rained without remission; a cold, dense, lashing rain; now and again there blew a puff of wind, but these sheets of falling water kept it down. Bottle and all, it was a sad and silent drive as far as Penicuik, where they were to spend the evening. They stopped once, to hide their implements in a thick bush not far from the churchyard; and once again at the Fisher's Tryst, to have a toast before the kitchen fire, and vary their nips of whisky with a glass of ale. When they reached their journey's end the gig was housed, the horse was fed and comforted, and the two young doctors, in a private room, sat down to the best dinner and the best wine the house afforded. The lights, the fire, the beating rain upon the window, the cold, incongruous work that lay before them, added zest to their enjoyment of the meal. With every glass their cordiality increased. Soon Macfarlane handed a little pile of gold to his companion.

'A compliment,' he said. 'Between friends these little d —d accommodations ought to fly like pipe-lights.'

Fettes pocketed the money, and applauded the sentiment to the echo. 'You are a philosopher,' he cried. 'I was an ass till I knew you. You and K — between you, by the Lord Harry, but you'll make a man of me.'

'Of course we shall,' applauded Macfarlane. 'A man? I'll tell you it required a man to back me up the other morning. There are some big, brawling, forty-year-old cowards would have turned sick at the look of the d —d thing; but not you – you kept your head. I watched you.'

'Well, and why not?' Fettes thus vaunted himself. 'It was no affair of mine. There was nothing to gain on the one side but disturbance, and on the other I could count on your gratitude, don't you see?' And he slapped his pocket till the gold pieces rang.

Macfarlane somehow felt a certain touch of alarm at these unpleasant words; he may have regretted that he had taught his young companion so successfully; but he had no time to interfere, for the other noisily continued in this boastful strain.

'The great thing is not to be afraid. Now, between you and me, I don't want to hang – that's practical – but for all cant, Macfarlane, I was born with a contempt. Hell, God, devil, right, wrong, sin, crime, and all that old gallery of curiosities – they may frighten boys, but men of the world, like you and me, despise them. Here's to the memory of Gray!'

It was by this time growing somewhat late. The gig, according to order, was brought round to the door with both lamps brightly shining, and the young men had to pay their bill and take the road. They announced that they were bound for Peebles, drove in that direction till they were clear of the last houses of the town; then, extinguishing the lamps, returned upon their course, and followed a by-road towards Glencorse. There was no sound but that of their own passage, and the incessant, strident pouring of the rain. It was pitch dark; here and there a white gate or a white stone in the wall guided them for a short space across the night; but for the most part it was at a foot's pace, and almost groping, that they picked their way through that resonant blackness to their solemn and isolated destination. In the sunken roads that traverse the neighbourhood of the burying-ground the last glimmer failed them, and it became necessary to kindle a match and reillume one of the lanterns of the gig. Thus, under the dripping trees, and environed by huge and moving shadows, they reached the scene of their unhallowed labours.

They were both experienced in such affairs, and powerful with the spade; and they had scarce been twenty minutes at their task before they were rewarded by a dull rattle on the coffin lid. At the same moment Macfarlane, having hurt his hand upon a stone, flung it carelessly above his head. The grave, in which they now stood almost to the shoulders, was close to the edge of the plateau of the graveyard; and the gig lamp had been propped, the better to illuminate their labours, against a tree, and on the immediate verge of the steep bank descending to the stream. Chance had taken a sure aim with the stone. Then came a clang of broken glass; night fell upon them; sounds alternately dull and ringing announced the bounding of the lantern down the bank, and its occasional collision with the trees; a stone or two, which it had dislodged in its descent, rattled behind it into the profundities of the glen; and then silence, like night, resumed its sway; and they might bend their hearing to its utmost pitch but nought was to be heard except the rain, now marching to the wind, now steadily falling over miles of open country.

They were so nearly at an end of their abhorred task that they judged it wiser to complete it in the dark. The coffin was exhumed and broken open; the body inserted in the dripping sack and carried between them to the gig; one mounted, to keep it in its place, and the other, taking the horse by the mouth, groped along by wall and bush, until they reached the wider road by the Fisher's Tryst. Here was a faint, diffused radiancy which they hailed like daylight; by that they pushed the horse to a good pace and began to rattle almost merrily in the direction of the town.

They had both been wetted to the skin during their operations, and now, as the gig jumped among the deep ruts, the thing that stood propped between them fell now upon the one and now upon the other. At every repetition of the horrid contact each instinctively repelled it with the greater haste; and the process, natural although it was, began to tell upon the nerves of the companions. Macfarlane made some ill-favoured jest about the farmer's wife, but it came hollowly from his lips, and was allowed to drop in silence. Still their unnatural burden bumped from side to side, and now the head would be laid, as if in confidence, upon their shoulders, and now the drenching sackcloth would flap icily about their faces. A creeping chill began to possess the soul of Fettes. He peered at the bundle, and it seemed somehow larger than at first. All over the countryside, and from every degree of distance, the farm dogs accompanied their passage with tragic ululations; and it grew and grew upon his mind that some unnatural miracle had been accomplished, that some nameless change had befallen the dead body, and that it was in fear of their unholy burden that the dogs were howling.

'For God's sake,' said he, making a great effort to arrive at speech, 'for God's sake let's have a light.'

Seemingly Macfarlane was affected in the same direction; for, though he made no reply, he stopped the horse, passed the reins to his companion, got down, and proceeded to kindle the remaining lamp. They had by that time got no farther than the cross road down to Auchenclinny. The rain still poured, as though the deluge were returning, and it was no easy matter to make a light in such a world of wet and darkness. When at last the flickering blue flame had been transferred to the wick, and began to expand and clarify, and shed a wide circle of misty brightness round the gig, it became possible for the two young men to see each other and the thing they had along with them. The rain had moulded the rough sacking to the outlines of the body underneath; the head was distinct from the trunk, the shoulders plainly modelled; something at once spectral and human riveted their eyes upon the ghastly comrade of their drive.

For some time Macfarlane stood motionless, holding up the hand. A nameless dread was swathed, like a wet sheet, about the body, and tightened the white skin upon the face of Fettes; a fear that was meaningless, a horror of what could not be, kept mounting in his brain. Another beat of the watch, and he had spoken; but his comrade forestalled him.

'That is not a woman,' said Macfarlane, in a hushed voice.

'It was a woman when we put her in,' whispered Fettes.

'Hold that lamp,' said the other; 'I must see her face.'

And as Fettes took the lamp his companion untied the fastenings of the sack and drew down the cover from the head. The light fell very clear upon the dark, well-moulded features and smooth-shaven cheeks of a too familiar countenance, often beheld in dreams by both of these young men. A wild yell rang up into the night; each leaped from his own side into the roadway; the lamp fell, broke, and was extinguished; and the horse, terrified by this unusual commotion, bounded and went off towards Edinburgh at the gallop, bearing along with it, sole occupant of the gig, the body of the long dead and long dissected Gray.

OLALLA

Olalla

'Now,' said the doctor, 'my part is done, and, I may say, with some vanity, well done. It remains only to get you out of this cold and poisonous city, and to give you two months of a pure air[1] and an easy conscience. The last is your affair. To the first I think I can help you. It falls indeed rather oddly; it was but the other day the Padre came in from the country; and as he and I are old friends, although of contrary professions,[2] he applied to me in a matter of distress among some of his parishioners. This was a family – but you are ignorant of Spain, and even the names of our grandees are hardly known to you; suffice it, then, that they were once great people, and are now fallen to the brink of destitution. Nothing now belongs to them but the residencia, and certain leagues of desert mountain, in the greater part of which not even a goat could support life. But the house is a fine old place, and stands at a great height among the hills, and most salubriously; and I had no sooner heard my friend's tale, than I remembered you. I told him I had a wounded officer, wounded in the good cause,[3] who was now able to make a change; and I proposed that his friends should take you for a lodger. Instantly the Padre's face grew dark, as I had maliciously foreseen it would. It was out of the question, he said. Then let them starve, said I, for I have no sympathy with tatterdemalion pride.[4] Thereupon we separated, not very content with one another; but yesterday, to my wonder, the Padre returned and made a submission: the difficulty, he said, he had found upon inquiry to be less than he had feared; or, in other words, these proud people had put their pride in their pocket. I closed with the offer; and, subject to your approval, I have taken rooms for you in the residencia.

The air of these mountains will renew your blood; and the quiet in which you will there live is worth all the medicines in the world.'

'Doctor,' said I, 'you have been throughout my good angel, and your advice is a command. But tell me, if you please, something of the family with which I am to reside.'

'I am coming to that,' replied my friend; 'and, indeed, there is a difficulty in the way. These beggars are, as I have said, of very high descent and swollen with the most baseless vanity; they have lived for some generations in a growing isolation, drawing away, on either hand, from the rich who had now become too high for them, and from the poor, whom they still regarded as too low; and even today, when poverty forces them to unfasten their door to a guest, they cannot do so without a most ungracious stipulation. You are to remain, they say, a stranger; they will give you attendance, but they refuse from the first the idea of the smallest intimacy.'

I will not deny that I was piqued, and perhaps the feeling strengthened my desire to go, for I was confident that I could break down that barrier if I desired. 'There is nothing offensive in such a stipulation,' said I; 'and I even sympathize with the feeling that inspired it.'

'It is true they have never seen you,' returned the doctor politely; 'and if they knew you were the handsomest and the most pleasant man that ever came from England (where I am told that handsome men are common, but pleasant ones not so much so), they would doubtless make you welcome with a better grace. But since you take the thing so well, it matters not. To me, indeed, it seems discourteous. But you will find yourself the gainer. The family will not much tempt you. A mother, a son, and a daughter; an old woman said to be half-witted, a country lout, and a country girl, who stands very high with her confessor, and is, therefore,' chuckled the physician, 'most likely plain; there is not much in that to attract the fancy of a dashing officer.'

'And yet you say they are high-born,' I objected.

'Well, as to that, I should distinguish,' returned the doctor. 'The mother is; not so the children. The mother was the last representative of a princely stock, degenerate both in parts and fortune.[5] Her father was not only poor, he was mad: and the girl ran wild about the residencia till his death. Then, much of the fortune having died with him, and the family being quite extinct, the girl ran wilder than ever, until at last she married, Heaven knows whom, a muleteer some say, others a smuggler; while there are some who uphold there was no marriage at all, and that Felipe and Olalla are bastards. The union, such as it was, was tragically dissolved some years ago; but they live in such seclusion, and the country at that time was in so much disorder, that the precise manner of the man's end is known only to the priest – if even to him.'

'I begin to think I shall have strange experiences,' said I.

'I would not romance, if I were you,' replied the doctor; 'you will find, I fear, a very grovelling and commonplace reality. Felipe, for instance, I have seen. And what am I to say? He is very rustic, very cunning, very loutish, and, I should say, an innocent;[6] the others are probably to match. No, no, Señor Commandante, you must seek congenial society among the great sights of our mountains; and in these at least, if you are at all a lover of the works of nature, I promise you will not be disappointed.'

The next day Felipe came for me in a rough country cart, drawn by a mule; and a little before the stroke of noon, after I had said farewell to the doctor, the innkeeper, and different good souls who had befriended me during my sickness, we set forth out of the city by the Eastern gate, and began to ascend into the Sierra. I had been so long a prisoner, since I was left behind for dying after the loss of the convoy, that the mere smell of the earth set me smiling. The country through which we went was wild and rocky, partially covered with rough woods, now of the cork-tree, and now of the great Spanish chestnut, and frequently intersected by the beds of mountain torrents. The sun shone, the wind rustled joyously; and we had advanced some miles, and the city had already shrunk into an inconsiderable knoll upon the plain behind us, before my attention began to be diverted to the companion of my drive. To the eye, he seemed but a diminutive, loutish, well-made country lad, such as the doctor had described, mighty quick and active, but devoid of any culture; and this first impression was with most observers final. What began to strike me was his familiar, chattering talk; so strangely inconsistent with the terms on which I was to be received; and partly from his imperfect enunciation, partly from the sprightly incoherence of the matter, so very difficult to follow clearly without an effort of the mind. It is true I had before talked with persons of a similar mental constitution; persons who seemed to live (as he did) by the senses, taken and possessed by the visual object of the moment and unable to discharge their minds of that impression. His seemed to me (as I sat, distantly giving ear) a kind of conversation proper to drivers, who pass much of their time in a great vacancy of the intellect and threading the sights of a familiar country. But this was not the case of Felipe; by his own account, he was a home-keeper; 'I wish I was there now,' he said; and then, spying a tree by the wayside, he broke off to tell me that he had once seen a crow among its branches.

'A crow?' I repeated, struck by the ineptitude of the remark, and thinking I had heard imperfectly.

But by this time he was already filled with a new idea; hearkening with a rapt intentness, his head on one side, his face puckered; and he struck me rudely, to make me hold my peace. Then he smiled and shook his head.

'What did you hear?' I asked.

'O, it is all right,' he said; and began encouraging his mule with cries that echoed unhumanly up the mountain walls.

I looked at him more closely. He was superlatively well-built, light, and lithe and strong; he was well-featured; his yellow eyes were very large, though, perhaps, not very expressive; take him altogether, he was a pleasant-looking lad, and I had no fault to find with him, beyond that he was of a dusky hue, and inclined to hairyness;[7] two characteristics that I disliked. It was his mind that puzzled, and yet attracted me. The doctor's phrase – an innocent – came back to me; and I was wondering if that were, after all, the true description, when the road began to go down into the narrow and naked chasm of a torrent. The waters thundered tumultuously in the bottom; and the ravine was filled full of the sound, the thin spray, and the claps of wind, that accompanied their descent. The scene was certainly impressive; but the road was in that part very securely walled in; the mule went steadily forward; and I was astonished to perceive the paleness of terror in the face of my companion. The voice of that wild river was inconstant, now sinking lower as if in weariness, now doubling its hoarse tones; momentary freshets seemed to swell its volume, sweeping down the gorge, raving and booming against the barrier walls; and I observed it was at each of these accessions to the clamour, that my driver more particularly winced and blanched. Some thoughts of Scottish superstition and the river Kelpie[8] passed across my mind; I wondered if perchance the like were prevalent in that part of Spain; and turning to Felipe, sought to draw him out.

'What is the matter?' I asked.

'O, I am afraid,' he replied.

'Of what are you afraid?' I returned. 'This seems one of the safest places on this very dangerous road.'

'It makes a noise,' he said, with a simplicity of awe that set my doubts at rest.

The lad was but a child in intellect; his mind was like his body, active and swift, but stunted in development; and I began from that time forth to regard him with a measure of pity, and to listen at first with indulgence, and at last even with pleasure, to his disjointed babble.

By about four in the afternoon we had crossed the summit of the mountain line, said farewell to the western sunshine, and began to go down upon the other side, skirting the edge of many ravines and moving through the shadow of dusky woods. There rose upon all sides the voice of falling water, not condensed and formidable as in the gorge of the river, but scattered and sounding gaily and musically from glen to glen. Here, too, the spirits of my driver mended, and he began to sing aloud in a falsetto voice, and with a singular bluntness of musical perception, never true either to melody or key, but wandering at will, and yet somehow with an effect that was natural and pleasing, like that of the song of birds. As the dusk increased, I fell more and more under the spell of this artless warbling, listening and waiting for some articulate air, and still disappointed; and when at last I asked him what it was he sang – 'O,' cried he, 'I am just singing!' Above all, I was taken with a trick he had of unweariedly repeating the same note at little intervals; it was not so monotonous as you would think, or, at least, not disagreeable; and it seemed to breathe a wonderful contentment with what is, such as we love to fancy in the attitude of trees, or the quiescence of a pool.

Night had fallen dark before we came out upon a plateau, and drew up a little after, before a certain lump of superior blackness which I could only conjecture to be the residencia. Here, my guide, getting down from the cart, hooted and whistled for a long time in vain; until at last an old peasant man came towards us from somewhere in the surrounding dark, carrying a candle in his hand. By the light of this I was able to perceive a great arched doorway of a Moorish character: it was closed by iron-studded gates, in one of the leaves of which Felipe opened a wicket. The peasant carried off the cart to some out-building; but my guide and I passed through the wicket, which was closed again behind us; and by the glimmer of the candle, passed through a court, up a stone stair, along a section of an open gallery, and up more stairs again, until we came at last to the door of a great and somewhat bare apartment. This room, which I understood was to be mine, was pierced by three windows, lined with some lustrous wood disposed in panels, and carpeted with the skins of many savage animals. A bright fire burned in the chimney, and shed abroad a changeful flicker; close up to the blaze there was drawn a table, laid for supper; and in the far end a bed stood ready. I was pleased by these preparations, and said so to Felipe; and he, with the same simplicity of disposition that I had already remarked on him, warmly re-echoed my praises. 'A fine room,' he said; 'a very fine room. And fire, too; fire is good; it melts out the pleasure in your bones. And the bed,' he continued, carrying over the candle in that direction – 'see what fine sheets – how soft, how smooth, smooth;' and he passed his hand again and again over their texture, and then laid down his head and rubbed his cheeks among them with a grossness of content that somehow offended me. I took the candle from his hand (for I feared he would set the bed on fire) and walked back to the supper-table, where, perceiving a measure of wine, I poured out a cup and called to him to come and drink of it. He started to his feet at once and ran to me with a strong expression of hope; but when he saw the wine, he visibly shuddered.

'Oh, no,' he said, 'not that; that is for you. I hate it.'

'Very well, Señor,' said I; 'then I will drink to your good health, and to the prosperity of your house and family. Speaking of which,' I added, after I had drunk, 'shall I not have the pleasure of laying my salutations in person at the feet of the Señora, your mother?'

But at these words all the childishness passed out of his face, and was succeeded by a look of indescribable cunning and secrecy. He backed away from me at the same time, as though I were an animal about to leap or some dangerous fellow with a weapon, and when he had got near the door, glowered at me suddenly with contracted pupils. 'No,' he said at last, and the next moment was gone noiselessly out of the room; and I heard his footing die away downstairs as light as rainfall, and silence closed over the house.

After I had supped I drew up the table nearer to the bed and began to prepare for rest; but in the new position of the light, I was struck by a picture on the wall. It represented a woman, still young. To judge by her costume and the mellow unity which reigned over the canvas, she had long been dead; to judge by the vivacity of the attitude, the eyes and the features, I might have been beholding in a mirror the image of life. Her figure was very slim and strong, and of a just proportion; red tresses lay like a crown over her brow; her eyes, of a very golden brown, held mine with a look; and her face, which was perfectly shaped, was yet marred by a cruel, sullen, and sensual expression. Something in both face and figure, something exquisitely intangible, like the echo of an echo, suggested the features and bearing of my guide; and I stood awhile, unpleasantly attracted and wondering at the oddity of the resemblance. The common, carnal stock of that race, which had been originally designed for such high dames as the one now looking on me from the canvas, had fallen to baser uses, wearing country clothes, sitting on the shaft and holding the reins of a mule cart, to bring home a lodger. Perhaps an actual link subsisted; perhaps some scruple of the delicate flesh that was once clothed upon with the satin and brocade of the dead lady, now winced at the rude contact of Felipe's frieze.

The first light of the morning shone full upon the portrait, and, as I lay awake, my eyes continued to dwell upon it with growing complacency; its beauty crept about my heart insidiously, silencing my scruples one after another; and while I knew that to love such a woman were to sign and seal one's own sentence of degeneration, I still knew that, if she were alive, I should love her. Day after day the double knowledge of her wickedness and of my weakness grew clearer. She came to be the heroine of many day-dreams, in which her eyes led on to, and sufficiently rewarded, crimes. She cast a dark shadow on my fancy; and when I was out in the free air of heaven, taking vigorous exercise and healthily renewing the current of my blood, it was often a glad thought to me that my enchantress was safe in the grave, her wand of beauty broken, her lips closed in silence, her philtre spilt. And yet I had a half-lingering terror that she might not be dead after all, but re-arisen in the body of some descendant.

Felipe served my meals in my own apartment; and his resemblance to the portrait haunted me. At times it was not; at times, upon some change of attitude or flash of expression, it would leap out upon me like a ghost. It was above all in his ill tempers that the likeness triumphed. He certainly liked me; he was proud of my notice, which he sought to engage by many simple and childlike devices; he loved to sit close before my fire, talking his broken talk or singing his odd, endless, wordless songs, and sometimes drawing his hand over my clothes with an affectionate manner of caressing that never failed to cause in me an embarrassment of which I was ashamed. But for all that, he was capable of flashes of causeless anger and fits of sturdy sullenness. At a word of reproof, I have seen him upset the dish of which I was about to eat, and this not surreptitiously, but with defiance; and similarly at a hint of inquisition. I was not unnaturally curious, being in a strange place and surrounded by strange people; but at the shadow of a question, he shrank back, lowering and dangerous. Then it was that, for a fraction of a second, this rough lad might have been the brother of the lady in the frame. But these humours were swift to pass; and the resemblance died along with them.

In these first days I saw nothing of anyone but Felipe, unless the portrait is to be counted; and since the lad was plainly of weak mind, and had moments of passion, it may be wondered that I bore his dangerous neighbourhood with equanimity. As a matter of fact, it was for some time irksome; but it happened before long that I obtained over him so complete a mastery as set my disquietude at rest.

It fell in this way. He was by nature slothful, and much of a vagabond, and yet he kept by the house, and not only waited upon my wants, but laboured every day in the garden or small farm to the south of the residencia. Here he would be joined by the peasant whom I had seen on the night of my arrival, and who dwelt at the far end of the enclosure, about half a mile away, in a rude out-house; but it was plain to me that, of these two, it was Felipe who did most; and though I would sometimes see him throw down his spade and go to sleep among the very plants he had been digging, his constancy and energy were admirable in themselves, and still more so since I was well assured they were foreign to his disposition and the fruit of an ungrateful effort. But while I admired, I wondered what had called forth in a lad so shuttle-witted this enduring sense of duty. How was it sustained? I asked myself, and to what length did it prevail over his instincts? The priest was possibly his inspirer; but the priest came one day to the residencia. I saw him both come and go after an interval of close upon an hour, from a knoll where I was sketching, and all that time Felipe continued to labour undisturbed in the garden.

At last, in a very unworthy spirit, I determined to debauch the lad from his good resolutions, and, waylaying him at the gate, easily persuaded him to join me in a ramble. It was a fine day, and the woods to which I led him were green and pleasant and sweet-smelling and alive with the hum of insects. Here he discovered himself in a fresh character, mounting up to heights of gaiety that abashed me, and displaying an energy and grace of movement that delighted the eye. He leaped, he ran round me in mere glee; he would stop, and look and listen, and seem to drink in the world like a cordial; and then he would suddenly spring into a tree with one bound, and hang and gambol there like one at home. Little as he said to me, and that of not much import, I have rarely enjoyed more stirring company; the sight of his delight was a continual feast; the speed and accuracy of his movements pleased me to the heart; and I might have been so thoughtlessly unkind as to make a habit of these walks, had not chance prepared a very rude conclusion to my pleasure. By some swiftness or dexterity the lad captured a squirrel in a tree top. He was then some way ahead of me, but I saw him drop to the ground and crouch there, crying aloud for pleasure like a child. The sound stirred my sympathies, it was so fresh and innocent; but as I bettered my pace to draw near, the cry of the squirrel knocked upon my heart. I have heard and seen much of the cruelty of lads, and above all of peasants; but what I now beheld struck me into a passion of anger. I thrust the fellow aside, plucked the poor brute out of his hands, and with swift mercy killed it. Then I turned upon the torturer, spoke to him long out of the heart of my indignation, calling him names at which he seemed to wither; and at length, pointing toward the residencia, bade him begone and leave me, for I chose to walk with men, not with vermin. He fell upon his knees, and, the words coming to him with more clearness than usual, poured out a stream of the most touching supplications, begging me in mercy to forgive him, to forget what he had done, to look to the future. 'O, I try so hard,' he said. 'O, Commandante, bear with Felipe this once; he will never be a brute again!' Thereupon, much more affected than I cared to show, I suffered myself to be persuaded, and at last shook hands with him and made it up. But the squirrel, by way of penance, I made him bury; speaking of the poor thing's beauty, telling him what pains it had suffered, and how base a thing was the abuse of strength. 'See, Felipe,' said I, 'you are strong indeed; but in my hands you are as helpless as that poor thing of the trees. Give me your hand in mine. You cannot remove it. Now suppose that I were cruel like you, and took a pleasure in pain. I only tighten my hold, and see how you suffer.' He screamed aloud, his face stricken ashy and dotted with needle points of sweat; and when I set him free, he fell to the earth and nursed his hand and moaned over it like a baby. But he took the lesson in good part; and whether from that, or from what I had said to him, or the higher notion he now had of my bodily strength, his original affection was changed into a dog-like, adoring fidelity.

Meanwhile I gained rapidly in health. The residencia stood on the crown of a stony plateau; on every side the mountains hemmed it about; only from the roof, where was a bartizan, there might be seen between two peaks, a small segment of plain, blue with extreme distance. The air in these altitudes moved freely and largely; great clouds congregated there, and were broken up by the wind and left in tatters on the hilltops; a hoarse, and yet faint rumbling of torrents rose from all round; and one could there study all the ruder and more ancient characters of nature in something of their pristine force. I delighted from the first in the vigorous scenery and changeful weather; nor less in the antique and dilapidated mansion where I dwelt. This was a large oblong, flanked at two opposite corners by bastion-like projections, one of which commanded the door, while both were loopholed for musketry. The lower storey was, besides, naked of windows, so that the building, if garrisoned, could not be carried without artillery. It enclosed an open court planted with pomegranate trees. From this a broad flight of marble stairs ascended to an open gallery, running all round and resting, towards the court, on slender pillars. Thence again, several enclosed stairs led to the upper storeys of the house, which were thus broken up into distinct divisions. The windows, both within and without, were closely shuttered; some of the stone-work in the upper parts had fallen; the roof, in one place, had been wrecked in one of the flurries of wind which were common in these mountains; and the whole house, in the strong, beating sunlight, and standing out above a grove of stunted cork-trees, thickly laden and discoloured with dust, looked like the sleeping palace of the legend.[9] The court, in particular, seemed the very home of slumber. A hoarse cooing of doves haunted about the eaves; the winds were excluded, but when they blew outside, the mountain dust fell here as thick as rain, and veiled the red bloom of the pomegranates; shuttered windows and the closed doors of numerous cellars, and the vacant arches of the gallery, enclosed it; and all day long the sun made broken profiles on the four sides, and paraded the shadow of the pillars on the gallery floor. At the ground level there was, however, a certain pillared recess, which bore the marks of human habitation. Though it was open in front upon the court, it was yet provided with a chimney, where a wood fire would be always prettily blazing; and the tile floor was littered with the skins of animals.

It was in this place that I first saw my hostess. She had drawn one of the skins forward and sat in the sun, leaning against a pillar. It was her dress that struck me first of all, for it was rich and brightly coloured, and shone out in that dusty courtyard with something of the same relief as the flowers of the pomegranates. At a second look it was her beauty of person that took hold of me. As she sat back – watching me, I thought, though with invisible eyes – and wearing at the same time an expression of almost imbecile good-humour and contentment, she showed a perfectness of feature and a quiet nobility of attitude that were beyond a statue's. I took off my hat to her in passing, and her face puckered with suspicion as swiftly and lightly as a pool ruffles in the breeze; but she paid no heed to my courtesy. I went forth on my customary walk a trifle daunted, her idol-like impassivity haunting me; and when I returned, although she was still in much the same posture, I was half surprised to see that she had moved as far as the next pillar, following the sunshine. This time, however, she addressed me with some trivial salutation, civilly enough conceived, and uttered in the same deep-chested, and yet indistinct and lisping tones, that had already baffled the utmost niceness of my hearing from her son. I answered rather at a venture; for not only did I fail to take her meaning with precision, but the sudden disclosure of her eyes disturbed me. They were unusually large, the iris golden like Felipe's, but the pupil at that moment so distended that they seemed almost black; and what affected me was not so much their size as (what was perhaps its consequence) the singular insignificance of their regard. A look more blankly stupid I have never met. My eyes dropped before it even as I spoke, and I went on my way upstairs to my own room, at once baffled and embarrassed. Yet, when I came there and saw the face of the portrait, I was again reminded of the miracle of family descent. My hostess was, indeed, both older and fuller in person; her eyes were of a different colour; her face, besides, was not only free from the ill-significance that offended and attracted me in the painting; it was devoid of either good or bad – a moral blank expressing literally naught. And yet there was a likeness, not so much speaking as imma-nent, not so much in any particular feature as upon the whole. It should seem, I thought, as if when the master set his signature to that grave canvas, he had not only caught the image of one smiling and false-eyed woman, but stamped the essential quality of a race.

From that day forth, whether I came or went, I was sure to find the Señora seated in the sun against a pillar, or stretched on a rug before the fire; only at times she would shift her station to the top round of the stone staircase, where she lay with the same nonchalance right across my path. In all these days, I never knew her to display the least spark of energy beyond what she expended in brushing and re-brushing her copious copper-coloured hair, or in lisping out, in the rich and broken hoarseness of her voice, her customary idle salutations to myself. These, I think, were her two chief pleasures, beyond that of mere quiescence. She seemed always proud of her remarks, as though they had been witticisms: and, indeed, though they were empty enough, like the conversation of many respectable persons, and turned on a very narrow range of subjects, they were never meaningless or incoherent; nay, they had a certain beauty of their own, breathing, as they did, of her entire contentment. Now she would speak of the warmth, in which (like her son) she greatly delighted; now of the flowers of the pomegranate trees, and now of the white doves and long-winged swallows that fanned the air of the court. The birds excited her. As they raked the eaves in their swift flight, or skimmed sidelong past her with a rush of wind, she would sometimes stir, and sit a little up, and seem to awaken from her doze of satisfaction. But for the rest of her days she lay luxuriously folded on herself and sunk in sloth and pleasure. Her invincible content at first annoyed me, but I came gradually to find repose in the spectacle, until at last it grew to be my habit to sit down beside her four times in the day, both coming and going, and to talk with her sleepily, I scarce knew of what. I had come to like her dull, almost animal neighbourhood; her beauty and her stupidity soothed and amused me. I began to find a kind of transcendental good sense in her remarks, and her unfathomable good nature moved me to admiration and envy. The liking was returned; she enjoyed my presence half-unconsciously, as a man in deep medi- tation may enjoy the babbling of a brook. I can scarce say she brightened when I came, for satisfaction was written on her face eternally, as on some foolish statue's; but I was made conscious of her pleasure by some more intimate communication than the sight. And one day, as I sat within reach of her on the marble step, she suddenly shot forth one of her hands and patted mine. The thing was done, and she was back in her accustomed attitude, before my mind had received intelligence of the caress; and when I turned to look her in the face I could perceive no answerable sentiment. It was plain she attached no moment to the act, and I blamed myself for my own more uneasy consciousness.

The sight and (if I may so call it) the acquaintance of the mother confirmed the view I had already taken of the son. The family blood had been impoverished, perhaps by long inbreeding, which I knew to be a common error among the proud and the exclusive.[10] No decline, indeed, was to be traced in the body, which had been handed down unimpaired in shapeliness and strength; and the faces of today were struck as sharply from the mint, as the face of two centuries ago that smiled upon me from the portrait. But the intelligence (that more precious heirloom) was degenerate; the treasure of ancestral memory ran low; and it had required the potent, plebeian crossing of a muleteer or mountain contrabandista[11] to raise, what approached hebetude[12] in the mother, into the active oddity of the son. Yet of the two, it was the mother I preferred. Of Felipe, vengeful and placable, full of starts and shyings, inconstant as a hare, I could even conceive as a creature possibly noxious. Of the mother I had no thoughts but those of kindness. And indeed, as spectators are apt ignorantly to take sides, I grew something of a partisan in the enmity which I perceived to smoulder between them. True, it seemed mostly on the mother's part. She would sometimes draw in her breath as he came near, and the pupils of her vacant eyes would contract as if with horror or fear. Her emotions, such as they were, were much upon the surface and readily shared; and this latent repulsion occupied my mind, and kept me wondering on what grounds it rested, and whether the son was certainly in fault.

I had been about ten days in the residencia, when there sprang up a high and harsh wind, carrying clouds of dust. It came out of malarious lowlands, and over several snowy sierras. The nerves of those on whom it blew were strung and jangled; their eyes smarted with the dust; their legs ached under the burden of their body; and the touch of one hand upon another grew to be odious. The wind, besides, came down the gullies of the hills and stormed about the house with a great, hollow buzzing and whistling that was wearisome to the ear and dismally depressing to the mind. It did not so much blow in gusts as with the steady sweep of a waterfall, so that there was no remission of discomfort while it blew. But higher upon the mountain, it was probably of a more variable strength, with accesses of fury; for there came down at times a far-off wailing, infinitely grievous to hear; and at times, on one of the high shelves or terraces, there would start up, and then disperse, a tower of dust, like the smoke of an explosion.

I no sooner awoke in bed than I was conscious of the nervous tension and depression of the weather, and the effect grew stronger as the day proceeded. It was in vain that I resisted; in vain that I set forth upon my customary morning's walk; the irrational, unchanging fury of the storm had soon beat down my strength and wrecked my temper; and I returned to the residencia, glowing with dry heat, and foul and gritty with dust. The court had a forlorn appearance; now and then a glimmer of sun fled over it; now and then the wind swooped down upon the pomegranates, and scattered the blossoms, and set the window shutters clapping on the wall. In the recess the Señora was pacing to and fro with a flushed countenance and bright eyes; I thought, too, she was speaking to herself, like one in anger. But when I addressed her with my customary salutation, she only replied by a sharp gesture and continued her walk. The weather had distempered even this impassive creature; and as I went on upstairs I was the less ashamed of my own discomposure.

All day the wind continued; and I sat in my room and made a feint of reading, or walked up and down, and listened to the riot overhead. Night fell, and I had not so much as a candle. I began to long for some society, and stole down to the court. It was now plunged in the blue of the first darkness; but the recess was redly lighted by the fire. The wood had been piled high, and was crowned by a shock of flames, which the draught of the chimney brandished to and fro. In this strong and shaken brightness the Señora continued pacing from wall to wall with disconnected gestures, clasping her hands, stretching forth her arms, throwing back her head as in appeal to heaven. In these disordered movements the beauty and grace of the woman showed more clearly; but there was a light in her eye that struck on me unpleasantly; and when I had looked on awhile in silence, and seemingly unobserved,

I turned tail as I had come, and groped my way back again to my own chamber.

By the time Felipe brought my supper and lights, my nerve was utterly gone; and, had the lad been such as I was used to seeing him, I should have kept him (even by force had that been necessary) to take off the edge from my distasteful solitude. But on Felipe, also, the wind had exercised its influence. He had been feverish all day; now that the night had come he was fallen into a low and tremulous humour that reacted on my own. The sight of his scared face, his starts and pallors and sudden harkenings, unstrung me; and when he dropped and broke a dish, I fairly leaped out of my seat.

'I think we are all mad today,' said I, affecting to laugh.

'It is the black wind,' he replied dolefully. 'You feel as if you must do something, and you don't know what it is.'

I noted the aptness of the description; but, indeed, Felipe had sometimes a strange felicity in rendering into words the sensations of the body. 'And your mother, too,' said I; 'she seems to feel this weather much. Do you not fear she may be unwell?'

He stared at me a little, and then said, 'No,' almost defiantly; and the next moment, carrying his hand to his brow, cried out lamentably on the wind and the noise that made his head go round like a millwheel. 'Who can be well?' he cried; and, indeed, I could only echo his question, for I was disturbed enough myself.

I went to bed early, wearied with day-long restlessness; but the poisonous nature of the wind, and its ungodly and unintermittent uproar, would not suffer me to sleep. I lay there and tossed, my nerves and senses on the stretch. At times I would doze, dream horribly, and wake again; and these snatches of oblivion confused me as to time. But it must have been late on in the night, when I was suddenly startled by an outbreak of pitiable and hateful cries. I leaped from my bed, supposing I had dreamed; but the cries still continued to fill the house, cries of pain, I thought, but certainly of rage also, and so savage and discordant that they shocked the heart. It was no illusion; some living thing, some lunatic or some wild animal, was being foully tortured. The thought of Felipe and the squirrel flashed into my mind, and I ran to the door, but it had been locked from the outside; and I might shake it as I pleased, I was a fast prisoner. Still the cries continued. Now they would dwindle down into a moaning that seemed to be articulate, and at these times I made sure they must be human; and again they would break forth and fill the house with ravings worthy of hell. I stood at the door and gave ear to them, till at last they died away. Long after that, I still lingered and still continued to hear them mingle in fancy with the storming of the wind; and when at last I crept to my bed, it was with a deadly sickness and a blackness of horror on my heart.

It was little wonder if I slept no more. Why had I been locked in? What had passed? Who was the author of these indescribable and shocking cries? A human being? It was inconceivable. A beast? The cries were scarce quite bestial; and what animal, short of a lion or a tiger, could thus shake the solid walls of the residencia? And while I was thus turning over the elements of the mystery, it came into my mind that I had not yet set eyes upon the daughter of the house. What was more probable than that the daughter of the Señora, and the sister of Felipe, should be herself insane? Or, what more likely than that these ignorant and half-witted people should seek to manage an afflicted kinswoman by violence? Here was a solution; and yet when I called to mind the cries (which I never did without a shuddering chill) it seemed altogether insufficient: not even cruelty could wring such cries from madness. But of one thing I was sure: I could not live in a house where such a thing was half conceivable, and not probe the matter home and, if necessary, interfere.

The next day came, the wind had blown itself out, and there was nothing to remind me of the business of the night. Felipe came to my bedside with obvious cheerfulness; as I passed through the court, the Señora was sunning herself with her accustomed immobility; and when I issued from the gateway, I found the whole face of nature austerely smiling, the heavens of a cold blue, and sown with great cloud islands, and the mountainsides mapped forth into provinces of light and shadow. A short walk restored me to myself, and renewed within me the resolve to plumb this mystery; and when, from the vantage of my knoll, I had seen Felipe pass forth to his labours in the garden, I returned at once to the residencia to put my design in practice. The Señora appeared plunged in slumber; I stood awhile and marked her, but she did not stir; even if my design were indiscreet, I had little to fear from such a guardian; and turning away, I mounted to the gallery and began my exploration of the house.

All morning I went from one door to another, and entered spacious and faded chambers, some rudely shuttered, some receiving their full charge of daylight, all empty and unhomely. It was a rich house, on which Time had breathed his tarnish and dust had scattered disillusion. The spider swung there; the bloated tarantula scampered on the cornices; ants had their crowded highways on the floor of halls of audience; the big and foul fly, that lives on carrion and is often the messenger of death, had set up his nest in the rotten woodwork, and buzzed heavily about the rooms. Here and there a stool or two, a couch, a bed, or a great carved chair remained behind, like islets on the bare floors, to testify of man's bygone habitation; and everywhere the walls were set with the portraits of the dead. I could judge, by these decaying effigies, in the house of what a great and what a handsome race I was then wandering. Many of the men wore orders on their breasts and had the port of noble offices; the women were all richly attired; the canvases most of them by famous hands. But it was not so much these evidences of greatness that took hold upon my mind, even contrasted, as they were, with the present depopulation and decay of that great house. It was rather the parable of family life that I read in this succession of fair faces and shapely bodies. Never before had I so realized the miracle of the continued race, the creation and recreation, the weaving and changing and handing down of fleshly elements. That a child should be born of its mother, that it should grow and clothe itself (we know not how) with humanity, and put on inherited looks, and turn its head with the manner of one ascendant, and offer its hand with the gesture of another, are wonders dulled for us by repetition. But in the singular unity of look, in the common features and common bearing, of all these painted generations on the walls of the residencia, the miracle started out and looked me in the face. And an ancient mirror falling opportunely in my way, I stood and read my own features a long while, tracing out on either hand the filaments of descent and the bonds that knit me with my family.[13]

At last, in the course of these investigations, I opened the door of a chamber that bore the marks of habitation. It was of large proportions and faced to the north, where the mountains were most wildly figured. The embers of a fire smouldered and smoked upon the hearth, to which a chair had been drawn close. And yet the aspect of the chamber was ascetic to the degree of sternness; the chair was uncushioned; the floor and walls were naked; and beyond the books which lay here and there in some confusion, there was no instrument of either work or pleasure. The sight of books in the house of such a family exceedingly amazed me; and I began with a great hurry, and in momentary fear of interruption, to go from one to another and hastily inspect their character. They were of all sorts, devotional, historical, and scientific, but mostly of a great age and in the Latin tongue. Some I could see to bear the marks of constant study; others had been torn across and tossed aside as if in petulance or disapproval. Lastly, as I cruised about that empty chamber, I espied some papers written upon with pencil on a table near the window. An unthinking curiosity led me to take one up. It bore a copy of verses, very roughly metred in the original Spanish, and which I may render somewhat thus –

> Pleasure approached with pain and shame,
> Grief with a wreath of lilies came.
> Pleasure showed the lovely sun;
> Jesu dear, how sweet it shone!
> Grief with her worn hand pointed on,
> > Jesu dear, to thee!

Shame and confusion at once fell on me; and, laying down the paper, I beat an immediate retreat from the apartment. Neither Felipe nor his mother could have read the book nor written these rough but feeling verses. It was plain I had stumbled with sacrilegious feet into the room of the daughter of the house. God knows, my own heart most sharply punished me for my indiscretion. The thought that I had thus secretly pushed my way into the confidence of a girl so strangely situated, and the fear that she might somehow come to hear of it, oppressed me like guilt. I blamed myself besides for my suspicions of the night before; wondered that I should ever have attributed those shocking cries to one of whom I now conceived as of a saint, spectral of mien, wasted with maceration, bound up in the practices of a mechanical devotion, and dwelling in a great isolation of soul with her incongruous relatives; and as I leaned on the balustrade of the gallery and looked down into the bright close of pomegranates and at the gaily dressed and somnolent woman, who just then stretched herself and delicately licked her lips as in the very sensuality of sloth, my mind swiftly compared the scene with the cold chamber looking northward on the mountains, where the daughter dwelt.

That same afternoon, as I sat upon my knoll, I saw the Padre enter the gates of the residencia. The revelation of the daughter's character had struck home to my fancy, and almost blotted out the horrors of the night before; but at sight of this worthy man the memory revived. I descended, then, from the knoll, and making a circuit among the woods, posted myself by the wayside to await his passage. As soon as he appeared I stepped forth and introduced myself as the lodger of the residencia. He had a very strong, honest countenance, on which it was easy to read the mingled emotions with which he regarded me, as a foreigner, a heretic, and yet one who had been wounded for the good cause. Of the family at the residencia he spoke with reserve, and yet with respect. I mentioned that I had not yet seen the daughter, whereupon he remarked that that was as it should be, and looked at me a little askance. Lastly, I plucked up courage to refer to the cries that had disturbed me in the night. He heard me out in silence, and then stopped and partly turned about, as though to mark beyond doubt that he was dismissing me.

'Do you take tobacco powder?' said he, offering his snuff-box; and then, when I had refused, 'I am an old man,' he added, 'and I may be allowed to remind you that you are a guest.'

'I have, then, your authority,' I returned, firmly enough, although I flushed at the implied reproof, 'to let things take their course, and not to interfere?'

He said 'yes,' and with a somewhat uneasy salute turned and left me where I was. But he had done two things: he had set my conscience at rest, and he had awakened my delicacy. I made a great effort, once more dismissed the recollections of the night, and fell once more to brooding on my saintly poetess. At the same time, I could not quite forget that I had been locked in, and that night when Felipe brought me my supper I attacked him warily on both points of interest.

'I never see your sister,' said I casually.

'Oh, no,' said he; 'she is a good, good girl,' and his mind instantly veered to something else.

'Your sister is pious, I suppose?' I asked in the next pause.

'Oh!' he cried, joining his hands with extreme fervour, 'a saint; it is she that keeps me up.'

'You are very fortunate,' said I, 'for the most of us, I am afraid, and myself among the number, are better at going down.'

'Señor,' said Felipe earnestly, 'I would not say that. You should not tempt your angel. If one goes down, where is he to stop?'

'Why, Felipe,' said I, 'I had no guess you were a preacher, and I may say a good one; but I suppose that is your sister's doing?'

He nodded at me with round eyes.

'Well, then,' I continued, 'she has doubtless reproved you for your sin of cruelty?'

'Twelve times!' he cried; for this was the phrase by which the odd creature expressed the sense of frequency. 'And I told her you had done so – I remembered that,' he added proudly – 'and she was pleased.'

'Then, Felipe,' said I, 'what were those cries that I heard last night for surely they were cries of some creature in suffering.'

'The wind,' returned Felipe, looking in the fire.

I took his hand in mine, at which, thinking it to be a caress, he smiled with a brightness of pleasure that came near disarming my resolve. But I trod the weakness down. 'The wind,' I repeated; 'and yet I think it was this hand,' holding it up, 'that had first locked me in.' The lad shook visibly, but answered never a word. 'Well,' said I, 'I am a stranger and a guest. It is not my part either to meddle or to judge in your affairs; in these you shall take your sister's counsel, which I cannot doubt to be excellent. But in so far as concerns my own I will be no man's prisoner, and I demand that key.' Half an hour later my door was suddenly thrown open, and the key tossed ringing on the floor.

A day or two after I came in from a walk a little before the point of noon. The Señora was lying lapped in slumber on the threshold of the recess; the pigeons dozed below the caves like snowdrifts; the house was under a deep spell of noontide quiet; and only a wandering and gentle wind from the mountain stole round the galleries, rustled among the pomegranates, and pleasantly stirred the shadows. Something in the stillness moved me to imitation, and I went very lightly across the court and up the marble staircase. My foot was on the topmost round, when a door opened, and I found myself face to face with Olalla. Surprise transfixed me; her loveliness struck to my heart; she glowed in the deep shadow of the gallery, a gem of colour; her eyes took hold upon mine and clung there, and bound us together like the joining of hands; and the moments we thus stood face to face, drinking each other in, were sacramental and the wedding of souls. I know not how long it was before I awoke out of a deep trance, and, hastily bowing, passed on into the upper stair. She did not move, but followed me with her great, thirsting eyes; and as I passed out of sight it seemed to me as if she paled and faded.

In my own room, I opened the window and looked out, and could not think what change had come upon that austere field of mountains that it should thus sing and shine under the lofty heaven. I had seen her – Olalla! And the stone crags answered, Olalla! and the dumb, unfathomable azure answered, Olalla! The pale saint of my dreams had vanished for ever; and in her place I beheld this maiden on whom God had lavished the richest colours and the most exuberant energies of life, whom he had made active as a deer, slender as a reed, and in whose great eyes he had lighted the torches of the soul. The thrill of her young life, strung like a wild animal's, had entered into me; the force of soul that had looked out from her eyes and conquered mine, mantled about my heart and sprang to my lips in singing. She passed through my veins: she was one with me.

I will not say that this enthusiasm declined; rather my soul held out in its ecstasy as in a strong castle, and was there besieged by cold and sorrowful considerations. I could not doubt but that I loved her at first sight, and already with a quivering ardour that was strange to my experience. What then was to follow? She was a child of an afflicted house,[14] the Señora's daughter, the sister of Felipe; she bore it even in her beauty. She had the lightness and swiftness of the one, swift as an arrow, light as dew; like the other, she shone on the pale background of the world with the brilliancy of flowers. I could not call by the name of brother that half-witted lad, nor by the name of mother that immovable and lovely thing of flesh, whose silly eyes and perpetual simper now recurred to my mind like something hateful. And if I could not marry, what then? She was helplessly unprotected; her eyes, in that single and long glance which had been all our intercourse, had confessed a weakness equal to my own; but in my heart I knew her for the student of the cold northern chamber, and the writer of the sorrowful lines; and this was a knowledge to disarm a brute. To flee was more than I could find courage for; but I registered a vow of unsleeping circumspection.

As I turned from the window, my eyes alighted on the portrait. It had fallen dead, like a candle after sunrise; it followed me with eyes of paint. I knew it to be like, and marvelled at the tenacity of type in that declining race; but the likeness was swallowed up in difference. I remembered how it had seemed to me a thing unapproachable in the life, a creature rather of the painter's craft than of the modesty of nature, and I marvelled at the thought, and exulted in the image of Olalla. Beauty I had seen before, and not been charmed, and I had been often drawn to women, who were not beautiful except to me; but in Olalla all that I desired and had not dared to imagine was united.

I did not see her the next day, and my heart ached and my eyes longed for her, as men long for morning. But the day after, when I returned, about my usual hour, she was once more on the gallery, and our looks once more met and embraced. I would have spoken, I would have drawn near to her; but strongly as she plucked at my heart, drawing me like a magnet, something yet more imperious withheld me; and I could only bow and pass by; and she, leaving my salutation unanswered, only followed me with her noble eyes.

I had now her image by rote, and as I conned the traits in memory it seemed as if I read her very heart. She was dressed with something of her mother's coquetry, and love of positive colour. Her robe, which I knew she must have made with her own hands, clung about her with a cunning grace. After the fashion of that country, besides, her bodice stood open in the middle, in a long slit, and here, in spite of the poverty of the house, a gold coin, hanging by a ribbon, lay on her brown bosom. These were proofs, had any been needed, of her inborn delight in life and her own loveliness. On the other hand, in her eyes that hung upon mine, I could read depth beyond depth of passion and sadness, lights of poetry and hope, blacknesses of despair, and thoughts that were above the earth. It was a lovely body, but the inmate, the soul, was more than worthy of that lodging. Should I leave this incomparable flower to wither unseen on these rough mountains? Should I despise the great gift offered me in the eloquent silence of her eyes? Here was a soul immured; should I not burst its prison? All side considerations fell off from me; were she the child of Herod I swore I should make her mine; and that very evening I set myself, with a mingled sense of treachery and disgrace, to captivate the brother. Perhaps I read him with more favourable eyes, perhaps the thought of his sister always summoned up the better qualities of that imperfect soul; but he had never seemed to me so amiable, and his very likeness to Olalla, while it annoyed, yet softened me.

A third day passed in vain – an empty desert of hours. I would not lose a chance, and loitered all afternoon in the court where (to give myself a countenance) I spoke more than usual with the Señora. God knows it was with a most tender and sincere interest that I now studied her; and even as for Felipe, so now for the mother, I was conscious of a growing warmth of toleration. And yet I wondered. Even while I spoke with her, she would doze off into a little sleep, and presently awake again without embarrassment; and this composure staggered me. And again, as I marked her make infinitesimal changes in her posture, savouring and lingering on the bodily pleasure of the move-ment, I was driven to wonder at this depth of passive sensuality. She lived in her body; and her consciousness was all sunk into and disseminated through her members, where it luxuriously dwelt. Lastly, I could not grow accustomed to her eyes. Each time she turned on me these great beautiful and meaningless orbs, wide open to the day, but closed against human inquiry – each time I had occasion to observe the lively changes of her pupils which expanded and contracted in a breath – I know not what it was came over me, I can find no name for the mingled feeling of disappointment, annoyance, and distaste that jarred along my nerves. I tried her on a variety of subjects, equally in vain; and at last led the talk to her daughter. But even there she proved indifferent; said she was pretty, which (as with children) was her highest word of commendation, but was plainly incapable of any higher thought; and when I remarked that Olalla seemed silent, merely yawned in my face and replied that speech was of no great use when you had nothing to say. 'People speak much, very much,' she added, looking at me with expanded pupils; and then again yawned, and again showed me a mouth that was as dainty as a toy. This time I took the hint, and, leaving her to her repose, went up into my own chamber to sit by the open window, looking on the hills and not beholding them, sunk in lustrous and deep dreams, and hearkening in fancy to the note of a voice that I had never heard.

I awoke on the fifth morning with a brightness of anticipation that seemed to challenge fate. I was sure of myself, light of heart and foot, and resolved to put my love incontinently to the touch of knowledge. It should lie no longer under the bonds of silence, a dumb thing, living by the eye only, like the love of beasts; but should not put on the spirit, and enter upon the joys of the complete human intimacy. I thought of it with wild hopes, like a voyager to El Dorado;[15] into that unknown and lovely country of her soul, I no longer trembled to adventure. Yet when I did indeed encounter her, the same force of passion descended on me and at once submerged my mind; speech seemed to drop away from me like a childish habit; and I but drew near to her as the giddy man draws near to the margin of a gulf. She drew back from me a little as I came; but her eyes did not waver from mine, and these lured me forward. At last, when I was already within reach of her, I stopped. Words were denied me; if I advanced I could but clasp her to my heart in silence; and all that was sane in me, all that was still uncon-quered, revolted against the thought of such an accost. So we stood for a second, all our life in our eyes, exchanging salvos of attraction and yet each resisting; and then, with a great effort of the will, and conscious at the same time of a sudden bitterness of disappointment, I turned and went away in the same silence.

What power lay upon me that I could not speak? And she, why was she also silent? Why did she draw away before me dumbly, with fascinated eyes? Was this love? or was it a mere brute attraction, mindless and inevitable, like that of the magnet for the steel? We had never spoken, we were wholly strangers; and yet an influence, strong as the grasp of a giant, swept us silently together. On my side, it filled me with impatience; and yet I was sure that she was worthy; I had seen her books, read her verses, and thus, in a sense, divined the soul of my mistress. But on her side, it struck me almost cold. Of me, she knew nothing but my bodily favour; she was drawn to me as stones fall to the earth; the laws that rule the earth conducted her, uncon-senting, to my arms; and I drew back at the thought of such a bridal, and began to be jealous for myself. It was not thus that I desired to be loved. And then I began to fall into a great pity for the girl herself. I thought how sharp must be her mortification, that she, the student, the recluse, Felipe's saintly monitress, should have thus confessed an overweening weakness for a man with whom she had never exchanged a word. And at the coming of pity, all other thoughts were swallowed up; and I longed only to find and console and reassure her; to tell her how wholly her love was returned on my side, and how her choice, even if blindly made, was not unworthy.

The next day it was glorious weather; depth upon depth of blue over-canopied the mountains; the sun shone wide; and the wind in the trees and the many falling torrents in the mountains filled the air with delicate and haunting music. Yet I was prostrated with sadness. My heart wept for the sight of Olalla, as a child weeps for its mother. I sat down on a boulder on the verge of the low cliffs that bound the plateau to the north. Thence I looked down into the wooded valley of a stream, where no foot came. In the mood I was in, it was even touching to behold the place untenanted; it lacked Olalla; and I thought of the delight and glory of a life passed wholly with her in that strong air, and among these rugged and lovely surroundings, at first with a whimpering sentiment, and then again with such a fiery joy that I seemed to grow in strength and stature, like a Samson.[16]

And then suddenly I was aware of Olalla drawing near. She appeared out of a grove of cork-trees, and came straight towards me;

and I stood up and waited. She seemed in her walking a creature of such life and fire and lightness as amazed me; yet she came quietly and slowly. Her energy was in the slowness; but for inimitable strength, I felt she would have run, she would have flown to me. Still, as she approached, she kept her eyes lowered to the ground; and when she had drawn quite near, it was without one glance that she addressed me. At the first note of her voice I started. It was for this I had been waiting; this was the last test of my love. And lo, her enunciation was precise and clear, not lisping and incomplete like that of her family; and the voice, though deeper than usual with women, was still both youthful and womanly. She spoke in a rich chord; golden contralto strains mingled with hoarseness, as the red threads were mingled with the brown among her tresses. It was not only a voice that spoke to my heart directly; but it spoke to me of her. And yet her words immediately plunged me back upon despair.

'You will go away,' she said, 'today.'

Her example broke the bonds of my speech; I felt as lightened of a weight, or as if a spell had been dissolved. I know not in what words I answered; but, standing before her on the cliffs, I poured out the whole ardour of my love, telling her that I lived upon the thought of her, slept only to dream of her loveliness, and would gladly forswear my country, my language, and my friends, to live for ever by her side. And then, strongly commanding myself, I changed the note; I reassured, I comforted her; I told her I had divined in her a pious and heroic spirit, with which I was worthy to sympathize, and which I longed to share and lighten. 'Nature,' I told her, 'was the voice of God, which men disobey at peril; and if we were thus dumbly drawn together, ay, even as by a miracle of love, it must imply a divine fitness in our souls; we must be made,' I said – 'made for one another. We should be mad rebels,' I cried out – 'mad rebels against God, not to obey this instinct.'

She shook her head. 'You will go today,' she repeated, and then with a gesture, and in a sudden, sharp note – 'No, not today,' she cried, 'tomorrow!'

But at this sign of relenting, power came in upon me in a tide. I stretched out my arms and called upon her name; and she leaped to me and clung to me. The hills rocked about us, the earth quailed; a shock as of a blow went through me and left me blind and dizzy. And the next moment she had thrust me back, broken rudely from my arms, and fled with the speed of a deer among the cork-trees.

I stood and shouted to the mountains; I turned and went back towards the residencia, walking upon air. She sent me away, and yet I had but to call upon her name and she came to me. These were but the weaknesses of girls, from which even she, the strangest of her sex, was not exempted. Go? Not I, Olalla – O, not I, Olalla, my Olalla! A bird sang near by; and in that season, birds were rare. It bade me be of good cheer. And once more the whole countenance of nature, from the ponderous and stable mountains down to the lightest leaf and the smallest darting fly in the shadow of the groves, began to stir before me and to put on the lineaments of life and wear a face of awful joy. The sunshine struck upon the hills, strong as a hammer on the anvil, and the hills shook; the earth, under that vigorous insolation, yielded up heady scents; the woods smouldered in the blaze. I felt the thrill of travail and delight run through the earth. Something elemental, something rude, violent, and savage, in the love that sang in my heart, was like a key to nature's secrets; and the very stones that rattled under my feet appeared alive and friendly. Olalla! Her touch had quickened, and renewed, and strung me up to the old pitch of concert with the rugged earth, to a swelling of the soul that men learn to forget in their polite assemblies. Love burned in me like rage; tenderness waxed fierce; I hated, I adored, I pitied, I revered her with ecstasy. She seemed the link that bound me in with dead things on the one hand, and with our pure and pitying God upon the other: a thing brutal and divine, and akin at once to the innocence and to the unbridled forces of the earth.

My head thus reeling, I came into the courtyard of the residencia, and the sight of the mother struck me like a revelation. She sat there, all sloth and contentment, blinking under the strong sunshine, branded with a passive enjoyment, a creature set quite apart, before whom my ardour fell away like a thing ashamed. I stopped a moment, and, commanding such shaken tones as I was able, said a word or two. She looked at me with her unfathomable kindness; her voice in reply sounded vaguely out of the realm of peace in which she slumbered, and there fell on my mind, for the first time, a sense of respect for one so uniformly innocent and happy, and I passed on in a kind of wonder at myself, that I should be so much disquieted.

On my table there lay a piece of the same yellow paper I had seen in the north room; it was written on with pencil in the same hand, Olalla's hand, and I picked it up with a sudden sinking of alarm, and read, 'If you have any kindness for Olalla, if you have any chivalry for a creature sorely wrought, go from here today; in pity, in honour, for the sake of Him who died, I supplicate that you shall go.' I looked at this awhile in mere stupidity, then I began to awaken to a weariness and horror of life; the sunshine darkened outside on the bare hills, and I began to shake like a man in terror. The vacancy thus suddenly opened in my life unmanned me like a physical void. It was not my heart, it was not my happiness, it was life itself that was involved. I could not lose her. I said so, and stood repeating it. And then, like one in a dream, I moved to the window, put forth my hand to open the casement, and thrust it through the pane. The blood spurted from my wrist; and with an instantaneous quietude and command of myself, I pressed my thumb on the little leaping fountain, and reflected what to do. In that empty room there was nothing to my purpose; I felt, besides, that I required assistance. There shot into my mind a hope that Olalla herself might be my helper, and I turned and went down stairs, still keeping my thumb upon the wound.

There was no sign of either Olalla or Felipe, and I addressed myself to the recess, whither the Señora had not drawn quite back and sat dozing close before the fire, for no degree of heat appeared too much for her.

'Pardon me,' said I, 'if I disturb you, but I must apply to you for help.'

She looked up sleepily and asked me what it was, and with the very words I thought she drew in her breath with a widening of the nostrils and seemed to come suddenly and fully alive.

'I have cut myself,' I said, 'and rather badly. See!' And I held out my two hands from which the blood was oozing and dripping.

Her great eyes opened wide, the pupils shrank into points;[17] a veil seemed to fall from her face, and leave it sharply expressive and yet inscrutable. And as I still stood, marvelling a little at her disturbance, she came swiftly up to me, and stooped and caught me by the hand; and the next moment my hand was at her mouth, and she had bitten me to the bone. The pang of the bite, the sudden spurting of blood, and the monstrous horror of the act, flashed through me all in one, and I beat her back; and she sprang at me again and again, with bestial cries, cries that I recognized, such cries as had awakened me on the night of the high wind. Her strength was like that of madness; mine was rapidly ebbing with the loss of blood; my mind besides was whirling with the abhorrent strangeness of the onslaught, and I was already forced against the wall, when Olalla ran betwixt us, and Felipe, following at a bound, pinned down his mother on the floor.

A trance-like weakness fell upon me; I saw, heard, and felt, but I was incapable of movement. I heard the struggle roll to and fro upon the floor, the yells of that catamount ringing up to Heaven as she strove to reach me. I felt Olalla clasp me in her arms, her hair falling on my face, and, with the strength of a man, raise and half drag, half carry me upstairs into my own room, where she cast me down upon the bed. Then I saw her hasten to the door and lock it, and stand an instant listening to the savage cries that shook the residencia. And then, swift and light as a thought, she was again beside me, binding up my hand, laying it in her bosom, moaning and mourning over it with dove-like sounds. They were not words that came to her, they were sounds more beautiful than speech, infinitely touching, infinitely tender; and yet as I lay there, a thought stung to my heart, a thought wounded me like a sword, a thought, like a worm in a flower, profaned the holiness of my love. Yes, they were beautiful sounds, and they were inspired by human tenderness; but was their beauty human?

All day I lay there. For a long time the cries of that nameless female thing, as she struggled with her half-witted whelp, resounded through the house, and pierced me with despairing sorrow and disgust. They were the death-cry of my love; my love was murdered; it was not only dead, but an offence to me; and yet, think as I pleased, feel as I must, it still swelled within me like a storm of sweetness, and my heart melted at her looks and touch. This horror that had sprung out, this doubt upon Olalla, this savage and bestial strain that ran not only through the whole behaviour of her family, but found a place in the very foundations and story of our love – though it appalled, though it shocked and sickened me, was yet not of power to break the knot of my infatuation.

When the cries had ceased, there came a scraping at the door, by which I knew Felipe was without; and Olalla went and spoke to him – I know not what. With that exception, she stayed close beside me, now kneeling by my bed and fervently praying, now sitting with her eyes upon mine. So then, for these six hours I drank in her beauty, and silently perused the story in her face. I saw the golden coin hover on her breasts; I saw her eyes darken and brighten, and still speak no language but that of an unfathomable kindness; I saw the faultless face, and, through the robe, the lines of the faultless body. Night came at last, and in the growing darkness of the chamber, the sight of her slowly melted; but even then the touch of her smooth hand lingered in mine and talked with me. To lie thus in deadly weakness and drink in the traits of the beloved, is to reawake to love from whatever shock of disillusion. I reasoned with myself; and I shut my eyes on horrors, and again I was very bold to accept the worst. What mattered it, if that imperious sentiment survived; if her eyes still beckoned and attached me; if now, even as before, every fibre of my dull body yearned and turned to her? Late on in the night some strength revived in me, and I spoke:

'Olalla,' I said, 'nothing matters; I ask nothing; I am content; I love you.'

She knelt down awhile and prayed, and I devoutly respected her devotions. The moon had begun to shine in upon one side of each of the three windows, and make a misty clearness in the room, by which I saw her indistinctly. When she re-arose she made the sign of the cross.

'It is for me to speak,' she said, 'and for you to listen. I know; you can but guess. I prayed, how I prayed for you to leave this place. I begged it of you, and I know you would have granted me even this; or if not, O let me think so!'

'I love you,' I said.

'And yet you have lived in the world,' she said; after a pause, 'you are a man and wise; and I am but a child. Forgive me, if I seem to teach, who am as ignorant as the trees of the mountain; but those who learn much do but skim the face of knowledge; they seize the laws, they conceive the dignity of the design – the horror of the living fact fades from their memory. It is we who sit at home with evil who remember, I think, and are warned and pity. Go, rather, go now, and keep me in mind. So I shall have a life in the cherished places of your memory: a life as much my own, as that which I lead in this body.'

'I love you,' I said once more; and reaching out my weak hand, took hers, and carried it to my lips, and kissed it. Nor did she resist, but winced a little; and I could see her look upon me with a frown that was not unkindly, only sad and baffled. And then it seemed she made a call upon her resolution; plucked my hand towards her, herself at the same time leaning somewhat forward, and laid it on the beating of her heart. 'There,' she cried, 'you feel the very footfall of my life. It only moves for you; it is yours. But is it even mine? It is mine indeed to offer you, as I might take the coin from my neck, as I might break a live branch from a tree, and give it you. And yet not mine! I dwell, or I think I dwell (if I exist at all), somewhere apart, an impotent prisoner, and carried about and deafened by a mob that I disown. This capsule, such as throbs against the sides of animals, knows you at a touch for its master; ay, it loves you! But my soul, does my soul? I think not; I know not, fearing to ask. Yet when you spoke to me your words were of the soul; it is of the soul that you ask – it is only from the soul that you would take me.'

'Olalla,' I said, 'the soul and the body are one, and mostly so in love. What the body chooses, the soul loves; where the body clings, the soul cleaves; body for body, soul to soul, they come together at God's signal; and the lower part (if we can call aught low) is only the footstool and foundation of the highest.'

'Have you,' she said, 'seen the portraits in the house of my fathers? Have you looked at my mother or at Felipe? Have your eyes never rested on that picture that hangs by your bed? She who sat for it died ages ago; and she did evil in her life. But, look again: there is my hand to the least line, there are my eyes and my hair. What is mine, then, and what am I? If not a curve in this poor body of mine (which you love, and for the sake of which you dotingly dream that you love me) not a gesture that I can frame, not a tone of my voice, not any look from my eyes, no, not even now when I speak to him I love, but has belonged to others? Others, ages dead, have wooed other men with my eyes; other men have heard the pleading of the same voice that now sounds in your ears. The hands of the dead are in my bosom; they move me, they pluck me, they guide me; I am a puppet at their command; and I but reinform features and attributes that have long been laid aside from evil in the quiet of the grave. Is it me you love, friend? or the race that made me? The girl who does not know and cannot answer for the least portion of herself? or the stream of which she is a transitory eddy, the tree of which she is the passing fruit? The race exists; it is old, it is ever young, it carries its eternal destiny in its bosom; upon it, like waves upon the sea, individual succeeds to individual, mocked with a semblance of self-control, but they are nothing. We speak of the soul, but the soul is in the race.'

'You fret against the common law,' I said. 'You rebel against the voice of God, which he has made so winning to convince, so imperious to command. Hear it, and how it speaks between us! Your hand clings to mine, your heart leaps at my touch, the unknown elements of which we are compounded awake and run together at a look; the clay of the earth remembers its independent life and yearns to join us; we are drawn together as the stars are turned about in space, or as the tides ebb and flow, by things older and greater than we ourselves.'

'Alas!' she said, 'what can I say to you? My fathers, eight hundred years ago, ruled all this province: they were wise, great, cunning, and cruel; they were a picked race of the Spanish; their flags led in war; the king called them his cousin; the people, when the rope was slung for them or when they returned and found their hovels smoking, blasphemed their name. Presently a change began. Man has risen; if he has sprung from the brutes, he can descend again to the same level. The breath of weariness blew on their humanity and the cords relaxed; they began to go down; their minds fell on sleep, their passions awoke in gusts, heady and senseless like the wind in the gutters of the mountains; beauty was still handed down, but no longer the guiding wit nor the human heart; the seed passed on, it was wrapped in flesh, the flesh covered the bones, but they were the bones and the flesh of brutes, and their mind was as the mind of flies. I speak to you as I dare; but you have seen for yourself how the wheel has gone backward with my doomed race. I stand, as it were, upon a little rising ground in this desperate descent, and see both before and behind, both what we have lost and to what we are condemned to go farther downward. And shall I – I that dwell apart in the house of the dead, my body, loathing its ways – shall I repeat the spell? Shall I bind another spirit, reluctant as my own, into this bewitched and tempest-broken tenement that I now suffer in? Shall I hand down this cursed vessel of humanity, charge it with fresh life as with fresh poison, and dash it, like a fire, in the faces of posterity? But my vow has been given; the race shall cease from off the earth.[18] At this hour my brother is making ready; his foot will soon be on the stair; and you will go with him and pass out of my sight for ever. Think of me sometimes as one to whom the lesson of life was very harshly told, but who heard it with courage; as one who loved you indeed, but who hated herself so deeply that her love was hateful to her; as one who sent you away and yet would have longed to keep you for ever; who had no dearer hope than to forget you, and no greater fear than to be forgotten.'

She had drawn towards the door as she spoke, her rich voice sounding softer and farther away; and with the last word she was gone, and I lay alone in the moonlit chamber. What I might have done had not I lain bound by my extreme weakness, I know not; but as it was there fell upon me a great and blank despair. It was not long before there shone in at the door the ruddy glimmer of a lantern, and Felipe coming, charged me without a word upon his shoulders, and carried me down to the great gate, where the cart was waiting. In the moonlight the hills stood out sharply, as if they were of cardboard; on the glimmering surface of the plateau, and from among the low trees which swung together and sparkled in the wind, the great black cube of the residencia stood out bulkily, its mass only broken by three dimly lighted windows in the northern front above the gate. They were Olalla's windows, and as the cart jolted onwards I kept my eyes fixed upon them till, where the road dipped into a valley, they were lost to my view for ever. Felipe walked in silence beside the shafts, but from time to time he would check the mule and seem to look back upon me; and at length drew quite near and laid his hand upon my head. There was such kindness in the touch, and such a simplicity, as of the brutes, that tears broke from me like the bursting of an artery.

'Felipe,' I said, 'take me where they will ask no questions.'

He said never a word, but he turned his mule about, end for end, retraced some part of the way we had gone, and, striking into another path, led me to the mountain village, which was, as we say in Scotland, the kirkton[19] of that thinly peopled district. Some broken memories dwell in my mind of the day breaking over the plain, of the cart stopping, of arms that helped me down, of a bare room into which I was carried, and of a swoon that fell upon me like sleep.

The next day and the days following the old priest was often at my side with his snuff-box and prayer book, and after a while, when I began to pick up strength, he told me that I was now on a fair way to recovery, and must as soon as possible hurry my departure; whereupon, without naming any reason, he took snuff and looked at me sideways. I did not affect ignorance; I knew he must have seen Olalla. 'Sir,' said I, 'you know that I do not ask in wantonness. What of that family?'

He said they were very unfortunate; that it seemed a declining race, and that they were very poor and had been much neglected.

'But she has not,' I said. 'Thanks, doubtless, to yourself, she is instructed and wise beyond the use of women.'

'Yes,' he said; 'the Señorita is well-informed. But the family has been neglected.'

'The mother?' I queried.

'Yes, the mother too,' said the Padre, taking snuff. 'But Felipe is a well-intentioned lad.

'The mother is odd?' I asked.

'Very odd,' replied the priest.

'I think, sir, we beat about the bush,' said I. 'You must know more of my affairs than you allow. You must know my curiosity to be justified on many grounds. Will you not be frank with me?'

'My son,' said the old gentleman, 'I will be very frank with you on matters within my competence; on those of which I know nothing it does not require much discretion to be silent. I will not fence with you, I take your meaning perfectly; and what can I say, but that we are all in God's hands, and that His ways are not as our ways? I have even advised with my superiors in the church, but they, too, were dumb. It is a great mystery.'

'Is she mad?' I asked.

'I will answer you according to my belief. She is not,' returned the Padre, 'or she was not. When she was young – God help me, I fear I neglected that wild lamb – she was surely sane; and yet, although it did not run to such heights, the same strain was already notable; it had been so before her in her father, ay, and before him, and this inclined me, perhaps, to think too lightly of it. But these things go on growing, not only in the individual but in the race.'

'When she was young,' I began, and my voice failed me for a moment, and it was only with a great effort that I was able to add, 'was she like Olalla?'

'Now God forbid!' exclaimed the Padre. 'God forbid that any man should think so slightingly of my favourite penitent. No, no; the Señorita (but for her beauty, which I wish most honestly she had less of) has not a hair's resemblance to what her mother was at the same age. I could not bear to have you think so; though, Heaven knows, it were, perhaps, better that you should.'

At this, I raised myself in bed, and opened my heart to the old man; telling him of our love and of her decision, owning my own horrors, my own passing fancies, but telling him that these were at an end; and with something more than a purely formal submission, appealing to his judgement.

He heard me very patiently and without surprise; and when I had done, he sat for some time silent. Then he began: 'The church,' and instantly broke off again to apologize. 'I had forgotten, my child, that you were not a Christian,'[20] said he. 'And indeed, upon a point so highly unusual, even the church can scarce be said to have decided. But would you have my opinion? The Señorita is, in a matter of this kind, the best judge; I would accept her judgement.'

On the back of that he went away, nor was he thenceforward so assiduous in his visits; indeed, even when I began to get about again, he plainly feared and deprecated my society, not as in distaste but much as a man might be disposed to flee from the riddling sphinx. The villagers, too, avoided me; they were unwilling to be my guides upon the mountain. I thought they looked at me askance, and I made sure that the more superstitious crossed themselves on my approach.[21] At first I set this down to my heretical opinions; but it began at length to dawn upon me that if I was thus redoubted it was because I had stayed at the residencia. All men despise the savage notions of such peasantry; and yet I was conscious of a chill shadow that seemed to fall and dwell upon my love. It did not conquer, but I may not deny that it restrained my ardour.

Some miles westward of the village there was a gap in the sierra, from which the eye plunged direct upon the residencia; and thither it became my daily habit to repair. A wood crowned the summit; and just where the pathway issued from its fringes, it was overhung by a considerable shelf of rock, and that, in its turn, was surmounted by a crucifix of the size of life and more than usually painful in design. This was my perch; thence, day after day, I looked down upon the plateau, and the great old house, and could see Felipe, no bigger than a fly, going to and fro about the garden. Sometimes mists would draw across the view, and be broken up again by mountain winds; sometimes the plain slumbered below me in unbroken sunshine; it would sometimes be all blotted out by rain. This distant post, these interrupted sights of the place where my life had been so strangely changed, suited the indecision of my humour. I passed whole days there, debating with myself the various elements of our position; now leaning to the sugges-tions of love, now giving an ear to prudence, and in the end halting irresolute between the two.

One day, as I was sitting on my rock, there came by that way a somewhat gaunt peasant wrapped in a mantle. He was a stranger, and plainly did not know me even by repute; for, instead of keeping the other side, he drew near and sat down beside me, and we had soon fallen in talk. Among other things he told me he had been a muleteer, and in former years had much frequented these mountains; later on, he had followed the army with his mules, had realized a competence, and was now living retired with his family.

'Do you know that house?' I inquired, at last, pointing to the residencia, for I readily wearied of any talk that kept me from the thought of Olalla.

He looked at me darkly and crossed himself.

'Too well,' he said, 'it was there that one of my comrades sold himself to Satan; the Virgin shield us from temptations! He has paid the price; he is now burning in the reddest place in Hell!'

A fear came upon me; I could answer nothing; and presently the man resumed, as if to himself: 'Yes,' he said, 'O yes, I know it. I have passed its doors. There was snow upon the pass, the wind was driving it; sure enough there was death that night upon the mountains, but there was worse beside the hearth. I took him by the arm, Señor, and dragged him to the gate; I conjured him, by all he loved and respected, to go forth with me; I went on my knees before him in the snow; and I could see he was moved by my entreaty. And just then she came out on the gallery, and called him by his name; and he turned, and there was she standing with a lamp in her hand and smiling on him to come back. I cried out aloud to God, and threw my arms about him, but he put me by, and left me alone. He had made his choice; God help us. I would pray for him, but to what end? there are sins that not even the Pope can loose.'

'And your friend,' I asked, 'what became of him?'

'Nay, God knows,' said the muleteer. 'If all be true that we hear, his end was like his sin, a thing to raise the hair.'

'Do you mean that he was killed?' I asked.

'Sure enough, he was killed,' returned the man. 'But how? Ay, how? But these are things that it is sin to speak of.'

'The people of that house . . .' I began.

But he interrupted me with a savage outburst. 'The people?' he cried. 'What people? There are neither men nor women in that house of Satan's! What? Have you lived here so long, and never heard?' And here he put his mouth to my ear and whispered, as if even the fowls of the mountain might have overheard and been stricken with horror.

What he told me was not true, nor was it even original; being, indeed, but a new edition, vamped up again by village ignorance and superstition, of stories nearly as ancient as the race of man. It was rather the application that appalled me. In the old days, he said, the church would have burned out that nest of basilisks; but the arm of the church was now shortened; his friend Miguel had been unpunished by the hands of men, and left to the more awful judgment of an offended God. This was wrong; but it should be so no more. The Padre was sunk in age; he was even bewitched himself; but the eyes of his flock were now awake to their own danger; and some day – ay, and before long – the smoke of that house should go up to heaven.

He left me filled with horror and fear. Which way to turn I knew not; whether first to warn the Padre, or to carry my ill-news direct to the threatened inhabitants of the residencia. Fate was to decide for me; for, while I was still hesitating, I beheld the veiled figure of a woman drawing near to me up the pathway. No veil could deceive my penetration; by every line and every movement I recognized Olalla; and keeping hidden behind a corner of the rock, I suffered her to gain the summit. Then I came forward. She knew me and paused, but did not speak; I, too, remained silent; and we continued for some time to gaze upon each other with a passionate sadness.

'I thought you had gone,' she said at length. 'It is all that you can do for me – to go. It is all I ever asked of you. And you still stay. But do you know, that every day heaps up the peril of death, not only on your head, but on ours? A report has gone about the mountain; it is thought you love me, and the people will not suffer it.'

I saw she was already informed of her danger, and I rejoiced at it. 'Olalla,' I said, 'I am ready to go this day, this very hour, but not alone.'

She stepped aside and knelt down before the crucifix to pray, and I stood by and looked now at her and now at the object of her adoration, now at the living figure of the penitent, and now at the ghastly, daubed countenance, the painted wounds, and the projected ribs of the image. The silence was only broken by the wailing of some large birds that circled sidelong, as if in surprise or alarm, about the summit of the hills. Presently Olalla rose again, turned towards me, raised her veil, and, still leaning with one hand on the shaft of the crucifix, looked upon me with a pale and sorrowful countenance.

'I have laid my hand upon the cross,' she said. 'The Padre says you are no Christian; but look up for a moment with my eyes, and behold the face of the Man of Sorrows. We are all such as He was – the inheritors of sin; we must all bear and expiate a past which was not ours; there is in all of us – ay, even in me – a sparkle of the divine. Like Him, we must endure for a little while, until morning returns bringing peace. Suffer me to pass on upon my way alone; it is thus that I shall be least lonely, counting for my friend Him who is the friend of all the distressed; it is thus that I shall be the most happy, having taken my farewell of earthly happiness, and willingly accepted sorrow for my portion.'

I looked at the face of the crucifix, and, though I was no friend to images, and despised that imitative and grimacing art of which it was a rude example, some sense of what the thing implied was carried home to my intelligence. The face looked down upon me with a painful and deadly contraction; but the rays of a glory encircled it, and reminded me that the sacrifice was voluntary. It stood there, crowning the rock, as it still stands on so many highway sides, vainly preaching to passers-by, an emblem of sad and noble truths: that pleasure is not an end, but an accident; that pain is the choice of the magnanimous; that it is best to suffer all things and do well. I turned and went down the mountain in silence; and when I looked back for the last time before the wood closed about my path, I saw Olalla still leaning on the crucifix.

A CHAPTER ON DREAMS

(abridged)

A Chapter on Dreams

(abridged)

... There are some among us who claim to have lived longer and more richly than their neighbours; when they lay asleep they claim they were still active; and among the treasures of memory that all men review for their amusement, these count in no second place the harvests of their dreams. There is one of this kind whom I have in my eye, and whose case is perhaps unusual enough to be described. He was from a child an ardent and uncomfortable dreamer. When he had a touch of fever at night, and the room swelled and shrank, and his clothes, hanging on a nail, now loomed up instant to the bigness of a church, and now drew away into a horror of infinite distance and infinite littleness, the poor soul was very well aware of what must follow, and struggled hard against the approaches of that slumber which was the beginning of sorrows. But his struggles were in vain; sooner or later the night-hag would have him by the throat, and pluck him, strangling and screaming, from his sleep.

... And then, while he was yet a student, there came to him a dream-adventure which he has no anxiety to repeat; he began, that is to say, to dream in sequence and thus to lead a double life – one of the day, one of the night[1] – one that he had every reason to believe was the true one, another that he had no means of proving to be false. I should have said he studied, or was by way of studying, at Edinburgh College, which (it may be supposed) was how I came to know him. Well, in his dream-life he passed a long day in the surgical theatre, his heart in his mouth, his teeth on edge, seeing monstrous malformations and the abhorred dexterity of surgeons. In a heavy, rainy, foggy evening he came forth into the South Bridge, turned up the High

Street, and entered the door of a tall *land*, at the top of which he supposed himself to lodge. All night long, in his wet clothes, he climbed the stairs, stair after stair in endless series, and at every second flight a flaring lamp with a reflector. All night long he brushed by single persons passing downward – beggarly women of the street, great, weary, muddy labourers, poor scarecrows of men, pale parodies of women – but all drowsy and weary like himself, and all single, and all brushing against him as they passed. In the end, out of a northern window, he would see day beginning to whiten over the Firth, give up the ascent, turn to descend, and in a breath be back again upon the streets, in his wet clothes, in the wet, haggard dawn, trudging to another day of monstrosities and operations.

. . . This honest fellow had long been in the custom of setting himself to sleep with tales, and so had his father before him; but these were irresponsible inventions, told for the teller's pleasure, with no eye to the crass public or the thwart reviewer: tales where a thread might be dropped, or one adventure quitted for another, on fancy's least suggestion. So that the little people who manage man's internal theatre had not as yet received a very rigorous training; and played upon their stage like children who should have slipped into the house and found it empty, rather than like drilled actors performing a set piece to a huge hall of faces. But presently my dreamer began to turn his former amusement of story-telling to (what is called) account; by which I mean that he began to write and sell his tales. Here was he, and here were the little people who did that part of his business, in quite new conditions. The stories must now be trimmed and pared and set upon all-fours, they must run from a beginning to an end and fit (after a manner) with the laws of life; the pleasure, in one word, had become a business; and that not only for the dreamer, but for the little people of his theatre. These understood the change as well as he. When he lay down to prepare himself for sleep, he no longer sought amusement, but printable and profitable tales; and after he had dozed off in his box-seat, his little people continued their evolutions with the same mercantile designs. All other forms of dream deserted him but two: he still occasionally reads the most delightful books, he still visits at times the most delightful places; and it is perhaps worthy of note that to these same places, and to one in particular, he returns at intervals of months and years, finding new field-paths, visiting new neighbours, beholding that happy valley under new effects of noon and dawn and sunset. But all the rest of the family of visions is quite lost to him: the common, mangled version of yesterday's affairs, the raw-head-and-bloody-bones nightmare, rumoured to be the child of toasted cheese – these and their like are gone; and, for the most part, whether awake or asleep, he is simply occupied – he or his little people – in consciously making stories for the market.[2] This dreamer (like many other persons) has encountered some trifling vicissitudes of fortune. When the bank begins to send letters and the butcher to linger at the back gate, he sets to belabouring his brains after a story, for that is his readiest money-winner; and, behold! at once the little people begin to bestir themselves in the same quest, and labour all night long, and all night long set before him truncheons of tales upon their lighted theatre. No fear of his being frightened now; the flying heart and the frozen scalp are things bygone; applause, growing applause, growing interest, growing exultation in his own cleverness (for he takes all the credit), and at last a jubilant leap to wakefulness, with the cry, 'I have it, that'll do!' upon his lips: with such and similar emotions he sits at these nocturnal dramas, with such outbreaks, like Claudius in the play,[3] he scatters the performance in the midst. Often enough the waking is a disappointment: he has been too deep asleep, as I explain the thing; drowsiness has gained his little people, they were gone stumbling and maundering through their parts; and the play, to the awakened mind, is seen to be a tissue of absurdities. And yet how often have these sleepless Brownies[4] done him honest service, and given him, as he sat idly taking his pleasure in the boxes, better tales than he could fashion for himself.

. . . The more I think of it, the more I am moved to press upon the world my question: Who are the Little People? They are near connections of the dreamer's, beyond doubt; they share in his financial worries and have an eye to the bank-book; they share plainly in his training; they have plainly learned like him to build the scheme of a considerate story and to arrange emotion in progressive order; only I think they have more talent; and one thing is beyond doubt, they can tell him a story piece by piece, like a serial, and keep him all the while in ignorance of where they aim. Who are they, then? and who is the dreamer?

Well, as regards the dreamer, I can answer that, for he is no less a person than myself; – as I might have told you from the beginning, only that the critics murmur over my consistent egotism; – and as I am positively forced to tell you now, or I could advance but little further with my story. And for the Little People, what shall I say they are but just my Brownies, God bless them! who do one-half my work for me while I am fast asleep, and in all human likelihood, do the rest for me as well, when I am wide awake and fondly suppose I do it for myself. That part which is done while I am sleeping is the Brownies' part beyond contention; but that which is done when I am up and about is by no means necessarily mine, since all goes to show the Brownies have a hand in it even then. Here is a doubt that much concerns my conscience. For myself – what I call I, my conscious ego, the denizen of the pineal gland unless he has changed his residence since Descartes,[5] the man with the conscience and the variable bank-account, the man with the hat and the boots, and the privilege of voting and not carrying his candidate at the general elections – I am sometimes tempted to suppose is no story-teller at all, but a creature as matter of fact as any cheesemonger or any cheese, and a realist bemired up to the ears in actuality; so that, by that account, the whole of my published fiction should be the single-handed product of some Brownie, some Familiar, some unseen collaborator, whom I keep locked in a back garret, while I get all the praise and he but a share (which I cannot prevent him getting) of the pudding. I am an excellent adviser, something like Molière's servant.[6] I pull back and I cut down; and I dress the whole in the best words and sentences that I can find and make; I hold the pen, too; and I do the sitting at the table, which is about the worst of it; and when all is done, I make up the manuscript and pay for the registration; so that, on the whole, I have some claim to share, though not so largely as I do, in the profits of our common enterprise.

I can but give an instance or so of what part is done sleeping and what part awake, and leave the reader to share what laurels there are, at his own nod, between myself and my collaborators; and to do this I will first take a book that a number of persons have been polite enough to read, 'The Strange Case of Dr Jekyll and Mr Hyde'. I had long been trying to write a story on this subject, to find a body, a vehicle, for that strong sense of man's double being which must at times come in upon and overwhelm the mind of every thinking creature. I had even written one, 'The Travelling Companion', which was returned by an editor on the plea that it was a work of genius and indecent, and which I burned the other day on the ground that it was not a work of genius, and that 'Jekyll' had supplanted it. Then came one of those financial fluctuations to which (with an elegant modesty) I have hitherto referred in the third person. For two days I went about racking my brains for a plot of any sort; and on the second night I dreamed the scene at the window, and a scene afterward split in two, in which Hyde, pursued for some crime, took the powder and underwent the change in the presence of his pursuers.[7] All the rest was made awake, and consciously, although I think I can trace in much of it the manner of my Brownies. The meaning of the tale is therefore mine, and had long pre-existed in my garden of Adonis,[8] and tried one body after another in vain; indeed, I do most of the morality, worse luck! and my Brownies have not a rudiment of what we call a conscience. Mine, too, is the setting, mine the characters. All that was given me was the matter of three scenes, and the central idea of a voluntary change becoming involuntary. Will it be thought ungenerous, after I have been so liberally ladling out praise to my unseen collaborators, if I here toss them over, bound hand and foot, into the arena of the critics? For the business of the powders, which so many have censured, is, I am relieved to say, not mine at all, but the Brownies'. Of another tale, in case the reader should have glanced at it, I may say a word: the not very defensible story of 'Olalla'. Here the court, the mother, the mother's niche, Olalla, Olalla's chamber, the meetings on the stair, the broken window, the ugly scene of the bite, were all given me in bulk and detail as I have tried to write them; to this I added only the external scenery (for in my dream I never was beyond the court), the portrait, the characters of Felipe and the priest, the moral, such as it is, and the last pages, such as, alas! they are. And

I may even say that is this case the moral itself was given me; for it arose immediately on a comparison of the mother and the daughter, and from the hideous trick of atavism[9] in the first. Sometimes a parabolic sense is still more undeniably present in a dream; sometimes I cannot but suppose my Brownies have been aping Bunyan,[10] and yet in no case with what would possibly be called a moral in a tract; never with the ethical narrowness; conveying hints instead of life's larger limitations and that sort of sense which we seem to perceive in the arabesque of time and space . . .

DIAGNOSING JEKYLL:

The Scientific Context to Dr Jekyll's Experiment
and Mr Hyde's Embodiment

By Robert Mighall

Diagnosing Jekyll: The Scientific Context to Dr Jekyll's Experiment and Mr Hyde's Embodiment

Dr Jekyll and Mr Hyde is presented as a 'case' in the legal sense, but it is also partly a fictional case-study in what was known at the time as 'morbid psychology'. A number of contemporary readers responded to this aspect of Stevenson's tale. A reviewer from *The Times* wondered whether it was 'a flash of intuitive psychological research', and explains that its denouement 'accounts for everything upon strictly scientific grounds, though the science of problematical futurity'. Stevenson's friend John Addington Symonds complained that his story made an artistic contribution to a process taking place in the 'physical and biological science[s]' of 'reducing individual freedom to zero, and weakening the sense of responsibility'.[1] And Oscar Wilde's Vivian observed that 'the transformation of Dr Jekyll reads dangerously like something out of the *Lancet*'.[2] However fantastic or melodramatic we might find the chemical transformation, Stevenson's representation of abnormal psychology was plausible enough to engage or unnerve his original readers. Indeed, Stevenson's wife Fanny recalled many years later how her husband had been 'deeply impressed by a paper he had read in a French scientific journal on sub-consciousness [which] had given him the germ of the idea'.[3] As these scientific themes play an important role in the *Strange Case*, it is worth exploring this body of knowledge, and establishing the scientific context for Jekyll's experiment and Mr Hyde's embodiment. For as was suggested in the Introduction, although Stevenson's story has had an enormous influence on both fictional and cinematic practitioners in horror, its most far-reaching legacy has perhaps been in the contribution made by its central 'idea', and this specifically in the area of popular psychology.

'Jekyll and Hyde', has an independent life beyond the pages or screens of the horror industry, and it is worth examining the historical conditions of the formation of an idea that struck an immediate chord with its contemporaries, and also enjoys this unnatural life a hundred years after its original conception. To do this we must return to the scientific, and principally the psychiatric, literature of the time. Whilst I have touched on this in the Introduction, a much fuller investigation of this context allows us to identify ideas that resonate through Stevenson's text. The following is a short essay on the psychiatric, criminological and sexological literature of the late-Victorian period, designed to enable the modern reader to understand Stevenson's 'psychological' speculations historically, by providing extended annotation to the relevant passages from the text. It is hoped that readers will find this useful for illuminating Stevenson's tale, and of historical interest in its own right.

(1) Double-consciousness

Man is not truly one, but truly two

At the core of Stevenson's *Strange Case* is a concern with the doubleness or even plurality of the self. Jekyll recognizes 'the thorough and primitive duality of man' through an awareness of the conflicts within his moral life: 'I saw that, of the two natures that contended in the field of my consciousness, even if I could rightly be said to be either, it was only because I was radically both.' It is his 'almost morbid sense of shame' at the promptings of what he considers his lower self, that encourages him to pursue his scientific studies. His researches might have included Theodule Ribot's *Diseases of Memory* from 1882. Jekyll referred to himself as being a 'compound', similarly Ribot asserts that 'conscious personality [is] a compound resultant of very complex states'.[4] And, like Jekyll, he imposes an hierarchical structure on this, referring to a 'highest state' which in time 'succumbs' and is replaced by another. Ribot is principally describing a normal process here, but comes closer to Henry Jekyll's case when he discusses the characteristics of 'periodic amnesia' or memory loss. Where he finds '*an evolution of two memories*. In extreme cases . . . the two memories are independent of one another; when one appears the other disappears . . . As a result of this discerption of memory, the individual appears – at least to others – to be living a double life.' Jekyll's researches explore a similar territory, situated on the very frontier of knowledge about the mind and its disorders.[5] His chemical experiment achieves what Ribot observes in extreme pathological cases: 'when one appears the other disappears' – the very premise of Jekyll's use of Hyde: 'Think of it – I did not even exist.' This *pathological* emphasis in the scientific literature is an important consideration when exploring the context for *Strange Case of Jekyll and Hyde*. For Stevenson employs the fantastic plot device of chemical transformation to effect what were described in the psychiatric literature as dysfunctional phenomena. This can be understood more fully by considering how nineteenth-century psychiatry brought scientific models to 'moral' problems, and how the category of 'moral insanity' enables us to diagnose Jekyll according to contemporary criteria.

(2) Moral Insanity

It was on the moral side, and in my own person, that I learned to recognize the thorough and primitive duality of man

If Dr Lanyon, who learns of 'the moral turpitude that man unveiled to me', chose to diagnose Jekyll, chances are he would have found him suffering from some form of 'moral insanity'. This notion became a central concern of mental pathologists, or 'alienists' as they were known, in the second half of the nineteenth century, and was used to pathologize eccentric or inappropriate behaviour. 'Moral' here does not *necessarily* point to an established code of ethics (although in practice that was often what informed diagnoses), but refers more broadly to 'behavioural' anomalies, and was devised to classify phenomena that were increasingly considered pathological in the modern industrialized society. The foundations of this category were established by James

Cowles Prichard in his highly influential *Treatise on Insanity and Other Disorders Affecting the Mind* from 1835. Prichard's 'Case No. 3' bears a striking resemblance to Jekyll's own:

A gentleman of good connexions, of good education, and of mental capabilities far above the general average, was brought up under the most advantageous circumstances that wealth can command, to the surgical branch of our profession . . . Educated as a gentleman, he possessed what is essential to the character – the highest moral and religious principles . . . and the strictest regard for the correct conduct which is due to those of his own rank in society. An unfortunate excess to which he was seduced when his duties in London were fulfilled, laid the foundation for a complete subversion of his character. He became reckless in his habits, negligent of his person, careless of the society he fell into, addicted to drinking, suspicious of his friends, wantonly extravagant, perverse in disposition, irritable, and overbearing.[6]

Observed by others, Jekyll, who comes from an identical background, also becomes 'careless of the society he fell into' and appears to be 'suspicious of his friends', refusing to trust Utterson with his secret and locking himself away. Both Utterson and Lanyon are concerned about Jekyll's eccentric behaviour, his apparent taste for low company, and begin to fear for his sanity. In a 'Case' compiled by lawyers and doctors it is not surprising that these ideas are entertained. Jekyll's own behaviour conforms to a pattern of temptation, compulsion to debauch, followed by a horror at what Hyde was capable of, and an attempt at complete reformation when 'Dr Jekyll is Quite at Ease', followed by further 'thirsts' and relapses as 'an ordinary secret sinner', with a final uncontrollable descent into Hyde. Case 3 follows a similar pattern; for as Prichard explains:

Excepting at these times [of drunken excess], this gentleman's habits are most abstemious . . . When, however, this thirst for ardent spirits comes on, a fondness for low society accompanies it. On these occasions he repairs to a *pot-house*, [and] takes his mixture amidst the lowest of mankind . . . This continues from twenty to thirty hours, when he awakes to the horrors of his situation, and to the mortification arising from his folly. (p. 58)

We see here a divided being; causing his friends dismay at the low company he keeps, and himself acutely aware, on recovery, of the duplicity of his conduct. If his interests had been like Jekyll's, more chemical than surgical, he might also have devised a potion to segregate the 'incongruous' denizens of his self.

Prichard's case helps us to identify an important aspect of the idea of Moral Insanity, that is also essential to our understanding of Jekyll's own case. For Jekyll's 'insanity', as suspected by his friends, is largely consequent upon his position in society. The first thing we learn about Case 3 is that he is a 'gentleman of good connexions . . . [and] most advantageous circumstances'. It is principally this that makes his compulsion to 'slum' pathological. Jekyll was also born 'to a large fortune, endowed besides with excellent parts, inclined by nature to industry, fond of the respect of the wise and good among my fellow-men, and thus, as might have been supposed, with every guarantee of an honourable and distinguished future'. That which makes him the subject of a Case is also his compulsion to act in ways opposed to his class identity. Hyde's embodiment could be seen as a way for Jekyll to avoid acting in a morally insane way: 'If each, I told myself, could be housed in separate identities, life would be relieved of all that was unbearable.' He 'houses' Hyde both figuratively and in practice: in a lower body, and in a lower district of the city. We meet with numerous Jekylls in the textbooks of Victorian psychiatry;[7] perhaps it is only the supernatural element makes his case 'strange'.

(3) Criminal Responsibility

It was Hyde, after all, and Hyde alone that was guilty

Once separated and segregated Jekyll explicitly diagnoses Hyde as himself morally insane. As he states of the Carew murder:

I declare at least, before God, no man morally sane could have been guilty of that crime upon so pitiful a provocation; and I struck in no more reasonable spirit than that in which a sick child may break a plaything.

Jekyll, the physician, wields his diagnostic prerogative. But his use of the first person in the very same sentence implicates him in this deed and in the diagnosis, collapsing the divisions he sought to effect. His 'Case' is ultimately a self-diagnosis, with him acting in his professional capacity as a physician and an expert in psychology. For the role of deciding whether a culprit was mad or bad, a criminal or a victim of mental illness, increasingly fell to medical experts towards the end of the nineteenth century. Jekyll claims that Hyde, in his later days, is motivated by a fear of the gallows, implying that his responsibility for the Carew murder would be evident; and yet his own diagnosis of Hyde as morally insane might very well have been accepted, and he would have been incarcerated in a special prison instead. Indeed, John Addington Symonds in the letter quoted earlier, asserts that 'The doors of Broadmoor would have closed on Mr Hyde' if he had been given up to justice (Maixner, 1981, p. 211). The idea of 'diminished responsibility' is familiar to us now, but it was a concept that had to be proven, and was fought for long and hard by mental pathologists throughout the century. Such concerns might throw light on Jekyll's motives for leaving his 'Full Statement of the Case'. For when he 'bring[s] the life of that unhappy Henry Jekyll to an end', he is referring to the *narrative*, the written account of his life, as much as his own life. He does not know what the outcome will be for Hyde. He may very well be leaving his confession to be read by his medical colleagues so that they can judge Hyde/Jekyll's responsibility, and perhaps allow him to escape the 'scaffold'.[8] After all, he drew up a will to enable him to enjoy a form of after life in the person of Hyde, why not a case-study in moral insanity addressed to his lawyer, testifying to diminished criminal responsibility?

Let us consider it as such, and view what we know of Jekyll's and Hyde's case in the light of medico-legal writings on criminality. I have touched on these issues in the Introduction to this edition where I showed how the depiction of the simian, dwarfish 'hardly human' Hyde could be regarded as a typical embodiment of the type of the atavistic criminal. It is worth expanding on these ideas and examining other factors that point to Hyde being a subject for psychiatric or criminological Darwinism. His relative youthfulness perhaps reflects his atavistic status; a cause or effect of his immorality. It was believed by a number of eminent authorities that the individual 'recapitulated' in his or her own development (from foetus to adult) an abbreviated record of the various states of evolutionary growth through which the human species had evolved; ontogeny recapitulating phylogeny as the biologists put it.[9] This meant that the human child was considered to be closer to less evolved life forms – 'primitives' and animals, but also criminals and lunatics. This logic was interchangeable; if the criminal or lunatic was a product of arrested mental development, so he or she was also 'arrested' at an early stage of individual (as much as species) growth. This was a tenet of Cesare Lombroso's criminal anthropology (the first school of scientific criminology), and is spelt out by his daughter in her introduction to her father's work published in 1911:

the germs of moral insanity and criminality are found normally in mankind in the first stages of his existence, in the same way as forms considered monstrous when exhibited by adults frequently exist in the foetus . . . The child, like certain adults, whose abnormality consists in a lack of moral sense, represents what is known to alienists as a morally insane being and to criminologists as a born criminal, and it certainly resembles these types in its impetuous violence.[10]

Jekyll's protestation that 'no man morally sane could have been guilty [of Carew's murder] . . . I struck in no more reasonable spirit than that in which a sick child may break a plaything', supports Lombroso's reasoning, pointing to his less-evolved status.

Even Hyde's repellent aspect finds a 'scientific' endorsement in contemporary criminology. The eminent psychiatrist Henry Maudsley provides one of the best articulations of this idea from a British observer. For him, there is 'a distinct criminal class of beings [which] constitutes a degenerate or morbid variety of mankind, marked by peculiar low physical and mental characteristics . . . They are scrofulous, not seldom deformed, with badly-shaped angular heads; are stupid, sullen, sluggish, deficient in vital energy, and sometimes afflicted with epilepsy.[11] Everyone, including Jekyll, remarks on Hyde's ugliness and deformity, and on their instinctive aversion to his person.

Both Lanyon's and Utterson's responses to this are instructive. The former is 'struck . . . with the shocking expression of his face'; and, finding 'something seizing, surprising and revolting' in the creature that faces him, attempts to turn him into a case-study in abnormality. Utterson the lawyer also betrays what might be called a 'professional' interest in Hyde. Hearing of Hyde's violent character,

there sprang up and grew apace in the lawyer's mind a singularly strong, almost inordinate, curiosity to behold the features of the real Mr Hyde. If he could but once set eyes on him, he thought the mystery would lighten and perhaps roll altogether away . . . And at least it would be a face worth seeing: the face of a man who was without bowels of mercy . . .

Utterson attempts to solve the mystery by seeing Hyde, but, failing that, he has a lurid, or perhaps scientific or professional curiosity to see the face of this violent thug. He was far from being alone in this. Lombroso included vast photographic galleries of convicted criminals in his works, supposedly demonstrating the distinctive anthropological features of various criminal types. And Francis Galton devised a system of 'composite photography' which he used to capture the visual 'essence' of criminality, and provide tangible proof of this hypothesis. He published the results of his experiments in *Inquiries into Human Faculty* (1883), and they make interesting reading for our purposes.

Galton, a cousin of Charles Darwin and a founder of the 'science' of eugenics (the promotion of healthy populations by applying scientific principles to selective reproduction), was very much a pioneer of sociological method. As part of his project to isolate various tendencies within the human genus, he attempted to identify various 'types' by their essential features. To do this he applied the rigours of statistics to photography, collecting images of various social types – races, classes, but also healthy specimens, consumptives and criminals – and attempted to determine the physiognomic average of each type. To achieve this he aligned a number of representative portraits and exposed a photographic plate with each image in turn for a fraction of the time needed for a full exposure. With eight photographs each image was given one eighth of the full exposure time, until a photographic 'average' was produced on the plate. Galton's first experiments were on criminals. As he explains:

The photographs from which they were made are taken from two large groups. One are those of men undergoing severe sentences for murder and other crimes connected with violence; the other of thieves. They were reprints from those taken by order of the prison authorities for purposes of identification . . . It is unhappily a fact that fairly distinct types of criminals breeding true to their kind have become established, and are one of the saddest disfigurements of modern civilisation.[12]

Galton's search for the type of criminality can be characterized as a pursuit of Mr Hyde. For Hyde represents the *essence* of evil, reflected in his repellent features. Galton attempts to capture this 'disfigurement' on camera, whilst experiencing an emotion very similar to those who behold Hyde when he contemplates the many photographs he used in his experiments. As he asserts, with the photos of criminals 'I did not adequately appreciate the degradation of their expressions for some time; at last the sense of it took firm hold of me, and I cannot now handle the portraits without overcoming by an effort the aversion they suggest' (pp. 12–13). This is natural, according to the logic of *Jekyll and Hyde*; for he like Jekyll has devised an experiment to isolate, extract and give an independent 'identity' to the very type of evil. Jekyll refers to the 'stamping efficacy' of evil, suggesting that it acts like a printing press in producing the visual imprint of Hyde's 'character'. Galton's own photographic process attempts something similar. Like Utterson he attempts to contemplate and display the image of a man (of men) 'without bowels of mercy', the essential type of violent humanity. However, again like Utterson, he experiences problems in adequate representation:

I have made numerous composites of various groups of convicts, which are interesting negatively rather than positively. They produce faces of a mean description, with no villainy written on them. The individual faces are villainous enough, but they are villainous in different ways, and when they are combined, the individual peculiarities disappear, and a common humanity of a low type is all that is left. (p. 10)

There is a note of disappointment here, an echo of Enfield protesting to Utterson that Hyde's trampling on the child 'sounds nothing to hear, but it was hellish to see'. Galton asserts that individually they were 'hellish to see', but has to admit that his own pursuit of the Hyde-like essence of evil cannot be reproduced satisfactorily. Galton's problems compare with those encountered by everyone who attempts to describe Mr Hyde. Enfield asserts that 'He is not easy to describe. There is something wrong with his appearance; something displeasing, something downright detestable. I never saw a man I so disliked, and yet I scarce know why . . . No, sir; I can make no hand of it; I can't describe him.' Galton very nearly admits as much. Despite the most advanced and ingenious technology, despite the most careful mathematical methods of research, and despite the most valiant attempts by observers, the Mr Hydes of fact and fiction, the visual expression of essential evil or criminality, must ultimately remain hidden.

(4) Sexual Perversion

My devil had been long caged, he came out roaring

In the same year that Stevenson's *Strange Case* was published, there appeared in German a book containing if anything even stranger cases. Richard Von Krafft-Ebing's, *Psychopathia Sexualis* (1886; first English edition 1892), was the first major textbook in sexology, a science that emerged from psychiatry towards the latter part of the nineteenth century. From lust-murderers and zoophiles to exhibitionists and hair-fetishists, this professor of psychiatry and neurology at the University of Vienna brought before his medical colleagues a bewildering array of sexual anomalies and aberrations. Like the psychiatric literature encountered above, sexology concentrated on that grey area between criminality and mental pathology, and was exclusively concerned with classifying perversions. The pathological approach to sexual crime or 'immoral behaviour' shifted the focus from the act in question, to a thorough investigation of the instigator. Causes were sought in the subject's ancestry, childhood or physical or mental constitution, laying the foundations for the psychopathological theories we recognize today. This was a new domain for science, and one that appeared to be ever widening as the number of strange cases proliferated with every new edition of Krafft-Ebing's book.

There are sufficient hints in the text, in its various forms, to encourage an exploration of the *Strange Case* of Jekyll and Hyde partly in terms of this context. Scattered comments appear to add up to this, despite Stevenson's protestations to the contrary.[13] Earlier drafts of the text certainly reveal a more explicit sexual content. In the earliest surviving draft Jekyll confesses that 'From a very early age, however, I became ~~in secret~~ the slave of disgraceful pleasures.' This phrase was later changed to 'From an early age, however, I became in secret the slave of certain appetites' in what is known as the 'Printer's Copy', which was again revised just prior to publication. We also find Jekyll referring in the earliest existing version to how 'as soon as night had fallen and I could shake off my friends, the iron hand of indurated habit plunged me once again into the mire of my vices. I will trouble you with these no further than to say that they were at once criminal in the sight of the law and abhorrent in themselves,' and that, when he had devised Hyde he 'began to plunge into a career of cruel, soulless and degrading vice'. These fragments add up to a conviction that Stevenson had earlier conceived of a significant erotic element in Jekyll's and Hyde's activities, and that these pointed towards 'perverted' forms as defined at the time. Their language is similar to that encountered in Krafft-Ebing's cases (many of which included confessions from his subjects which would begin like Jekyll's). Stevenson was clearly situating Jekyll's own case within this territory. The suggestion that from a very early age Jekyll had been addicted or a slave to disgraceful pleasures is almost an explicit confession to masturbation, which it would appear sowed the seeds of a later career in 'criminal' vice. With the pun on the iron 'hand' of habit, this confession would have meant only one thing to his original readers. The terms 'secret vice' and 'slave of disgraceful pleasures' to which the young were 'addicted' could have been taken straight out of any quack treatise on 'self-abuse' published between 1840 and 1900.[14] Stevenson wisely excised these overt references from his tale in the interests of narrative indeterminacy.[15] The later emphasis on 'certain appetites' is actually more damning, as this indicates perverse or perverted *propensities* over and above the more widespread 'vice' of self-abuse.

What Jekyll's own 'criminal' vices, or 'certain appetites' were it is idle to speculate, especially as the published version tones these references down quite considerably. Here we find Jekyll protesting that 'The pleasures which I made haste to seek in my disguise were, as I have said, undignified', no longer criminal and no longer disgraceful. Jekyll is but an *ordinary* secret sinner, not a case for a Viennese medico-jurist. But his view of Hyde does encourage us to take down the volume of sexology once more: 'But in the hands of Edward Hyde they soon began to turn towards the monstrous.' These take a specific form: Hyde drank 'pleasure with bestial avidity from any degree of torture to another', 'tast[ed] delight from every blow' that he inflicts on the unresisting body of Danvers Carew, and is later described as 'strung to the pitch of murder, lusting to inflict pain'. Hyde's behaviour comes close to describing 'sadism' as it would be classified that year by Krafft-Ebing in *Psychopathia Sexualis*. Taking the name from the Marquis de Sade (who described the erotic pleasures of inflicting pain in his novels and philosophical musings), Krafft-Ebing defined sadism as 'Association of Active Cruelty and Violence with Lust', and explained that:

Sadism is nothing else than an excessive and monstrous intensification of phenomena, – possible too, in normal conditions in rudimentary forms, – which accompany the psychical vita sexualis, particularly in males . . . the sadistic acts [sometimes] have the character of impulsive deeds . . . [and] vary in monstrousness with variation in the power of the perverse instinct over the individual afflicted, and with variation in the strength of the opposing ideas that might be present, which almost always are more or less weakened by original ethical defect, hereditary degeneracy, or moral insanity. (pp. 59–61)

The idea that sadism is a 'monstrous' expression of normal instincts recalls Jekyll's remarks about the way his own 'undignified' pleasures, which many a man would have blazoned in the public eye, turned 'monstrous' in Hyde's hands, presumably owing to Jekyll's own 'morbid' shame. Here we see the pathological intensification of the normal impulse which underlies the sexological classification of immorality. Hyde, like the sadist, also acts 'impulsively' in his brutality. There is the 'ape-like fury' with which he attacks Carew without (apparent) provocation, and we learn that 'Once a woman spoke to him, offering, I think, a box of lights. He smote her in the face, and she fled.' Hyde 'strung to the pitch of murder, lusting to inflict pain', is almost a text-book description of what was sometimes called 'lust-murder'. His acts turn towards the monstrous because Jekyll has renounced the 'opposing ideas' of moral restraint by allowing Hyde release: 'My devil had been long caged, he came out roaring.'

A devil perhaps very like Hyde came out roaring on to the streets of London two years after the publication of Stevenson's *Strange Case*, providing some observers with an opportunity to apply or consolidate his depiction of abnormal psychology. For, as was stated at the offset, perhaps the greatest influence of Stevenson's tale is the way Jekyll-and-Hyde is as much an idea as a fiction, becoming a part of popular legend almost immediately after the tale was published. Here we can witness its emergence. Between September and November 1888, when the incidents ceased and the culprit disappeared, a number of prostitutes were murdered in or around Whitechapel in the East End of London. Five of these have been attributed to one man: Jack the Ripper, as he is believed to have signed himself, a reference to the brutal method he employed in eviscerating his victims.[16] He was never caught, and theories about his identity multiplied during and subsequent to his career of atrocities. They continue to grow still. By briefly considering the formation and dissemination of one persistent and popular theory we can judge the true imaginative appeal of Stevenson's story, and its place within the medico-legal context that I have attempted to establish.

At first it was believed that the Whitechapel murderer was indigenous to the area, one of the poorest in London. Authorities were used to associating the urban slums with crime, and immediately assumed that the brutal murder of prostitutes was a further manifestation of the criminality and poverty of the district – the nemesis of neglect. However, an editorial from the *Pall Mall Gazette* (which had published

Stevenson's 'The Body Snatcher' four years earlier) for 8 September makes a number of intriguing suggestions:

The murder perpetrated this morning shows no indication of hurry or of alarm. He seems to have first killed the woman by cutting her throat so deeply as almost to sever her head from her shoulders, then to have disembowelled her, and then to have disposed of the viscera in a fashion recalling stories of Red Indian savagery . . .

This renewed reminder of the potentialities of revolting barbarity which lie latent in man will administer a salutary shock to the complacent optimism which assumes that the progress of civilization has rendered unnecessary the bolts and bars, social, moral, and legal, which keep the Mr Hyde of humanity from assuming visible shape among us. There certainly appears to be a tolerably realistic impersonification of Mr Hyde at large in Whitechapel. The savage of civilization which we are raising by the hundred in our slums is quite capable of bathing his hands in blood as any Sioux who ever scalped a foe.

It would appear that Jekyll's experiment in social segregation was successful. The culprit is imagined to be one of the atavistic criminal types encountered in the psychiatric literature – a savage in civilization: 'a reversion to an old savage type', as one expert put it, 'born in the 19th instead of a long-past century'.[17] One of 'hundreds', this Mr Hyde appears to be a necessary product of social circumstances. But, given that the writer chose to invoke Stevenson's authority, we must assume that if Hyde is there, Jekyll can't be far behind. The piece continues:

But we should not be surprised if the murderer in the present case should not be slum bred. The nature of the outrages and calling of the victims suggest that we have to look for a man who is animated by that mania for bloodthirsty cruelty which sometimes springs from the unbridled indulgence in the worst passions. We may have a plebeian Marquis DE SADE at large in Whitechapel. If so, and if he is not promptly apprehended, we shall not have long to wait for another addition to the ghastly catalogue of murder.

There appears to be a distinction between pure impulsive and appalling violence – the province of slum-bred degenerates – and sexual sadism, propensities that have identifiable (erotic) motivations, hence the fear that more murders would follow. The reorientation of the murderer's social class (plebeian is relative here, meaning merely a commoner) carries with it the suggestion that Hyde might really be, or be contained within, a Jekyll. This suggestion is further endorsed in the same paper two days later, when the 'Occasional Notes' section expressed the hope

that the police and their amateur assistants are not confining their attention to those who look like 'horrid ruffians'. Many of the occupants of the Chamber of Horrors look like local preachers, Members of Parliament, or monthly nurses. We incline on the whole to the belief which we expressed on Saturday that the murderer is a victim of erotic mania which often takes the awful shape of an uncontrollable taste for blood. Sadism, as it is termed from the maniac-marquis, . . . is happily so strange to the majority of our people that they find it difficult to credit the possibility of mere debauchery bearing such an awful fruitage. The Marquis de Sade, who died in a lunatic asylum at the age of seventy-four . . . was an amiable-looking gentleman, and, so, possibly enough, may be the Whitechapel murderer.[18]

The message is, stop looking for Mr Hyde – the visible incarnation of evil, expressed in physical ugliness – but look around you, even among the respectable. Never trust appearances – the central idea of Stevenson's tale had taken root, and pretty soon the Jekyll-and-Hyde theory for the Whitechapel murderer caught on. On Saturday 6 October, following two further murders, the *East London Advertiser* reasoned that

there is so much in this of a deeply thought-out plan that we have to consider whether the murderer is a maniac in the narrow sense of the word, and is not rather a man with a maniacal tendency, but with sufficient control over himself and of his faculties to impose upon his neighbours, and possibly to mix in respectable society unquestioned by a single soul. He is probably able to command solitude whenever he pleases, and that seems to be the only requisite for concealing his crimes.

The features of Mr Hyde are becoming less and less distinct as he retreats further and further into the ordinary-looking, respectable individual. The man with the maniacal tendency, which periodically erupts in an horrific way, and who then disappears to take his respect-able place among his neighbours – 'like the stain of breath upon a mirror', as Jekyll puts it – was replacing the easily recognizable slum-bred 'savage'. It is now Jekyll who serves as the most likely model. So, on 13 October the same paper observed how

Among the theories as to the Whitechapel murders, which start up one day and vanish the next, the one which is most in favour is the Jekyll and Hyde theory, namely, that the murderer is a man living a dual life, one respectable and even religious, and the other lawless and brutal; that he has two sets of chambers, and is probably a married man, and in every way a person whom you would not for a moment suspect.

And further:

Dr Gordon Browne's evidence at the inquest on the woman discovered in Mitre-Square establishes beyond a doubt the theory that the murderer is possessed of considerable anatomical skill . . . we now know for certain that *he is a skilled anatomist.* [my italics]

From atavistic thug to respectable individual, and then to a member of the medical profession: Jack's metamorphosis reverses Jekyll's, or replicates the spectacle witnessed by Lanyon. This 'Ripper as Mad Doctor' theory took hold, and proved, in Christopher Frayling's words, to be 'the most popular both in the press, and among commentators from the reading public at large'.[19] Whatever the truth, the notion that Jack the Ripper came from the West rather than the East End of London, and had some connection with the medical sciences has proved a lasting one.[20] Sightings of potential suspects started to conform to this type, a large bag like that carried by a doctor was generally an essential item. Indeed, a production of a play based upon Stevenson's tale had been playing in a London theatre since August, but was actually taken off possibly because it was fuelling speculation about the crimes. As the *Daily Telegraph* observed: 'Experience has taught this clever young actor that there is no taste in London just now for horrors on the stage. There is quite sufficient to make us shudder out of doors' (in Frayling, 1996, p. 213). The *Strange Case* had been eclipsed by its real-life counterpart. Stevenson's creation, partly reliant upon criminological and psychiatric theories, which moved, as one critic puts it, 'into the same terrain as the sexologists' of the time,[21] gave something back to medico-legal thought: the idea of a Jekyll-and-Hyde personality, the serial killer who lives a double life, was born.[22] It now lives an independent life from Stevenson's creation.

NOTES

Strange Case of Dr Jekyll and Mr Hyde

1. *Katherine de Mattos*: *née* Stevenson, a cousin and childhood friend.

STORY OF THE DOOR

1. *Cain's heresy*: Genesis 4:9 tells how Cain murdered his own brother Abel. When asked by God where Abel was he said 'Am I my brother's keeper?'

2. *It was a nut to crack for many, what these two could see in each other or what subject they could find in common*: This is just the first of many questions in a narrative full of speculations about appearances and relationships, and which is driven by the biggest 'nut to crack' – what Jekyll sees in Hyde.

3. *Juggernaut*: A Hindu god whose worshippers are said to display their devotion by throwing themselves in front of the car carrying the image of this god in a procession. Enfield compares this brutal encounter with these ancient rites.

4. *Sawbones:* A disrespectful slang term for a surgeon.

5. *harpies*: In classical mythology the harpies were winged monsters (with human female features) who usually avenged misdeeds.

6. *Coutts*: An old and distinguished banking house, established in 1672.

7. *apocryphal*: Unlikely, suspicious. The term is taken from the non-canonical books of the Bible called the Apocrypha.

8. *who do what they call good*: In retrospect, Enfield's qualification – doing 'what they call good', rather than Jekyll's actually doing good – might strike us as significant, subtly establishing a breach between public appearance and private reality.

9. *Queer Street*: To be in financial difficulties.

SEARCH FOR MR HYDE

1. MD, DCL, LLD, FRS, &c.,: Dr Jekyll's various professional qualifica-
tions, including doctor of medicine; doctor of civil laws; doctor of laws; fellow
of the Royal Society, establishing that he is an eminent and respected member
of his profession.

2. *Cavendish Square*: This is one of the few precise and identifiable London
locations in the story. First laid out in 1717, this square lies just north of Oxford
Circus and south-east of Marylebone High Street. It did indeed become a
'citadel of medicine' from the mid-nineteenth century, being the home of
more than one famous physician. Along with Wigmore, Wimpole and Harley
Streets, it is still associated with exclusive private medical practices and
cosmetic surgeons.

3. *Damon and Pythias*: Pythias (or Phintias) was condemned to death by Diony-
sius the Tyrant in the fourth century BC, but his friend Damon was allowed
to stand in his place while the former attended to important affairs, on the
understanding that he would die instead should Pythias not return. On his
return the Tyrant was so impressed by his devoted loyalty he allowed both
friends to live.

4. *labyrinths*: This was a conventional trope for representing the city, specifically
its older and poorer areas at the time. This dream image anticipates Utterson's
later visit to the 'dismal quarter of Soho' in search of Hyde, which he likens
to 'a district of some city in a nightmare'.

5. *If he could but once set eyes on him, he thought the mystery would lighten and perhaps
roll altogether away*: This desire to see Hyde has a specific significance, which
has been lost to us through Stevenson's revision of his story from initial
conception to its final form. In an earlier draft of the tale he was more explicit
about the form that Utterson's suspicions took. Initially he appears to entertain
two hypotheses: that Hyde is blackmailing Jekyll; and that Hyde is Jekyll's
illegitimate son. Both are covered by his fears that 'disgrace' explains his
actions. In what is called the 'Printer's Copy' of the text we find that, having
seen Hyde, Utterson decides: 'That could never be the face of his son, never
in this world' (Hirsch and Veeder, 1986, p. 23). Utterson, therefore, wanted
to see Hyde's face in order to determine if there is any family resemblance
between this 'young man', and his client who names him as his heir.

6. *Gaunt Street*: No such street existed in London at the time. The name is a
reflection on Utterson's self-mortifying character, the *OED* listing 'grim or
desolate' as well as 'abnormally lean, as from hunger' among the meanings
for this word. This 'allegorical' approach to London geography is typical of

Stevenson's technique in a novel with very few identifiable localities. In what is called the 'Printer's Copy' of the text he specifies that Utterson 'set forth eastward' from his own house to Jekyll's (Hirsch and Veeder, 1986, p. 20). But, without knowing where Jekyll's house is located this is of little help. Jekyll's area is described with much more care, but is also difficult to place exactly. Plainly it isn't in Soho, where Hyde has his other home for his debauched purposes, so this rules out Soho Square and Golden Square, both of which had fallen on hard times by the 1880s and been given over to trades and miscellaneous professions like those described. The houses are described as 'ancient', but this was used for anything up to the early eighteenth century by the (later) Victorians, who often seem to have regarded 'modernity' as beginning around 1750. Again, we can suspect that attempting to identify precise geography is pointless here as Jekyll's house provides another example of Stevenson's allegorical approach (see the Introduction for a discussion of this passage).

7. *he gave an impression of deformity without any nameable malformation*: Recourse to the unspeakable is a staple property of Gothic and fantastic fiction. Many of its practitioners, from Mrs Radcliffe to Arthur Machen, made conspicuous use of this suggestion. Stevenson is employing this rhetorical strategy to increase the mysterious, fearful and 'inhuman' attributes of Hyde.

8. *troglodytic*: Like a cave man. But a Troglodyte is also an anthropoid ape, such as a gorilla or chimpanzee (*OED*).

9. *Dr Fell*: An irrational hatred, and referring to a rendering of an epigram by Martial which contained the following reference to a seventeenth-century Dean of Christ Church, Oxford: 'I do not love thee, Dr Fell/The reason why I cannot tell/But this alone I know full well/I do not love thee Dr Fell'.

10. *pede claudo*: On halting foot, limping behind.

THE CAREW MURDER CASE

1. *not far from the river*: Where exactly? Again, Stevenson's geography is frustratingly imprecise. This is where the maid lives rather than works, so it is more likely to be a lower-class district. The MP Carew appears to be lost, a detail which supports this, with the reference to it being a 'lane' suggesting a narrow thoroughfare found in one of the older parts of the capital, Shadwell, Limehouse or Wapping or possibly the Borough or Bermondsey. But what would an elderly MP be doing late at night in any of these neighbourhoods (more appropriate to Hyde)? In this tale of double-lives and dubious appearances anything is possible.

2. *It seems she was romantically given*: The maid is fond of indulging in fancies deriving from Romantic literature, as indicated by her taste for moonlight and dreaming. As Richard Dury suggests, this casts doubt on the veracity of her testimony, introducing an element of 'fancy' which troubles the straight reportage of the incident. As he suggests, the passage might be read as 'an interpretation of events in terms of the "sensation novel" by the maid, who we have seen is linguistically influenced by the conventions of popular literature', Dury (1993), p. 117.

3. *ape-like fury*: A strong indication that Hyde should be read in terms of contemporary theories about evolutionary development, and its opposite, reversion. See the section of the Introduction entitled 'Apes and Angels', and 'Diagnosing Jekyll', section 3, for a discussion of this literature and its influence on the depiction of Hyde.

4. *Soho*: An area of about a mile square, situated to the south of Oxford Street, north of Piccadilly Circus and west of the Charring Cross Road. Its name derives from a hunting call, indicating that this was once a popular area for the chase when it was open fields. By the late seventeenth century it had become the refuge of French immigrants fleeing religious persecution. The 'low French eating house' testifies to this association, as do the 'foreign' mothers. Despite the stately mansions on Soho and Leicester Squares, this area had for a long time been associated with seediness and even criminality, bordering as it does on the notorious rookeries of St Giles and Seven Dials (where 'penny numbers' or penny dreadfuls were often sold). This area is still the centre of the capital's sex entertainment industry.

5. *had never been photographed*: The use of photography to assist criminal identification was becoming widespread at the time. See 'Diagnosing Jekyll'.

INCIDENT OF THE LETTER

1. *laboratory or the dissecting rooms*: The fact that the back door to Jekyll's house, which is associated with disreputable practices at odds with the 'respectable' frontage of the mansion, leads directly to an old dissecting room is significant. As those who read Stevenson's tale 'The Body Snatcher' will discover, this back door is where the former resident of the house, also a respectable physician, would have had contact with the clandestine trade in resurrected corpses, purchasing cadavers from professional body snatchers. This detail provides an intriguing link between the two tales published within two years of each other. Stevenson's characterization of the back door to Jekyll's house may well have been coloured by these circumstances and may partly reflect his imaginative engagement with that earlier tale of daylight respectability and dubious nocturnal transactions. See notes to 'The Body Snatcher' below.

2. *it put a better colour on the intimacy than he had looked for; and he blamed himself for some of his past suspicions*: For speculation on the form of 'intimacy' Utterson might have suspected, see the discussion in the 'Testimony' section of the Introduction.

REMARKABLE INCIDENT OF DOCTOR LANYON

1. *I have brought on myself a punishment and a danger that I cannot name*: This phrase recalls, and would certainly bring to mind in Utterson, friend of 'down-going men', language associated with two conditions which preoccupied medics and moralists at the time: syphilis, and the supposed pathological effects of masturbation, both of which were believed to be retribution for carnal indulgence. It is significant that this confession follows directly on from the revelation that the physician Lanyon knew some appalling secret about Jekyll. Might Jekyll have visited him professionally and revealed all about his 'unmanning' condition? Syphilis was a disease for which there was no effective cure at the time, and which was shrouded in mystery and silence. The first signs of it might not appear for years after infection, or might be kept in abeyance for a period and then return in later life. Utterson's comments later that Jekyll is 'plainly seized with one of those maladies that both torture and deform the sufferer; hence, for aught I know, the alteration of his voice; hence the mask and his avoidance of his friends; hence his eagerness to find this drug', reinforce this suggestion and might appear to provide the final conformation for this hypothesis for Utterson (seventh chapter). Both syphilis and the supposed consequences of 'self-abuse' would answer to this description, as the former disease could produce horrible disfigurements in the sufferer; whilst even more extravagant claims were made about the latter. This is how my favourite description of such a case ends: the sufferer 'experienced in the back of the neck such violent pains that he commonly raised, not cries merely, but howls . . . I learned of his condition; I visited him; I found less a living being than a corpse groaning upon the straw; emaciated, pale, filthy, exhaling an infectious odour . . . [he was now] a being far below the brute; a spectacle of which it is impossible to conceive the horror; one would with difficulty recognize that he had formerly belonged to the human species' (the case of 'L. D.', originating in Samuel Tissot's *Onanism* (1760), but used by at least three other writers in the nineteenth century). The principal 'cures' for both syphilis and masturbatory disorders (one real, the other imaginary, or possibly confused with the former), took the form of drugs: mercury and potassium iodide for syphilis, and patent medicines sold by the very quack doctors who terrified their patients, for the latter. Jekyll's eagerness to find the drug and reluctance to show himself in public would fit this pattern.

THE LAST NIGHT

1. *one of those maladies that both torture and deform the sufferer*: See note 1, p. 166.
2. *strong smell of kernals*: Arsenic has the smell of bitter almonds.

DOCTOR LANYON'S NARRATIVE

1. *10th December 18—*: There is a discrepancy between the date on the letter and the date on which Lanyon specified these events took place, 'On the ninth of January'. This is probably a mistake, one of the few resulting from the 'white-hot' pace in which Stevenson wrote the tale.
2. *bull's eye*: A type of lantern with a large thick glass lens, the centre of which resembles the centre of an archery target.
3. *our profession*: As it is Hyde talking here and not Jekyll, this is clearly a slip up.

HENRY JEKYLL'S FULL STATEMENT OF THE CASE

1. *war among my members*: An echo of James 4:1. 'Whence come wars and fightings among you? Come they not hence, even of your lusts that war in your members?'
2. *faggots*: Bundles of wood bound together.
3. *captives of Philippi*: Acts 16:26.
4. *Babylonian finger on the wall*: Daniel, 5:5–31. Whilst Belshazzar was feasting a hand appeared and pointed to words foretelling his doom written on the wall. The phrase 'the writing is on the wall' means that someone's downfall is now certain.
5. *Regent's Park*: First woodland, and later farmland, it became a park encircled by stately mansions designed by John Nash during the Regency period – hence its name. It lies to the north of Marylebone Road, and to the west of

Euston, not far from Lanyon's house. London's Zoological Gardens have been situated in the park since 1828.

6. *an hotel in Portland Street*: At the time a street on the south side of Oxford Street, bordering on Soho. This could easily be reached by cab from Regent's Park, and was but a few blocks away from Lanyon's house in Cavendish Square. However, why should Hyde risk coming so close to Soho, his old stomping ground? Great Portland Street, even closer to Regent's Park and Cavendish Square was once called Portland Street (although not by 1885), and there is Portland Place just north-east of Cavendish Square, a much safer and far likelier choice than a hotel in Soho for the fugitive Hyde. Stevenson, writing in bed in Bournemouth, may very well have confused these streets.

The Body Snatcher

1. *camlet cloak*: A waterproof garment made of either silk and camel's hair, or a cotton and wool mix.

2. *as if a man had risen from the dead*: This line is either an imaginative prefiguration of the action that follows or a joke in poor taste.

3. *rum and sin*: Excessive use of alcohol will indeed, after prolonged use, be indicated by the broken capillaries on and around the nose of the heavy drinker. The idea that 'sin' would also leave its traces on the face is a belief that was taken seriously when this story was first published. As Jekyll reasons when he first beholds the features of Hyde: 'Evil . . . had left on that body an imprint of deformity and decay.' This belief forms the basis of the plot of Oscar Wilde's tale of sin and hypocrisy, *The Picture of Dorian Gray* (1890/1), where by supernatural means the effects of Dorian's unspecified and clandestine debauchery leave their traces on his portrait rather than on his own face.

4. *Voltaire might have canted*: Recanted, would have renounced his atheistic believes if he had had the same experience as Fettes. Voltaire (Francois-Marie Arouet (1694–1778)) was a satirist and leading figure in the Enlightenment, infamous for his freethinking beliefs.

5. *fly*: A one-horse carriage.

6. *the letter K*— . . . *the mob that applauded at the execution of Burke called loudly for the blood of his employer*: 'K' can be positively identified as Robert Knox, the famous, and then infamous anatomy lecturer, whose reputation was ruined by his involvement with the murderers Burke and Hare. Stevenson's tale is openly based upon these well-publicised events, and a knowledge of them provides a useful historical background to his tale of terror. Body Snatchers, or 'Resurrection Men', made a living disinterring recently buried corpses from burial grounds and then selling them to anatomy schools, where they were dissected to instruct medical students in the rudiments of human anatomy. Before an Act of 1832 (brought about largely in response to the Burke and Hare murders, and which made provision for surgeons by entitling them to the bodies of those who died in workhouses), there was an enormous discrepancy between the number of corpses *legally* available for dissection, and the number of students who depended on their supply to complete their education as physicians or surgeons. Only the bodies of convicted murderers hanged on the gallows could be used for these purposes. The few legal corpses were allocated to the official anatomy schools, such as the Royal College of Surgeons in London, and the Medical School of the University in Edinburgh, where Stevenson's tale is set. Private schools, like that run by Knox, had to resort to other means for procuring all its 'subjects'. Often medical students, like those in Stevenson's tale, would supply their tutors, by visiting graveyards at night and disinterring corpses. But increasingly this was performed by professionals, who could earn as much as £10 in winter, and £8 in summer per corpse. Knox favoured Burke's and Hare's product because their corpses were so fresh. The reason for this was revealed in November 1828, when it was discovered that these corpses had never actually been buried, but that William Burke and William Hare had murdered up to fifteen unfortunates from the slums of Edinburgh and sold them to Knox as resurrected corpses. Although Burke and Hare had been equally guilty, Hare turned King's evidence and escaped sentence; only Burke was hanged in January 1829, his body, appropriately enough, being given to the Medical School for dissection, where his skeleton still hangs in the Anatomy Museum. The crowd did indeed clamour for Knox to account for his part in this scandal. Although he was cleared of any conscious collusion in the murders, Knox's reputation never recovered. He can however, be considered something of a scapegoat for practices that just about every anatomist working in England, Scotland and Ireland was implicated in. On Knox, see Isobel Rae, *Knox the Anatomist* (1964), on dissection see Ruth Richardson, *Death, Dissection and the Destitute* (1987), the definitive work on the subject.

7. *subjects*: Anatomical subjects, human bodies for dissection.

8. *wynd*: A Scottish dialect term for a narrow street or passage turning off a main thoroughfare (*OED*).

9. *He coveted besides a measure of consideration from his masters and his fellow-pupils . . . For his day of work he indemnified himself by nights of roaring blackguardly enjoyment*: Fettes resembles Jekyll in these details, and may have been something of a trial run for this more famous physician who was created the following year.

10. *quid pro quo*: Something in return for or consideration of something else.

11. *ghouls*: Spirits who feed on human corpses; metaphorically this is true, as these (supposed) body snatchers made a good living from selling resurrected cadavers to the anatomists.

12. *'God Almighty!' he cried, 'that is Jane Galbraith!'*: Stevenson draws upon historical circumstance here. The original for Jane Galbraith was Mary Patterson, a local prostitute, who was well-known on account of her fine looks, whom the students who received the corpse recognized. Burke explained that he had bought her corpse from an old lady after Mary had died of drink.

13. *Great Bashaw*: A corruption of Pasha, denoting a type of Eastern despot.

14. *cras tibi*: tomorrow you.

15. *precentor*: One who leads or directs the singing in a church (*OED*).

16. *a far different awakening*: A reference to the Christian belief that the dead will rise again from their graves to glory on the final Judgment Day.

Olalla

1. *get you out of this cold and poisonous city, and to give you two months of pure air . . .*: Robert Louis Stevenson, who suffered from the tuberculosis that ended his short life, spent most of his days in pursuit of this ideal. Born in wet and windy Scotland, he travelled to Southern France, California, Davos in Switzerland (Thomas Mann's 'Magic Mountain', a popular resort for consumptives) and finally the South Seas seeking relief from his condition.

2. *contrary professions*: A typical nineteenth-century observation. The rift between scientific and religious beliefs and principles widened increasingly in this century, particularly after the publication of Charles Darwin's *Origin of Species* (1859) which dealt a blow to scriptural teachings. This gulf would be deemed to be even wider when, as here, the priest is a Catholic.

3. *the good cause*: The 'Carlist Wars'. Spain was effectively under a state of civil war for the most of the middle decades of the nineteenth century.

4. *tatterdemalion pride*: Misplaced pride, because they are penniless, hence in tattered clothes. Pride is the dominant characteristic of aristocratic characters in Gothic tales, and it is generally depicted as their fatal flaw.

5. *degenerate both in parts and fortune*: The idea of degeneracy was a dominant motif in much late nineteenth-century thought and literature. It was often associated with the aristocracy and seen as the inevitable result of inbreeding within an exclusive circle (see note 10 below). Gothic fiction, from Walpole's *The Castle of Otranto* (1764) onwards, often depicted the last representatives of a degenerate line, a famous example being Edgar Alan Poe's 'The Fall of the House of Usher' (1839), a tale that might well have some influence on

Stevenson here. 'Usher' also starts with a journey to a distant and secluded mansion, where the narrator finds the last descendants of the once proud Usher family languishing in the last stages of a strange illness.

6. *innocent*: An idiot, one of the supposed manifestations of degeneracy through inbreeding.

7. *of a dusky hue, and inclined to hairyness*: It would appear that Stevenson had something against these characteristics. Mr Hyde is also described as being 'of a dusky pallor' and 'hairy', also signs of his 'degenerate' or atavistic status.

8. *Kelpie*: In Scottish fairy mythology the Kelpie lived in streams and, like the Dryads and mermaids, often drowned passers-by.

9. *the sleeping palace of the legend*: The story of the Sleeping Beauty, by Charles Perrault (1697), tells how a beautiful young princess is put under a spell that makes her sleep for a hundred years. She is eventually woken by the kiss of a valiant prince who hacks his way through the forest of thorns that surrounds her castle (a reference which provides a subtle prefiguration of some of the events of Stevenson's narrative). This tale was popular in the nineteenth century. Tennyson's poem 'The Day Dream' (1842) is based upon this legend, while the Pre-Raphaelite painter Edward Burne-Jones painted a series of vast canvases depicting this theme entitled 'The Briar Rose' (1870–90).

10. *The family blood had been impoverished, perhaps by long inbreeding, which I knew to be a common error among the proud and the exclusive*: J. F. Nisbet's *Marriage and Heredity* from 1889 stated: 'Privilege means exclusiveness, and exclusiveness means deterioration . . . As the result partly of luxurious living, partly of the in-and-in process of breeding, social castes develop, in course of time a neuropathic condition, which classes them among the unfit, and they die out like a family which has contracted too strong a taint of vice and insanity' (1889), pp. 137, 138.

11. *contrabandista*: A smuggler.

12. *hebetude*: Dullness or stupidity.

13. *everywhere the walls were set with the portraits of the dead . . . and the bonds that knit me with my own family*: The contemplation of ancestral portraits became a stock device in many Gothic tales, especially those which feature forms of hereditary curses and atavistic returns. Portraits feature in Horace Walpole's *The Castle of Otranto* (1764, recognized as the first Gothic novel), Nathaniel Hawthorne's *The House of the Seven Gables* (1851), and later in Oscar Wilde's *The Picture of Dorian Gray* (1890–91), and Arthur Conan Doyle's *The Hound of the Baskervilles* (1901–2). This particular passage most directly resembles the opening scene of the infamous 'Decadent' novel, *À Rebours* (Against Nature) by J. K. Huysmans, published in 1884, the year before Stevenson's tale appeared. 'Judging from the few portraits preserved in the Chateau de Lourps, the Floressas des Esseintes family has been composed in olden times of sturdy campaigners with forbidding faces ... [But] since then, the degeneration of this ancient house had clearly followed a regular course ... and over the last two hundred years, as if to complete the ruinous process, the Des Esseintes had taken to intermarrying among themselves, thus using up what little vigour they had left' (Huysmans, 1959, p. 17). Stevenson admired French literature which he read in the original, so he may very well have encountered Huysmans's novel. On the use and significance of ancestral portraits in Gothic fiction see Mighall, *A Geography of Victorian Fiction* (1999), chapter 3.

14. *She was the child of an afflicted house*: A character's burden of ancestry conflicting with his or her own romantic desires featured in a number of novels around the middle of the nineteenth century. It is the central plot of Jane Margaret Hopper's novel, *The House of Raby* (1854); Geraldine Jewsbury's *Constance Herbert* (1855), and Wilkie Collins's tale 'Mad Monkton' (1855). This novelistic interest coincided with the growing reliance on hereditary causes for mental and physical disorders in the medical sciences. By the time Stevenson wrote this tale heredity was the dominant aetiology in most works of mental pathology.

15. *El Dorado*: In Spanish this means 'the gilded', and refers to the legend that the king of Manoa was adorned with golden powder. It came to refer to the city of his kingdom, which stood as an idealized realm, a place to discover.

16. *Samson*: A covert reference to the danger which the narrator is in through his romantic enslavement by an unsuitable loved one. Judges 13–16 tells how Samson the extremely strong hero of the Israelites falls in love with Delilah, who betrays his secret of his great strength to the Philistine enemies. They cut his hair, thus rendering him powerless, and take him into captivity. The suggestion is that the narrator, who is there to recover his strength, and 'renew [his] blood', should learn from Samson's example and renounce his love for Olalla, the innocent inheritor of the diseased tendency that similarly 'enslaved' her own father.

17. *Her great eyes opened wide, the pupils shrank into points* ... : This description of the moment when the hostess reveals her 'vampiric' tendencies might have influenced a scene in Bram Stoker's *Dracula*, published twelve years later in 1897. The narrator is Jonathan Harker, who has also journeyed out to a remote castle in the mountains to see another last representative of a once noble race, and is also unlucky enough to cut himself in the presence of someone with a taste for blood: 'When the Count saw my face, [with blood on it from a shaving accident] his eyes blazed with a sort of demonic fury, and he suddenly made a grab for my throat.' Stoker may have read Stevenson's tale, for his description of a female vampire revealing her nature also echoes this passage from 'Olalla': 'As she looked [Lucy's] eyes blazed with unholy light', Bram Stoker, *Dracula*, edited by Maurice Hindle (1993), pp. 38, 271.

18. *the soul is in the race . . . the race shall cease from off the earth*: This passage outlining the principle of pathological atavism rings slightly false (as Stevenson admits, see 'A Chapter on Dreams'). For Olalla, the devout Catholic, delivers a highly informed lecture on hereditary determinism (or even eugenic principle) that would not disgrace the pages of materialists and agnostics such as Francis Galton or Henry Maudsley. Olalla appears to be a card-carrying materialist (on the side of the apes rather than the angels in this debate), despite her appeal to Christian doctrine.

19. *kirkton*: A Scottish dialect term for a small hamlet.

20. *you were not a Christian*: He means that the soldier was not a Roman Catholic, and therefore a heretic, despite his probable adherence to the Protestant faith.

21. *the more superstitious crossed themselves on my approach*: Another line that might have influenced Stoker in *Dracula*, where Harker encounters similar behaviour when he asks directions to the vampire's castle: 'both he and his wife crossed themselves . . . [and] simply refused to speak further' (1993), p. 11.

A Chapter on Dreams

Stevenson published this essay in *Scribner's Magazine* in January 1888. It is reproduced in abridged form here for the insights it provides into Stevenson's inspiration for writing *Jekyll and Hyde* and of his views of the role of imagination in the creative process. The essay, appearing in the magazine published by the house that published his *Strange Case* in the USA, is written in a characteristically playful and ironic way.

1. *lead a double life – one of the day, one of the night*: Of course the 'dreamer' in all these cases is Stevenson himself. This dream, whether true or not, touches on the theme of *Jekyll and Hyde*, and anticipates his later discussion of how his own 'divided' consciousness – his waking and sleeping sides – created that tale. The imagery of the endless stairs also recalls Utterson's half-dream of an endless succession of streets peopled with an endless succession of brutal Hydes. The ghastly scenes of the Edinburgh anatomy theatre also provide a link to 'The Body Snatcher'.

2. *making stories for the market*: This emphasis on the wholly commercial considerations of the artist's unconscious creative principle deals a slap in the face for
Romantic conceptions of creativity, which tended to stress the 'transcendent'
and even mystical origins of images drawn from the dreaming or drug-induced
state. To ally unconscious creativity with the demands of the cash nexus
deflates a sacred principle of Romantic aesthetic theory.

3. *Claudius in the play*: In Act III of Shakespeare's *Hamlet*, Claudius, his conscience caught by the events depicted in the 'Mousetrap' (which are contrived
to resemble his own treachery), breaks up the play by calling for 'Lights', and
hastily quits the scene.

4. *Brownies*: A friendly elfin spirit, who assists a family with its household tasks.
Stevenson internalizes these spirits and suggests that in his household they
assist his work as a writer.

5. *Descartes*: René Descartes (1596–1650), a French philosopher and mathema-
tician, who is regarded as the founder of modern philosophy for his development of rational methods and procedures for logical inquiry. His 'cogito' – I
think therefore I am – formed the basis of most philosophical and scientific
approaches to the problems of consciousness and the dualism of mind and
body for almost three centuries.

6. *Molière's servant*: Molière was the pseudonym of the French playwright
Jean-Baptiste Poquelin (1622–73). As servants feature in most of his plays it is
difficult to identify which one Stevenson intends.

7. *I dreamed the scene . . . pursuers*: There is a tradition of horror fiction deriving
from dreams. Horace Walpole claimed a central event in *The Castle of Otranto*
(1764), the first Gothic novel, originated in a dream, while Mary Shelley's
Frankenstein (1818) was also dream-inspired. With its central theme of the
creation of a monstrous individual that haunts its overreaching creator
Shelley's novel is clearly a forerunner of *Jekyll and Hyde*.

8. *garden of Adonis*: Adonis was a beautiful youth who spent his days hunting.
The phrase 'garden of Adonis' refers to one full of withered flowers, and
therefore makes a disparaging comment on the quality of his ideas before the
Brownies lent a hand.

9. *hideous trick of atavism*: Atavism comes from '*atavus*', meaning great-
grandfather, and derives from natural history, describing the tendency of
certain physical traits to skip a generation. The original use was morally
neutral, but increasingly, as the notion of progressive (social, cultural and
biological) evolution took hold of the scientific imagination, the term became
associated with pathological and anti-social phenomena. This latter use of the
idea of atavism features in *Jekyll and Hyde*, in the suggestion that Hyde is an
atavistic, 'hardly human', fragment of Jekyll's more evolved self.

10. *aping Bunyan*: John Bunyan's most famous work *The Pilgrim's Progress* (1678–84), was presented as a dream. Stevenson suggests that sometimes his dreams have a 'didactic' purpose, or at least appear to have, 'aping' that of Bunyan's earnest endeavours. 'Olalla' does appear to have a didactic element in its stress on the need for the renunciation of romantic desire when there is a hereditary taint – a pathological parable therefore.

Diagnosing Jekyll

1. From Maixner (1981), pp. 205, 211.

2. Wilde, 'The Decay of Lying', 1889, in Linda Dowling (ed.), *The Soul of Man Under Socialism and Other Critical Writings* (2001), p. 167.

3. Quoted in Frayling (1996), p. 140.

4. From *Diseases of Memory: An Essay in Positive Psychology* (1882), pp. 107–10.

5. According to Roger Swearingen, 'Stevenson told an interviewer in 1893 that he had never heard of any actual case of "double personality" when he wrote the book: "after the book was published I heard of the case of 'Louis V', the man in the hospital at Rochefort. Mr Myers sent it to me." ' Swearingen (1980), p. 101. This was a famous case which was first noticed in Britain in the very same month Stevenson's *Strange Case* was published, appearing in the 'Psychological Retrospect' section of the *Journal of Mental Science* for January 1886. Myers, who had been deeply impressed by Stevenson's tale, wrote an article on 'Multiplex Personality' giving details of Louis V's case, which he published in the *Nineteenth Century* for November 1886, and it was probably this that he sent to Stevenson. The case involves a young man whose personality changes and then reverts to its original a number of times following a severe shock. As with Jekyll there is a clear moral dichotomy between his states, which leads to what Myers refers to as his 'preaching, with *monkey-like impudence* rather than with reasoned clearness, radicalism in politics and atheism in religion', a phrase that might have been borrowed from Jekyll's reference to the 'ape-like tricks that [Hyde] would play me, scrawling in my own hand blasphemies on the pages of my books'. Myers also refers to Louis's case showing 'the *retrogressive* change of personality, the dissolution into incoordinate elements of the polity of our being', which recalls Jekyll's reference to man being 'a mere *polity* of multifarious, incongruous and independent denizens'. If Stevenson had not directly taken *from* this case, we can suspect that he might have given something to the writing up of it by Myers (1886), pp. 649, 654.

6. Prichard (1835), p. 57.

7. I shall confine myself to citing one of my favourites, which provides an hilarious variation on Jekyll/Hyde's blasphemous annotation of Jekyll's pious work. W. C. McIntosh's *On Morbid Impulse* from 1863 includes the case of 'a young gentleman who had an ungovernable propensity to run up into the organ loft during divine service, and play some well-known jocular tune, attached perhaps to profane and indecent words. It was impossible to prevent him, so suddenly was the act, and he voluntarily absented himself from Chapel' (1863), p. 8.

8. In Arthur Conan Doyle's most famous Sherlock Holmes case, *The Hound of the Baskervilles* (1901–2), we encounter Seldon, the Notting Hill murderer, whose 'death sentence' was commuted to imprisonment in Dartmoor 'due to some doubts as to his complete sanity, so atrocious was his conduct'. Seldon is described in similar terms to the 'troglodytic' Hyde, making it quite clear that he is also atavistic. This is Dr Watson's description: 'Over the rocks, in the crevice of which the candle burned, there was thrust out an evil yellow face, a terrible animal face, all seamed and scored with vile passions. Foul with mire, with a bristling beard, and hung with matted hair, it might well have belonged to one of those old savages who dwelt in the borrows on the hillsides', Doyle, edited by Christopher Frayling (2001) p. 96. Had Jekyll (or was it Hyde?) not killed himself, he might have ended up in the same institution.

9. This phrase describes something called the 'Biogenetic law', which was highly influential for a number of specialists in mental pathology, including Maudsley, Lombroso, Krafft-Ebing, Havelock Ellis and Sigmund Freud. It was formulated by the German biologist Ernst Haeckel, and is explained here: 'the series of forms through which the Individual Organism passes during its progress from the egg cell to its fully developed state, is a brief, compressed reproduction of the long series of forms through which the animal ancestors of that organism (or the ancestral form of the species) have passed from the earliest periods of so-called organic creation down to the present time', quoted by Laura Otis (1994), p. 7.

10. Gina Lombroso-Ferrero, *Criminal Man According to the Classifications of Cesare Lombroso* (1911), pp. 130–31.

11. Maudsley, *Responsibility in Mental Disease* (1874), pp. 29–30.

12. Galton, *Inquiries into Human Faculty*, 2nd edn (1906), p. 10.

13. Stevenson wrote to a friend complaining of a 'braying ass' of a reviewer (of a theatrical production of *Jekyll and Hyde* that had made the sexual elements of Hyde's acts more explicit): 'The harm was in Jekyll, because he was a hypocrite – not because he was fond of women; he says so himself; but people are so filled full of folly and inverted lust, that they can think of nothing but sexuality. The hypocrite let out the beast Hyde – who is no more sensual than another, but who is the essence of cruelty and malice, and selfishness and cowardice: these are the diabolic in man – not this poor wish to have a woman, that they make such a cry about.' (Maixner, p.231.) But, as Stephen Heath observes: 'The protest has a kind of self-defeating truth: if people *are* so filled full of folly and inverted lust, this must be central for what Hyde represents, all those "lower elements".' Stephen Heath (1986), p. 94.

14. On this literature, and its relation to Gothic literature and representation, see Mighall (1999), chapter 5, also Mighall, 'A Pestilence which Walketh in Darkness: Diagnosing the Victorian Vampire', in Byron and Punter (eds.), (1999), pp. 108–24.

15. There is an intriguing postscript to the suggestion that Stevenson may have been hinting at the effects of 'self-abuse' in his story. Two years after it was published a paper appeared in the *Journal of Mental Science* by an American psychiatrist and sexologist, Edward Charles Spitzka, entitled 'Cases of Masturbation (Masturbatic Insanity)'. This included the case of 'F.S.' who: 'was certainly one of the most singular-looking persons I have ever seen. The expression of his countenance was indescribable; in ordinary language it would be spoken of as at once repulsive, comical, and weird . . . Occasionally an expression of Satanic cunning would pass over his countenance; in the next moment it would look almost childishly open and appealing. His gait was sliding and swift, he appeared to pass along without steps . . . I could not resist the impression that the author of that ingeniously absurd romance, "Dr Jekyll and Mr Hyde", had some such person as my patient in mind when he described the repulsive influence exerted by the latter on persons passing him in the street. His complexion was ghastly' (Spitzka, 1888, p. 52). Spitzka is clearly fashioning F.S. in Hyde's image: from Satanic to appealing, he switches personality before the physician's eyes. He has Hyde's 'odd light footstep', and like him is ultimately indescribable. If Stevenson decided against hinting at this 'vice' as a candidate for Jekyll's supposed condition or for Hyde's repellent aspect in the revised form, he found at least one knowing interpreter who made the connection.

16. The attributed murders were as follows: Friday 31 August 1888, Mary Ann Nichols, Buck's Row, Whitechapel; Saturday 8 September 1888, Annie Chapman, back yard of 29 Hanbury Street, Spitalfields; Sunday 30 September 1888, Elizabeth Stride in a yard to the side of 40 Berner Street, St Georges-in-the-East, and Catherine Eddowes, Mitre Square, Aldgate, in the City of London; Friday 9 November 1888, Mary Jane Kelly, 13 Miller's Court, 26 Dorset Street, Spitalfields. According to the Metropolitan Police webpage devoted to the murders, 'The name "Jack the Ripper" is easy to explain. It was written at the end of a letter, dated 25 September 1888, and received by the Central News Agency on 27 September 1888. They, in turn, forwarded it to the Metropolitan Police on 29 September . . . The appended "trade name" of Jack the Ripper was then made public and further excited the imagination of the populace.' The most accessible and comprehensive source for contemporary materials on the murders, including police reports, medical reports, selective newspaper accounts and official documents unavailable elsewhere is the very useful *The Ultimate Jack the Ripper Sourcebook*, compiled by Steward P. Evans and Keith Skinner (2000).

17. Daniel Tuke (1885), p. 365.

18. The reference to the murderer being a 'victim' of sadism clearly indicates some familiarity with medico-legal thought and sexological practice. Krafft-Ebing had only formulated the category in a German textbook two years before. Jack himself appeared in later editions of *Psychopathia Sexualis*, and is referred to as a 'modern Bluebeard'.

19. Christopher Frayling, 'The House that Jack Built', in Tomaselli and Porter (eds.), (1986), p. 196. The *New York Times* of 9 September 1888 observed that 'Such a series of murders has not been known in London for a hundred years. There is a bare possibility that it may turn out to be something like a case of Jekyll and Hyde, as Joseph Taylor, a perfectly reliable man, who saw the suspected person this morning in a shabby dress, swears he has seen the same man coming out of a lodging house in Wilton-street very differently dressed. However that may be, the murders are certainly the most ghastly and mysterious known to English police history. What adds to the weird effect they exert on the London mind is the fact that they occur while everybody is talking about Mansfield's [play of] "Jekyll and Hyde" at the Lyceum.'

20. It is interesting to note that Edward Charles Spitzka (who had earlier compared one of his victims of 'masturbational insanity' with Mr Hyde, see note 15 above), concluded his address to the Society of Medical Jurisprudence in December 1888 on 'The Whitechapel Murders: Their Medico-Legal and Historical Aspects' (a catalogue of sadistic cases), with the observation: 'The wild beast . . . is slumbering in us all. It is not necessary always to invoke insanity to explain its awakening.' Dr Spitzka had obviously taken Stevenson's lesson to heart, and one can imagine the medical experts in his audience shifting uncomfortably in their seats. Spitzka 'Whitechapel Murders' (1888), p. 778.

21. Stephen Heath (1986).

22. On the formation and dissemination of this myth, see Deborah Cameron and Elizabeth Frazer, *The Lust to Kill: A Feminist Investigation of Sexual Murder* (1987), and Frayling (1996).